Operation Foreplay

Operation Foreplay

CHRISTINE HUGHES

FOREVER
YOURS

New York   Boston

Forever Yours
Hachette Book Group
1290 Avenue of the Americas
New York, NY 10104
hachettebookgroup.com
twitter.com/foreverromance

First published as an ebook and as a print on demand edition: November 2015

Forever Yours is an imprint of Grand Central Publishing.
The Forever Yours name and logo are trademarks of Hachette Book Group, Inc.

The publisher is not responsible for websites (or their content) that are not owned by the publisher.

The Hachette Speakers Bureau provides a wide range of authors for speaking events. To find out more, go to www.hachettespeakersbureau.com or call (866) 376-6591.

ISBN 978-1-4555-9002-5 (ebook edition)
ISBN 978-1-4555-9095-7 (print-on-demand edition)

For Tina and Jodi.
They can keep running around this circle but
they ain't getting in.

Acknowledgments

It seems that it's difficult for me to write my acknowledgments and not repeat myself! I am forever thankful for all the love and support I've received over the past five years from family, friends, and fans. It certainly makes my job easier when I know I have such amazing people surrounding me.

I always like to start by thanking my husband. He is truly an awesome human being and I seriously don't know what I ever did to deserve him but I won't question it. He makes me a better person and the influence he has on our boys is awe inspiring.

To my family, I love you all! You gave me the foundation I needed to follow my dreams.

To my awesome agent, Michelle Johnson—even if you are a night owl and I'm an early bird, we make a great team. And maybe my hubs is right, maybe we really do share a snarky brain with a slight ability to filter inappropriate thoughts and comments.

I have to thank Dana Hamilton for her awesome notes and insights into *Operation Foreplay*. She made editing the damn thing so much easier. Thank you, also, to Megha Parekh for her enthusiasm. It was so lovely to finally meet you in Dallas! Finally, thanks to Fareeda Bullert for help with publicity. I still owe you all some cocktails!

Leslie Wright, my boo! I am still so damn happy we are doing this together. Like I said, one day we'll end up in Miami as old ladies writing stories about hot men half our age. Can't wait.

Lastly, a HUGE thank you to all my readers—it's time to sit back, grab your favorite cocktail, and enjoy *Operation Foreplay* as you fall in love with Melody and Jared.

Operation Foreplay

Chapter One

When my biggest decision of the day is whether to bring red or white, I always bring both. And when those bottles are headed with me to Sarah's house, I buy two of each and tell the sales clerk to keep the change. Of course, since it's summer and summer can't start without a cold glass of pink lemonade, I picked up bottles of Prosecco and pink limoncello and was hoping Sarah had some raspberries.

Still dressed in a gray pinstriped pencil skirt, sleeveless silk tank, and a pair of bright red power heels, I couldn't wait to slip into nothing, crawl into bed, and sleep the night away. But tonight, that dream was going to have to wait. Sarah texted me earlier to let me know her brother Jared, who I hadn't seen in years, was moving back to New Jersey. Of course, many would wonder why he'd move from Georgia to the Garden State. I, on the other hand, didn't care. Not then. My plate was full enough with work, sleep, friends, and fucking my boss.

My feet started to cry as I made my way up to the fourth floor of Sarah's apartment building. Seriously, where was an elevator when you needed one? I must've looked like I needed rescuing from my choice in footwear when I heard a male voice behind me.

"Need some help?"

I tossed my hair over my shoulder and plastered on my you-better-be-hot smile. If he was going to save me from my stilettos then I kind of needed him to look good while doing it. I laughed and said, "Sure," as I turned to face the man. I nearly fell down the stairs as my knees gave out. Goddamn, he was hot. Dark hair, stubble, and big blue eyes. I envied his eyelashes and for a split second wondered how they'd feel on my skin.

"You okay?" He smiled as he grabbed my elbow and took one of the liquor store bags from me.

I slid my Prada bag high up on my shoulder and said, "Yeah. Thanks. My ass is gonna scream at me tomorrow after I climb all these stairs." He climbed up to the next step so he was one below me and we were eye level. Something in that face was familiar, but for the life of me I couldn't picture it anywhere but between my legs. I didn't like the fact that I was obviously flushed and caught off guard. I mean, honestly, the flirtation game is *my* bitch. I own it. I wrote the rules and I could bed a man faster than anyone else I'd ever met. But this guy had me thinking stupid the second he curved his lips and flashed his bright blues in my direction. "My name is Melody. Melody Ashford." I held out my hand.

"Nice to meet you, Melody. From what I saw, I'll be thanking these steps while your ass screams at you." He took my hand and I bit my lip, thinking it would quell the sudden throb between my thighs. For the first time, I wished I were wearing underwear.

I struggled to think of something clever to say but all I could think of was "Are you new?"

"I'm sorry?"

Oh my God. He had a dimple. *Where do I know this guy from?*

I handed him my bag and he climbed past me. "Are you new to the building?" His khakis fit his ass so well that my head tilted of its own accord and I licked my lips as if I were a lion on the Serengeti stalking my prey. If I had my way, and I always did, that man was about to be the new notch on my bedpost.

"Yeah. You could say that."

"I think I would have remembered you." I giggled. Inwardly, I rolled my eyes at myself. *Giggle? Really?*

"Would you now?" He continued up the next flight of stairs. "You have a good memory, then?"

"I'd like to think so." I scrambled to keep up. Damn shoes. "Um, fourth floor."

"Huh?" He called back down to me.

"I'm heading for the fourth floor."

"I know." He didn't look back at me. I felt like I was talking to the back of his head. It was annoying.

"You *know*? What are you, some kind of mind reader?" I seriously should have taken the heels off a floor and a half ago but I couldn't do that now. Not when I was stalking.

"Kind of." He answered vaguely.

My head popped in view of Sarah's door as he stepped onto the landing. My friend's door opened and she stepped out.

"What took you so long? The pizza's getting cold." She hugged the man who handed one of my liquor store bags to her. "You went to the liquor store? You shouldn't have!" She looked in the bag and pulled out the bottle of pink limoncello. "You bought this?"

The man looked confused, shrugged, and smiled.

"Um, no." I held up a finger as I teetered onto the landing. "That would be me. I went to the liquor store. I bought that. I bought the pink limoncello."

And suddenly I felt like a disheveled mess and Mr. Knight in a Pair of Khakis just tried to jack my party gift. Oh hell no.

I reached out and snatched—yes snatched—the other bag from him and handed it to Sarah while giving him the side eye as I leaned in to kiss her on the cheek. "Who's this guy?" I whispered and thumbed behind me.

"You don't know?" She laughed. "Well, it has been a long time. That's Jared. All grown-up."

Mother fuck.

All. Grown. Up. Indeed.

I turned slowly, horrified that the once skinny kid that was my friend's brother who thought it was funny to annoy the hell out of me so many years ago was suddenly hot. Still annoying but hot.

"Hey Mel." He chuckled and saluted.

"Ass Cheeks?" I said, bringing back the old nickname he earned when one of his high school Barbie doll girlfriends thought it would be funny to pants him at his graduation party. She grabbed the pockets of his jeans and instead of pulling his pants down, she ripped the ass right out of them. And he wasn't wearing any underwear. Hence the name. Ass cheeks. I had a fabulous time calling him that. He didn't like it so much.

"A Cup." He replied, reminding me of the moniker he and his not-so-funny friends used for me before my plastic surgeon enhanced my shortcomings.

"Nice. Obviously *that* is no longer an issue." I smiled and squared my shoulders. I had great tits. And I could tell he thought so, too.

"Apparently not. A little much, don't you think? As least your ass is still kickin'." He winked.

I wanted to be offended. To huff and throw drama around like glitter, but I couldn't bring myself to do anything but stand there with my mouth hanging open like an invitation. I remember when I didn't find him hilarious or adorable, just annoying and skinny. Then again, he was four years younger than me. How else was I supposed to look at him? He was some sort of Mr. Popular in his high school but when it came to his sister's college friends, he had no game. But as I stared at him I knew that he knew he had my nonexistent panties in a bunch and I didn't like it. Not one bit.

"Nice to know you've retained that high school charm. All the girls must love you." I rolled my eyes and stepped through Sarah's door.

"You two act like no time has passed." Sarah laughed as she walked to the kitchen and pulled wineglasses from the kitchen cabinet.

I dropped my purse on the table and took up my spot on the far barstool. I crossed my legs and pointed my toes, debating if I should take off the shoes. Then I saw Jared try not to notice. Fuck my feet. The heels were staying on.

"Just like old friends, right?" Jared reached across the counter and tweaked my nose.

I smacked his hand. "Don't do that. I didn't like it then and I don't like it now."

He cocked an eyebrow and smirked. "So what have you been up

to these past, what is it? Six years? I mean besides losing your sense of humor."

"Eight. And I'm in finance."

"Eight but who's counting?"

"Exactly." I took my glass from Sarah and downed the contents in one swallow.

Sarah snickered. "Melody has a sense of humor."

"Thanks." I raised my empty glass to her.

"Anytime. Excuse me."

Jared watched with what I could only assume was interest. "Nervous?" He refilled my glass as Sarah headed to the bathroom.

"No. What makes you think I'd be nervous?" I straightened my shoulders.

"Oh nothing. So finance, huh? Interesting. I'm in finance myself. Figured out early on I was a numbers guy. All those sixes and nines—"

I choked on my wine. "Excuse me?"

"Did I say something interesting?"

I opened my mouth to say something that I am sure would have been fantastically snarky but I was instead saved by the group of people suddenly entering the apartment. Jared rolled his shoulders and stood. I watched as he confidently walked over to Drew, Sarah's boyfriend, and shook his hand. I watched as Drew made the introductions. He started with Caroline and Brian. Caroline has been my friend for years and Brian has been Drew's friend just as long. Care and Brian began dating just before Christmas, after she had a quite memorable one night stand with Brian's former roommate. Next he introduced Berk and Danny, two of his close friends, and, finally, Brian's sister Siobhan. I watched and bristled when Siobhan's eyes grew as wide as saucers as she took in Jared's wide shoulders, bright eyes, and full lips. I nearly fell off my chair when he turned toward me and winked. And don't think I didn't notice Caroline mouthing "ohmygod" in my direction. Even Berk betrayed me when he noticed Jared's ass as he walked away.

"You okay, beautiful?" Jared interrupted the daggers I was throwing at Berk.

"Don't call me beautiful, Ass Cheeks. You knew who I was on the stairs and yet you pretended you didn't."

"Sue me." He took a long swallow of wine while keeping his eyes on me.

"I'd rather ignore you."

"You couldn't ignore me if you tried."

"Ha! You're full of yourself."

"You could be full of me, too. All you have to do is get rid of that RBF." He tweaked my nose again and walked back to the group.

"I do *not* have resting bitch face," I called to him.

"What's with tall, dark, and fuckable?" Berk pulled up a chair next to me.

"Jared? Hardly fuckable. He's too into himself."

"Sounds like someone we know," Caroline quipped.

"I am *not* into myself." I frowned when the two of them laughed. I handed Caroline a napkin to clean up the wine she spit all over the countertop. "Assholes."

"Goddamn that boy is hot!" Siobhan jumped in the conversation.

"Seriously. That's my brother," Sarah added as she returned from the bathroom. "He is off-limits."

Berk and Caroline saluted and giggled while Siobhan huffed. I ignored her. Not like I wanted any of what he had to offer anyway.

"Melody? That mostly means you."

"Me? Why would I want your brother?"

"Um, because he has a cock."

"I'm offended."

"No you aren't. Plus, he just broke up with his fiancée. He doesn't need a dose of Melody on top of it."

"Fine." I rolled my eyes.

"He was engaged?" Caroline pouted, clearly remembering her own broken engagement. "Poor guy."

"Oh, please. He's so full of himself, he's probably nailed half of New Jersey in the twelve hours he's been here."

"Jealous much?" Berk laughed.

"Ew. No." I sipped my wine. "He's not my type anyway. I have Zac."

"Zac is married." Sarah wrinkled her nose.

Yeah he was. And he was my boss. And because I was fucking my married boss I had no time for Jared and his shenanigans, no matter how good they looked in a pair of khakis.

Chapter Two

With nothing but a towel wrapped tightly around my head, I padded barefoot to the kitchen to open a bottle of wine. Turning up the music, I shimmied around the room as I searched the drawer for the bottle opener. I was giddy after checking the time; Zac would be at my apartment in an hour. For the first time since, well, the first time, he'd be on my turf. There would be no sneaking around the office, no stolen kisses when no one was looking. No rushing out of bed at three in the morning to take a cab to the train that would bring me home by four only to head back into the city by nine. He was coming to my place. My place. Sleeping over. Spending the night. Spending the weekend. And if I had a say in it, the weekend would be spent in bed.

I'd put on the slinkiest, smuttiest underwear I could find—purchased specifically for the occasion—perfected my barely there makeup, and dabbed on the expensive perfume he'd purchased for me during his last visit to France.

With thirty minutes to go, I pulled the towel off my head and used the diffuser to ensure the honey-blond curls he loved so much were intact and full. I lit candles, slipped on my slinky black dress in time to pay the Chinese delivery guy, whose eyes bugged out of his head when he saw the surgically enhanced cleavage I presented him with when I answered the door, and set the table. Looking around my ridiculously spacious apartment, I smiled because everything was perfect. Early dinner meant more time in bed. Or on the floor. Or in the shower.

After I polished off my second glass of wine, I shot Zac a text and picked at the dumplings. Within thirty minutes, there were none left and I was still starving. I checked out the market recap, then flipped through the channels until I landed on a sitcom that highlighted one of the characters turning thirty. I poured a third glass and lamented the fact that I'd be thirty in less than a month. I wasn't *not* looking forward to it, but I didn't see the big deal. Unfortunately my mother didn't agree. Especially since she'd learned my friends were moving in a direction I clearly was not. I mean, who cared if Caroline moved in with Brian? Why did it matter if Sarah was dating Drew regularly? Who said I needed any of that? I was an attractive young professional woman. I was successful. And I liked to have sex. Lots of it. Though over the past few months I'd pared down the number of bedfellows to one Zachary Waterman. My boss. The things that man could do with his hands. The thought gave me goose bumps.

I reached across my chocolate leather sofa and grabbed a pillow to rest my laptop on. Maybe he'd e-mailed. I'd eaten both eggrolls and emptied the last of the bottle into my glass by the time I finished perusing the spam and department store sales advertisements. It wasn't a total loss. I'd ordered a sexy new pair of peep toes to go with the entirely too expensive suit I'd purchased the week before.

I clicked off the television and walked to my bedroom, wine sloshing from my glass due partly to my overpour and partly to my impaired balance. I call it my drunken girl strut. Everyone has one.

Relighting a vanilla candle that had snuffed out, I picked up my never-used landline and dialed my cell phone to make sure it was still working. He was an hour and twenty minutes late. I took a deep breath and reminded myself not to panic. Of course, he was a busy man. He ran a multimillion-dollar company. There was no need to worry.

Refreshing my makeup, I told myself over and over again not to worry. The voice in my head, unfortunately, was growing more frantic by the minute. I was never one to get all swoony and girly over a man. I had no time for relationships, no time for anything other than casual and mutually mind-blowing sex. I had a black book. I had notches on my bedpost and a belt with more holes than I cared to admit. It's not that I didn't care about the guys I slept with, it's just that I cared more about myself and my orgasms. Not a bad thing. I certainly wasn't selfish—any bedmate could tell you. I just wasn't relationship material. And it pissed off my mother.

So why was I all keyed up over Zac? What the hell made him so special that I'd sit home and wait for him? It was because he was unavailable to me in the relationship department. His wife would agree with me. I'd been involved with my still-married-but-going-through-a-divorce boss for the past five months. Not exactly going through, per se. More like promising-to-end-it-but-hasn't-yet. My friends thought I needed a new hobby.

I dialed his number and was slightly surprised when it went straight to voice mail. I didn't bother leaving a message. Instead,

I threw the phone on my couch and slinked back to the kitchen to grab the second bottle. I sat on the floor between the hallway and the kitchen cracking fortune cookies that gave shitty advice. It wasn't until that second bottle of Pinot sat unopened in my lap, mascara stained my cheeks, and he was officially two and a half hours late that I realized he wasn't coming.

That isn't true.

I realized it when he didn't return my text.

Calmly I walked to my bedroom and stripped off the slinky black dress I'd picked out for the evening, now wet from wine spillage, and let it fall to the floor. I yanked on the rattiest pair of sweatpants I could find in my drawer and pulled my old college T-shirt over my head. Even that had holes in it. Perfect metaphor for my life at that moment. Full of holes. I was crying by the time I called Sarah. Her brother answered. *Great.*

"Why are you answering your sister's phone?" I had no time for small talk. I was in crisis.

"She's in the bathroom." They were out somewhere. I could hear other people talking in the background.

"Get her." The amount of panic I was feeling rose along with the pitch of my voice.

"You okay?"

"Jared, just get your sister." The whisper slid through my clenched jaw.

"Are you crying?"

"Son of a bitch, Jared." I had no fight in me.

"Geez, I'd tell you not to get your panties in a bunch but I know you don't wear any."

"Fuck you." Maybe I did.

"You wish." He chuckled.

Sarah came on the line. "Hey."

"He didn't come." Unsteadily I made my way back into my living room.

"Oh, sweetie. I'm sorry."

"I've eaten five dumplings and two eggrolls. I have a pile of fortune cookie crumbs in my hallway. I am going to open my second bottle of wine and eat the lo mein I ordered without a fork. I will gain ten pounds and I don't care."

"We'll be right there."

"I will stick my face in the lo mein and eat it like a caveman."

"Do not eat the lo mein like a caveman. We will be there in less than twenty minutes."

The best part about having two best friends was there were no questions when one of us was down. I didn't have to ask. They'd be there. They'd answer the phone. They'd respond to a text and, barring a life-threatening accident, they wouldn't be two and a half hours late.

I barely heard them come in my apartment. It wasn't until Sarah plopped down on the floor next to me that I opened my eyes. Thankfully, I never opened that second bottle.

"You okay?"

I rolled my head and rested it on her shoulder. "Yeah. I'm okay."

"Can I be blunt?"

"I don't think it's a good time to be blunt. Caring and understanding. Not blunt." Caroline settled on my other side and handed me a cup of coffee from my favorite place.

"It's okay," I reassured her, "I can take it." I sipped the strong black coffee and knew sooner rather than later, I'd be perked back up. I didn't want to be perked back up. I wanted to wallow and woe-is-me in the dark depths that only sleeping with a married man could bring you.

"How long are you going to keep doing this to yourself?"

"Oh, at least another dozen or so times."

Caroline was right. I didn't want to hear what Sarah, the constant voice of reason, had to say.

"He's married."

"I am more than aware." I rolled my eyes and tipped my empty wineglass, hoping to tease out one last drop.

"He's done this to you more than once. He's a no show. Doesn't call. Doesn't text."

"That isn't fair." With a bit of latent enthusiasm, I shot forward and pointed a perfectly manicured finger at her. "The last time his mother was in the hospital."

"And the time before that he was stuck in traffic and the time before that—"

"I think she gets it, Sarah. Just like I think it's time for you, my dear, to get dressed."

Caroline stood, scooped her hands under my arms, and pulled me to my feet.

"I am in no shape to go out. I'm drunk." My point needed a drunken girl arm flail but I was too tired to attempt it.

"It's nine o'clock. Since when does a bottle of wine stop you? You're fine. Besides, if you stay here, you'll be in a food coma. Jesus"—she walked over to the dining room table— "how much did you order?"

"A lot."

"Drunk is fine. Drunk and holed up in your apartment crying

about a married man who didn't show up is not. Don't be silly. We're just going to Murphy's. It's time for target practice." Sarah winked at Caroline. I had the feeling they'd been planning this for a while.

Target practice. Almost a year ago Caroline's fiancé of five years broke up with her in the douchiest way imaginable—she walked in on him banging the intern. Needless to say, she retreated, hid, gained ten pounds, and became a disheveled mess. Until Sarah and I stepped in and forced her to see herself without Steve. Target Practice: Operation One Night Stand was born. After a few bumps in the road, Caroline ended up with Brian, the owner of Murphy's Bar. He was supposed to be a rebound, someone to pull her out of her funk. Two weeks ago, they moved in together and bought a dog.

Go figure.

"I don't need target practice," I moaned as the girls walked me back to my room. "I don't need to get over anyone."

"No, you don't have to get over Zac, necessarily. Maybe you just need some time away to get some perspective on what's working and what's not working as far as your naughty bits go," Sarah piped in.

"My naughty bits are in perfect working order, thank you."

"They need to be distracted from their current trajectory," Sarah said.

"Operation Distraction?" Caroline said with too much enthusiasm.

"Maybe Operation Take a Break from Sex Altogether," Sarah added with a raised eyebrow.

"Right! Like that will ever happen." I shook my head and laughed. "Whatever. Your brother won't be there will he?"

"Jared?"

"Yeah."

"Actually, he picked up some chick and took off as I was leaving," Sarah answered as she looked through my closet.

"Of course he did." I rolled my eyes. I tensed at the thought of him with another woman and it irritated me. "He's been here a week and he's already trolling for—"

"Does it matter?" Sarah interrupted.

"Of course it doesn't. I just don't need him knowing my business."

"Because?"

"Because, honestly, he's a snarky little shit with an opinion."

"I swear the more I think about it, the more I think you and Jared are the same person," Caroline added with a smirk.

"Shut it." I flopped onto my bed.

That night, Sarah and Caroline convinced me to shower, dress, and head to Murphy's. They reminded me that they'd warned me numerous times that getting involved with Zac wasn't the brightest of my ideas, and eventually I had to agree. After much discussion, it was decided that I would stop sleeping with Zac or anyone else until I could figure a way out of my sexy-time funk. Of course, dodging calls and advances from Zac and solidifying the platonic work-only relationship was probably best but certainly not as fun.

With reluctance, I allowed Sarah to delete Zac's number from my phone, which would have been a catchall solution had I not worked so closely with him. And had he not been the definition of tall, dark, handsome, and fucking sexy as hell.

I just needed to get through the week.

Chapter Three

After scrubbing myself raw for more than forty minutes, I finally felt somewhat clean. At least cleaner than I had at four in the morning when I kicked what's-his-name out of my apartment. So far, Operation Distraction was a bust. With five missed calls from Zac, three texts from Sarah, and a voice mail from my mother, I'd say that morning, or the night before, wasn't necessarily something I'd write down in a memoir. A week ago, I was a sobbing mess, having been put on hold by him once again so he could attend to the needs of the wife he had promised to leave. But at least I made it through the week without ripping his clothes off.

Instead, I thoroughly wore out my favorite vibrator.

The night before, the girls and I had gone out for a few. After copious amounts of my new favorite and appropriately named drink, Adios Motherfucker, I was feeling a bit lonely and in need of a random romp, despite my earlier promises to hold off.

Gabe—I found out his name twenty minutes into our conversation—was the opposite of what I normally took home. His was well over six feet tall with sleeves of tattoos over heavily muscled arms. He was, quite possibly, the face of stereotypical New Jersey. I didn't care, though. All I needed was a target to distract me and he was the one.

He excused himself and Caroline slid onto the seat he vacated. "I thought you weren't going to sleep with anyone until you figured your shit out?"

I took a sip of my drink and shrugged. "I'm horny." I shuddered as I watched Jared walk through the door with a redhead on his arm. Just the way he walked through a room made me clench my jaw. Redhead aside, I was suddenly acutely aware of the seam of my jeans.

"Right, but we said you needed a distraction, not a tune up. Besides"—she twisted around to look for Gabe before turning back to me—"he's kind of scary looking."

"He's not my usual choice, I'll give you that, but what's wrong with him? He's tall, dark—"

"And has more oil in his hair than I have in my car," Sarah interrupted. "You are not supposed to be going home with anyone right now, Mel. You are supposed to figure out a way to distract yourself from Zac."

"I'm pretty sure this guy"—I thumbed toward him over my shoulder—"will help distract me from the screams and cries of my lonely lady cave."

"Lonely lady cave?"

I shrugged. "Sounded better than pussy." I took a sip of my drink.

"And why is he orange? Spray tan much?" Caroline crinkled her nose.

"Oh, shut it. I'm a grown woman in charge of my own—"

"Lonely lady cave?" Sarah asked.

"Yes. And the last thing I need is the vagina patrol fucking up my mojo." I tilted my head and checked Gabe out once more. "Besides, with hands that big, there is no way he isn't packing serious junk-age. Now, if you'll excuse me, I'm going to see if he would like to go somewhere not so crowded."

"What's up ladies?" Jared leaned into the bar, pressing his shoulder into my boobs.

"Excuse me." I huffed and looked around. "Where's the red-head?"

"Jealous?"

"Hardly." I hopped off my barstool and readied myself for the night's distraction.

"Drink this first." Sarah handed me a shot.

"What is it?" Like I cared.

Jared leaned back with his elbow on the bar and his shirt rode up a little bit. Giving me a peek at the small patch of hair that led from his belly button to below the waistband of his jeans. I sucked in a breath as the thought of my tongue trailing along his stomach flashed in my mind.

"It's called a One Night Stand. Brian thought it up after, well, you know."

"Perfect." I looked over at Jared and he winked at me while raising his beer bottle in salute. I couldn't understand why he unnerved me.

The girls and I clinked shot glasses and downed the creamy beverage before I saluted, elbowed my way from the bar, and grabbed Gabe by the arm.

"Hey you."

"Hey." His eyes narrowed and he leaned down to press his lips to mine.

I should have known then that the night was going to be a disappointment. It was like kissing two dead fish with a side of corn chips. But I was a grown-up. I could see past all the not-so-great nuances. After all, it was only for one night, only a distraction. I could avoid kissing him as long as his package was delivered directly to my door.

"Wanna get out of here?" I hitched my designer handbag over my shoulder and cocked my head toward the door.

"Absolutely." He growled and smacked my ass hard enough to leave a semipermanent handprint.

I screamed the requisite girly scream and giggled. My friends rolled their eyes in pseudo amusement. Jared's mouth dropped open. They were displeased with my choice for the evening. Served them right, I figured. In my heart, I knew Zac and I were meant to be together, but in my head, I knew it wouldn't work. I liked to say I was a no-relationship girl but let's face it, it's easy to say that when the one you want to be with is married, so there isn't much to hope for.

Jared pulled me aside. "You're going home with *this* guy?"

"Jealous?" I threw his words at him.

"Hardly." And he lobbed mine back at me.

"You *do* have a redhead to get back to."

"Yeah. I guess I do."

I couldn't read his face and I was ready to get into it with him when his redhead for the night curled against him. My stomach dropped. "You two have fun."

I looked to Gabe as he high-fived a few friends on the way out and said, "Let's go."

His large hands dwarfed mine. I smiled. I was ready to test out his equipment.

The walk home was short and my key was barely in the lock when Gabe's testosterone took over. Fine with me. If it got out of hand I could always spray him with mace and shove the heel of my pumps into his crotch.

He pressed up behind me and twisted my hair in his fist. Pulling my head back he leaned down and licked my neck, leaving hot nerves firing in my stomach. So far, so good. I reached behind and pulled him closer as I opened the door to my apartment. I threw my purse on the floor and grabbed him by the waistband of his jeans, pulling him toward my bedroom.

I pulled off his shirt and marveled at the amazingly chiseled abs he brought to the table. *So he has dead fish for lips*, I thought to myself, *with a body like that, who the fuck cares?*

He clumsily tripped over the shoes I'd just kicked off and fell on top of me. At least the bed caught our fall. He kissed my neck and pulled my shirt over my head. I fiddled with his belt until I was able to unfasten the thing and slid my hand under his pants and squeezed his ass. It was tight and hard. My kind of ass. He moaned before abandoning his clumsy attempt at unhooking my bra and settled on ham-handing my boobs out of the structured cups.

And then things got weird.

"You have great titties," he said between sucks that sorta, kinda felt like a dentist working on an extraction.

I could only mutter, "Thanks." There was good pain and there was bad pain. The Hoover job he was doing on my nipples was bad pain.

At that point I just wanted to get it over with, so I unbuttoned my own pants and slid them over my hips, kicking my legs until they flew across the room. Gabe took the gesture as an invitation to rip my underwear with his teeth. I squeezed my eyes shut. The gesture should have been a turn on, but those panties cost me thirty bucks and I wasn't sure he even appreciated them.

He settled between my thighs, the inefficient nipple foreplay his only attempt at revving my engine, which was still stuck in first.

I'm not quite sure what he thought he was doing down there but he clamped onto my clit and sucked. He didn't stop sucking. There was no licking, no finger-fucking, no ass-tickling. He was a straight up sucker and it, well, sucked. After a minute or so, I knew it was going to go nowhere so I did what any girl would do. I faked it.

Moaning like he was the best thing to happen to me since the last call sale at Neiman Marcus, I sang like an operatic songbird. Looking back, I don't think I should have been so emphatic. All it did was egg him on to suck harder. He sucked until I swore to God my clit was going to pop off and shoot down his throat like an errant pea.

Jesus Christ. I hated foreplay.

"Oh God! Gabe!" I gave it one last faux crescendoing moan and pulled his hair hard enough to remove him from my vagina. Once again, I needed to remind myself that just because a man couldn't perform with his mouth, there was no reason to think his cock couldn't win a championship. After all, sex was kind of like a relay race. A good rule of thumb is to pace yourself and when no one's looking, defy all expectations with a perfect closer. Or something like that. I never did make the track team, unless you counted the few members I met under the bleachers back in high school.

I clamped my legs together as he yanked his tighty whities down.

The world slammed painfully into a brick wall of what-the-fuck-ed-ness.

Gabe pulled out what could only be described as a mini cock.

And suddenly the slowest runner on the team began the last leg.

As big as Gabe was, one would expect no less than an average-sized dick. I checked out my big toe for a moment to confirm that it, indeed, was larger than the cocktail wiener he pulled from his underwear.

I looked at him and realized he didn't think he had a small dick. He gazed at it before looking at me hungrily, as if he thought it would satisfy the needs of anyone. Ever.

"You like it baby?" He jiggled the thing like it was something to be proud of. But it was small enough to attach to my keychain.

What was it with men and their cocks? If it is small, own it. Work on the technique. Whatever. Make the girl forget that your penis is smaller than the heel of her shoe.

He edged up, straddling my body with his nasty ass planted on my chest, and brought the thing to my face.

"Want a taste?" He held his unbelievably rock-solid appendage between his fingers as he guided it toward me. It was all I could do to not turn my face away.

I could only assume he wanted a blow job but I wasn't sure if I should attempt it. Then again, a blow job is a blow job. How bad could it be?

Thankfully, his penis was small enough that there was no gag reflex even when he did that weird guy thing. He grabbed the back of my head and pumped into my face. Yeah. He was a face fucker.

Most of the time I was able to slip his tiny penis in my cheek like I was a squirrel collecting really tiny nuts.

It wasn't long before I was bored with pretending to suck his dick so I pulled away and said with as much seduction as I could muster, "I want you inside me." Of course I was thinking, *Good luck reaching my vagina, buddy*.

I handed him a condom and watched as he rolled it on his penis. I stifled a giggle when it was clear there was more than ample room left at the tip.

"What?" he asked.

"Nothing. My nose just had a tickle." And I pretended to sneeze.

I had to psych myself up. After all, who cares about size? It's the motion of the ocean, right? The little voice in my head told me not to get my hopes up. I told her to shut her trap.

Gabe settled between my legs and we bumped uglies for a bit before I realized he hadn't even entered my body and I was about to get rug burn from his never-been-trimmed bush of seventies porn style man pubes. He jack-hammered away thinking he was doing me a favor.

Putting my gym visits to good use, I twisted my legs and rolled over until I was on top of him.

"Oh yeah. Fuck me hard, Melanie."

Son of a bitch got my name wrong.

I paused a moment and took a breath. "My name is Melody. With a d."

"What?"

"Melody. My fucking name is Melody. Not Melanie."

"Right. That's what I said. Yeah, Melody."

I rolled my eyes and probably should have severed the connection there, but I am a glutton for punishment and I needed a decent orgasm. Maybe I rely too much on orgasms getting me through life.

I held out hope he could give one to me. If not, I had a stash of battery-operated boyfriends that would do the trick nicely.

I wiggled my hips as I gripped him and guided myself down until I was sure he was in. Unfortunately, any time I bounced, he'd pop right out and I'd have to start the process over. I was getting tired of reaching between my own legs to guide his mini-me into my frustrated vagina.

Then I had the fabulous idea of rocking instead of bouncing.

Of course, that felt like little more than an annoyance that didn't quite reach interesting. He didn't even have the decency to allow me to fake it again before he blew his load with a giant lion yell and a fart.

Motherfucker farted as he came. I covered my nose with the back of my hand.

I'd had enough.

Time to go, big guy.

I hopped off and grabbed my bathrobe, tying it tight enough to give him a clue that whatever the fuck just happened wasn't going to happen again.

"Okay, thanks." I stretched. "Man, I'm tired."

I left him alone to dress and walked to the kitchen to pour myself a big glass of Cabernet. I stared at the full glass for a moment before I took a gulp from the bottle. There would never be enough wine to erase what just transpired. What I needed was brain bleach.

After I finished my first glass, Gabe still hadn't emerged, so I went looking for him. The smell from the hallway alone told me he was either taking a shit or I had a dead animal problem.

The bathroom door was closed, which gave me the answer I foolishly tried to dismiss. He was taking a dump.

In my apartment.

Less than ten minutes after his feeble attempt at, at…I don't know what.

Sitting crisscross applesauce on top on my granite countertop, I chugged from the bottle, having abandoned the need for my wineglass, when he finally appeared in the kitchen.

"Hey, baby." He nuzzled my neck. His hands covered mine, and I realized he hadn't washed them.

I jerked away and hopped off the counter.

"Well, thanks for, uh, *that*." I faked a yawn and clutched the neck of the wine bottle like it was life support. "I'm really tired." The fact that I had to repeat myself had my inner bitch elbowing her way to the front of the line.

"Give me a minute, baby. We can go again."

I thought I wasn't going to be able to force the vomit back down my throat.

"Aw, that's sweet. But I really am tired. Maybe another time."

He opened the fridge. "Hey, you wanna get something to eat? You ain't got nothing in here but a pile of carrots and hummus."

A pain stabbed me through the ear as he pronounced it *hoo-mus*.

"No, no." I shut the refrigerator door. Inner bitch was getting ready to make her appearance. I closed my eyes for a beat and took a breath. "Like I said, maybe another time. I'll call you." I calculated the distance between him and my purse in case I needed to pepper spray the fucker. Then again, I could always bash him over the head with my wine bottle.

I pushed him toward the door and opened it, all but shoving him into the dimly lit hallway of my apartment building.

"Hey, I didn't give you my number!"

"That's okay. I can figure it out." I slammed the door in his face and fastened the dead bolt.

After banging my head on the door for what seemed like an eternity, I downed the rest of the wine and walked over to the kitchen. I grabbed the air disinfectant that I keep under the sink and moved to the hallway.

I sprayed the hell out of the bathroom and hall before starting on my bedroom. I ripped all the sheets and blankets off my bed for fear that the stench had somehow seeped into the fabric, stuffed them in a black garbage bag, and placed them by the door. I wasn't sure if I should trash them, burn them, or let the dry cleaner have a go.

It was official. It was four in the morning and my first attempt at target practice was a dud. A one-night dud.

Chapter Four

Taking advantage of the beautiful day, I decided to walk my way to lunch with Caroline and Sarah. Passing the flower market, I reminded myself to pick up a fresh bunch of daisies on my way back. The apartment could use a bit of sprucing up. And maybe they'd do a little something with the stench left from Gabe the Tiny-Dicked Fart Machine. Maybe daisies wouldn't be quite potent enough. I shuddered at the thought.

As I'd promised, I deleted the messages from Zac without listening to them. The girls would be impressed with my fortitude, though I wasn't sure how long I'd be able to hold out. Deleting messages was one thing but seeing him at work was entirely another challenge. And if the past week was any indication, I was going to start spritzing myself in the face with cold water any time he walked in the room. Or I was going to have to start jacking off at work. That, of course, wasn't an option.

My mother, apparently, was less than pleased that I hadn't spoken to her in over a week and she wouldn't let me off the phone before I promised to carve out time to visit her. There really was no reason I didn't visit her more often; she was only down the turnpike in South Jersey. I guess it was time to be a better daughter. I wasn't getting any younger and neither was she. I just wished she'd stop asking me when I'd find a man, settle down, and give her grandkids. Not that I had anything against kids, they just weren't on my bucket list.

I turned the corner toward the restaurant and saw the girls already sitting at an outside table, deep in conversation.

"Hey, bitches." I made the rounds as I headed to my seat.

"You look nice." Caroline checked out my yellow sundress and strappy sandals.

"Thanks, doll! So do you." The orange tank she wore set off highlights in her hair that magically appeared whenever she spent time in the sun. I could achieve the same look only with foil and chemicals.

"Gorgeous as always," Siobhan complimented me when I leaned down to kiss her cheek.

Siobhan's gotten all mixed up with a creepy author Caroline was editing for and since that faux relationship went to shit, she hung out with us every now and then. She was a cute kid, green on the dating scene. She'd recently gotten a job reporting for a national celebrity tabloid. She always had the dirt.

"Hey, lady." I grabbed Sarah's boob because that's just how we greet each other.

As the waiter stopped over to fill my water glass, I noticed an extra place setting at the table. "Why the extra plate? Brian stopping by?" I eyeballed Caroline. I thought we'd made the decision to allow girl time without significant others.

"No. Relax. It's just Berk."

Berk was our friend by default. He originally ran with Brian and his friends, but since Caroline started dating Brian and Sarah began her not very serious but somewhat kinky relationship with Drew, Berk became one of the girls. I would never tell him, though I am sure he suspects he's allowed to intrude on our girl time only because he's gay. Of course, more times than not, we lament the fact that, in addition to being ridiculously attractive, he'd be the perfect boyfriend. I mean, for a few months he made the perfect work husband. Good-looking, great job, fabulous wardrobe, and more war stories than the three of us combined. Berk liked to date. A lot. However, as of late, he'd been more interested in becoming a one-man man. I secretly hoped that never happened. Who else would be my wing person?

Speaking of the devil, Berk arrived a fashionable fifteen minutes late with a bit more than a five o'clock shadow covering his face.

"What's this?" Sarah pointed to the growth.

"I was told I look too young."

"You are young." I added, "And I am really digging the beard."

"You would."

"I like to lick them."

"I know you do."

"I could lick yours if you want me to."

"Anyway"—he shook his head and rolled his eyes—"twenty-nine is not young. I'm a little over a month—sorry *we're* a little over a month"—he nodded toward me—"away from thirty."

"Don't remind me." I groaned. Berk and I, besides sharing the same taste in men, shared a birthday.

"Sorry, honey. We're entering a new decade. Embrace it. And besides, that's not what I meant." He raised his hand to get the waiter's attention.

"Then why do you need to look older? Isn't that the opposite of how people are supposed to react to aging?" Siobhan asked as she tore a piece of bread and popped it in her mouth. "I mean, isn't getting older what keeps plastic surgeons in business?"

"I, for one, am diving headfirst into the Botox movement when I start to get wrinkles."

"Sorry to be the one to tell you Mel—" Berk began.

"No!" I pulled out my compact and searched the mirror for wrinkles.

"Yes. But this isn't about your drama."

The waiter stopped at the table, took our orders, and filled our glasses with the Riesling Sarah ordered.

Berk and the young waiter shared a moment as they checked each other out. I snapped my fingers to bring the conversation back to what was important.

"Yes?" Berk raised his eyebrows at me as he took a sip of the wine and shifted in his seat.

"My drama? What drama?"

Caroline snorted in her glass, Sarah giggled, and Siobhan busied herself with her phone. That girl was always on the phone.

"Yes, dear, your drama. Always your drama. I want to talk about me and my issues for a moment. If it's okay with you, of course."

"Go ahead." I waved him on.

Caroline and Sarah laughed. I guess Berk was right. I had more drama in my life at the moment than the channel six soap opera.

"Okay, so." He paused as the waiter stopped by the table with a basket of crunchy breadsticks and salad plates. The pause was a bit longer than usual because the two men did nothing to hide the fact that they were making eyes at each other. Again. If Berk didn't get the guy's number before lunch was out, I was getting it for him. "I'm sorry, where was I?"

"Looking older," Sarah offered.

"Right. So, remember me telling you about that real estate agent I went out with a few times? David?"

"Yeah." I remembered because Berk and I placed bets on who that man was going home with. Berk won. Never go up against a gay guy when he says someone plays for his team.

"Well, David and I have been hanging out, like, a lot. And the other night, when we were in the city for that gallery opening I told you guys about, well, he introduced me to a few of his friends and one of them made a comment about David going through a midlife crisis to be dating such a boy toy."

"No." Siobhan was entranced. Berk's stories always had that effect on her.

"Yes! Anyway, I blew it off as a joke, but since then, David's been making strange comments about how I dress, who I hang out with. We argued a bit and then, get this, he said if I was going to surround myself with frat boys and their girlfriends, then he wasn't sure we were going to work out."

"What's wrong with the way you dress?" Siobhan took her face out of her phone for the moment.

"Frat boys and their girlfriends?" I glanced at him over my glass.

"And the beard will fix all that?" Sarah looked perplexed.

"A good beard fixes everything," I added.

"I, for one, am a bit put off by the fact that he thinks Brian is a frat boy. He is certainly *not* a frat boy." Caroline crossed her arms over her chest and huffed.

"Of course not, sweetie." He patted her hand before holding his up. "So what should I do?"

"Well, I think," Sarah began, "if David can't take you for who you are then screw him. He knew your friends before you guys started dating. He should know better."

"Right. But I think ever since he turned forty he's been more about settling down."

"Did you tell him you don't want to settle down?" Caroline took a bite of the breadstick and wiped the crumbs off her lap.

"No. And maybe I do. Or don't. But I guess he just figures since I'm younger or whatever—"

"Bullshit." I interrupted him. "You and David are great together, but I have to agree with Sarah. He should know better."

"I guess you're right." Berk leaned back as the waiter served our salads. "I'm just so tired of everyone I find having some excuse not to be with me. I'm starting to think it's me. I mean, I can't be anything more than fabulous, right?"

"It's not you." I speared a pear with my fork and dipped it in the vinaigrette I ordered on the side. "You *are* fabulous. Screw him. Get the waiter's number and call it a day."

"I can't do that."

"We've been watching you two eye-fuck each other since you sat down," Sarah said.

Berk made a face that told us we weren't crazy.

"Anyway," he began, "enough about my issues. Why don't we give Mel the floor? How did it go last night? What are we calling it? Operation Distraction?"

"Oh, well, you know Mel. How *was* the oily-haired love machine?"

"At least you lasted a week without sex, right?" *I love how Berk gets me.*

I stopped mid bite, closed my eyes, and tried to shake away the memory. "I did. And I would like to thank the rest of you for appreciating that fact. And we aren't calling it operation anything." I eyeballed the girls. "It went, and then I kicked it right out the door."

"You mean Jersey Shore Gabe didn't do it for you?" Caroline laughed.

"No. No, he did not." I leaned back and crossed my arms over my chest. "I thought I was going to have to plan a funeral for my vagina."

"Oh, look who's pouting. What's the matter, Mel? Did the big, bad man not perform for you?" Berk teased. "Did he swivel when he should have shook?"

"Did you slip on the grease from his hair?" Siobhan gigglesnorted.

The question gave us pause and we all stopped to stare at her.

"What?" She shrugged. "Sarah told me he had greasy hair."

"Well, since I wasn't dancing on his hair, I didn't slip on the grease but thanks for your concern."

"It was a valid question, Mel," Sarah pointed out.

"Shut up. You wanna know how it went? He fucking farted the whole fucking night. Then he farted as he blew his tiny-ass load out of his tiny-ass dick."

"Ew." Siobhan crinkled her nose.

Caroline spit bits of her apple walnut salad across the table. "I'm sorry!" She began wiping up her food laden spit with her cloth napkin. "He *farted*? While you were having sex?"

"I'm more interested in hearing about the tiny-ass load that came from his tiny-ass dick." Berk smiled and tore a piece of bread in half.

"Tiny. Very tiny. And yes he farted. His anal cannon was on full blast last night. Pun fucking intended. Not to mention the giant shit he decided to take less than five minutes after we finished."

"Oh, honey! Why the hell didn't you kick him out when you realized it wasn't going to be good?" Caroline tried to mask her disgust.

"I don't understand." Siobhan's eyes were wide.

"What don't you get, sweetie?"

"Why would he do that?"

"Why did you even bring him home?" Berk interjected. "I mean, we may sleep around, doll, but at least we have standards."

"I don't know. I thought, maybe…Hell, I have no idea what I thought."

"Was the sex good at least?" Berk covered his grin with his well-manicured hand.

"Stop smiling. Hard to have good sex with a dick the size of my big toe." I held up my foot and wiggled my toes.

"No!" Berk looked mortified. Sarah was laughing so hard no noise was coming out. Caroline had her hands on either side of her shocked face. Siobhan looked like someone stole her puppy.

"Yes. I checked. His dick was actually the size of my big toe. And don't even get me started on his lack of vaginal dexterity. The son of a bitch couldn't tell a clit from a freaking belly button. At one point, I thought he was going to remove it from my body and it would lodge in his throat."

"It?" Caroline asked.

"It. My clit. It almost popped off and shot down his throat."

"Ouch!" Sarah yelped and her hands flew to her crotch.

"Goddamn right 'ouch.' I had to fake it." I held up two fingers. "Twice."

"Mel." Sarah had finally composed herself. "Do you think that maybe you should have called it off? I mean, if you were so miserable, if he was so bad, then why go through with it? We wanted you to find a distraction, not a Vienna sausage."

"Please." I waved her off. "A Vienna sausage would have been a welcome substitution. God! I hate fucking foreplay. No one knows how to do it right."

"I know how to do it right." Berk smiled.

"But you never have bad sex." Siobhan tried to make sense of the situation.

Did I mention she lived vicariously through travels of my lady parts?

"Sucking dick and muff diving are two different things."

"I ate out a girl once." Berk mentioned it just like he would mention the weather.

The entire table screeched to a halt.

"What," Caroline managed to squeak out.

"The," Sarah followed Caroline's lead.

"Everloving fuck," I finished the thought.

"What? You never experimented before?" Berk took a sip of his wine.

"Well, yeah, but I never thought it worked the other way around," Sarah said.

I sat back in shock.

"Other what way around?" Berk folded his hands and placed them in his lap.

"I didn't know gays experimented with straights," Caroline whispered.

"Oh, like horny college girls hold the rights to trying something new." He waved her off.

"Did you like it?" Siobhan asked the obvious question.

"Eh." He tilted his hand side to side.

"Eh?" I mimicked.

"Yeah. It was weird."

"Weird how?" Siobhan asked.

"You never experimented in college?" I asked her.

"No. I mean, I kissed a girl but I never did *that*."

"Not everyone fucks anything with legs," Sarah pointed out.

"Are you calling me a whore?" I feigned insult.

"Of course not. I would never call you a whore. You're just more *adventurous* than most."

I shrugged. "I like to try new stuff."

"To answer Siobhan's question, it was like licking the flesh of a—"

"Peach." I finished for him.

"Yes. Peach. Only slimier and saltier. Actually, more like a shellfish, like a mussel. It wasn't so great."

"I don't know." I leaned back. "I don't remember it being so bad."

"Well, if you like that sort of thing. I don't know what my point was, but I thought I had one." Berk rolled his shoulders and winked at the waiter, who was taking the order of the people at the next table over.

"Well, my point is that foreplay sucks. It's never done right. I don't know."

"Maybe you should slow down. Instead of going right for the cock, take it slow. Enjoy the touches and the kisses—"

"Who has time for all that? I know what I like and I like when the man part is inside my lady part."

"Maybe you should take a break," Caroline said slowly.

"From?"

"Sex."

It was my turn to spit wine across the table. Berk joined me.

"I'm sorry, what?" He and I spoke in unison. Peas. Pod. Me and Berk.

"You don't seem to be having much luck and maybe if you concentrated on finding the right guy rather than the 'right now' guy—"

"Are you slut shaming her?" Berk grabbed the bottle and filled my glass.

"She certainly is not, but she does have a point," Sarah interjected.

"Must I remind you about the time Caroline walked in on Danny tying your ass up, what, a week after you met him?" A bit of wine sloshed onto my lap. Hand gestures and an overfilled piece of stemware aren't the best of friends.

"Two weeks after I met him. Not the point. Just think about it."

"I am *not* giving up sex."

"It was just a suggestion."

"Giving up sex is not a suggestion. It's a sentence. Like death," Berk challenged. "You should know better!" He waggled his finger at Caroline.

"I'm almost thirty, not three hundred. Sex keeps me young," I challenged. "Really. Look. Sex. I like that shit. And I'm not going to compromise my likes, dislikes, or general behavior because of this so you can take your fabulous idea of abstinence off the table. My vagina would revolt against me if I were to put her on hiatus and I love her and all the good feels she gives me entirely too much to do that to her. I mean, would you deny a blind man the gift of sight? Why deny her"—I actually pointed to my crotch—"a good dicking?"

"You need help. You need to slow the fuck down." Siobhan laughed.

"Maybe the distraction idea was a bad one. I miss Zac."

"Zac is married!" Sarah shouted before lowering her voice to repeat, "Zac is married."

"Soon to be divorced."

"So he says." Berk offered.

"So he will be."

"Then wait until he is," Sarah offered.

"What do you think?" I asked Caroline.

"Me? I don't think it matters what I think." She took a big mouthful of salad to avoid answering the question.

"It does. You know it does."

She held up a finger, making me wait while she chewed and thought through her next words. "I think you're happy when you talk about Zac. I also think that if he really is leaving his wife then you should wait. I also think you're too young to wait for someone who's been telling you he's leaving his wife for the past few months. I say you give Jared a shot."

"Jared? Where the fuck did that come from?" I dropped my fork and it rattled on my plate.

"Jared my brother?" Sarah yelped.

"Yeah. Why not? He's cute, available. I think he and Mel would be good together."

"Ha! No. Just no. Not gonna happen." Sarah held up her hands and waved off Caroline's suggestion.

"Should I be offended? And besides, Jared is less into commitment than I am!" I threw a broken breadstick at Caroline and laughed. "I'll figure it out."

"I don't know about that," Berk offered.

"Don't know about what? Jared? He's seems to be more into random one nighters than I am."

"If you say so." He held up his hands and shrugged his shoulders.

"I do say so. Like I said, I'll figure it out."

The truth was I wasn't sure if I was going to figure it out. Caroline was right. I was mostly happy whenever I thought about being with Zac. And Zac was the man I'd dreamed of my whole life. Powerful. Successful. And the things that man could do with his hands. Just a tiny smirk from him turned my knees to jelly. But he was married and the longer he and I messed around, the bigger that elephant in the room became. I questioned what we were. Of course, I never verbalized that to anyone. I didn't want a round of "I told you so's" from my friends. And I really didn't want to bring it up with Zac; I wasn't ready to give him an ultimatum.

And then Jared showed up. He threw me off my game, tilted me sideways. And my libido lost her mind. I wondered, briefly, what that meant. Then I threw the answer out of my head.

I returned to the conversation in time to hear Caroline describe how much she loved living with Brian. She'd moved in only two weeks ago and none of us have ever seen her happier. After seeing her with Steven for so long, none of us thought she'd ever be the same. But I'd learned one should never say never because she met Brian and, after six months together, knew he was right enough to give up her apartment with Sarah and move in with him. Couple that with their new dog and a stranger would think the two of them were made for each other.

I couldn't lie. I was jealous. I was happy for her, of course, but a tiny piece of me wondered why love wasn't as easy for me. I would never tell her. That secret was something I kept to myself. If you couldn't be happy for your best friend, then who could you be happy for?

My phone buzzed and I reached for it, but Berk grabbed it before I could.

"Melody's phone."

"Give me my phone!" He held up his finger to shush me.

"I'm sorry she isn't available right now. May I take a message?"

He pulled out a pen from his pocket and wrote on a napkin.

"Berk!"

"Yes, uh-huh." He pressed his finger to my lips. "Absolutely. I'll give her the message." He hung up and placed the phone in my hand.

"Who was that?"

"That was Zachary Waterman. He was calling to let you know you need to stay late tomorrow to finish the proposal. I wrote it all down." He playfully handed me the napkin as if he were handing me a note in math class.

"Zac's calling on a Sunday?" Sarah raised her eyebrows.

"That's not necessarily unusual." I read the note, noticed the tiny penis Berk drew next to Zac's name, folded it back up, and stuffed it in my purse.

"He couldn't wait till tomorrow to let you know?" Caroline asked.

"Look, he probably wanted to let me know so I would be prepared. Whenever we stay late, I bring more comfortable clothes with me so I don't have to wear a suit for a million hours."

"Comfortable like naked?" Berk laughed as I slapped his shoulder.

"No! Well, sometimes—"

"I knew it!" Berk pointed at me. "You have office sex!"

"Who hasn't?" Sarah offered.

"I haven't!" Caroline said. "And when have you? Don't tell me you do it in the classroom?"

"Ew, no. I've done it in the janitor's closet." Sarah's eyes widened as she shook her head.

"With who?" Caroline pulled out her credit card and handed it to the waiter.

"You don't know him and besides, we're talking about Melody."

Berk wiggled his finger. "Shame on you!"

Sarah pushed his finger away as I continued, "But I told you. I'm off Zac. You are right. The situation isn't good for me. I'll be sure to bring my rattiest sweatpants and holey T-shirt for my comfy after-work attire."

"Do you even own ratty sweatpants and a holey T-shirt?" Siobhan asked.

"Of course I don't."

I only hoped I had the actual resolve I forced into my voice. After-hours work meetings were definitely not good for staying away. Especially since Zac and I generally didn't get much actual work done in the hours after everyone else left the office.

"Ohmygod!" Siobhan squealed.

"What?" All four of us looked at her.

"I have to go. Picked up a scoop."

"Do tell." Berk leaned in.

"Well." Siobhan looked around before she said, "You know Cami Jax?"

"The actress?"

"Yeah. Well, my guy just told me she was spotted walking out of a hotel in Midtown holding hands with, get this, another woman."

"No!"

"The horror!" I feigned disgust.

"Yes. And that's not all. The goodbye kiss was apparently one for the record books." She leaned back, obviously pleased with herself.

"Well, ain't that something. Cami Jax is a vagitarian."

I snorted when Siobhan asked, "A vagina-what?"

"Vagitarian," Berk explained. "Carpet muncher." He rolled his eyes when the confusion refused to leave her face and said, "Lesbian."

"Oh. Right. Well, I gotta run. Scoop time!"

Lunch was over and we all stood, said our see-yas, and as we walked away from the restaurant, Berk said, "Hold on."

He ran over to the waiter and handed him a business card.

"What?" He asked as he returned. "Gotta keep my options open. Now, let's go buy you some new sexy comfy clothes because you and I both know you won't wear ratty sweatpants and holey T-shirts in front of Zac."

He knew me so well.

He put his arm around my shoulder as we said goodbye to Caroline and Sarah.

"Just so you know, I support whatever you decide about Zac. Just be careful. All I want is for you to be happy."

"I know." I looped my arm in his and leaned my head on his

shoulder. "When are you going to be my work husband again?"

"I told you, I have a job for you anytime you want to leave."

"But I miss you at *my* work."

"It wasn't for me, doll. You know that. Not enough room for me to spread my wings."

"I know. I just miss hanging with you at work."

"I miss you too, Mel. And I can still be your work husband. We just work at separate places."

"Defeats the purpose of a work husband."

"I know." He patted my hand. He was quiet for a bit before he said, "Maybe it's not a distraction you need."

"Tell me, what *do* I need?"

"Foreplay."

"What?"

"I mean it. You need that slow buildup. Those crazy feelings where you think you're going to lose your mind."

"You've lost your mind."

"I hereby rename the challenge Operation Foreplay." He shot off a text to the girls to let them in on his new idea.

I was going to do my best to refuse Zac's advances but who said I couldn't look good doing it? At least Berk understood. Being single was so much better than being in the wrong relationship.

"And for the record," he whispered, "I think Jared is perfect for you."

"Shut up." I secretly wondered if he was right.

"I'm just saying."

"You're always just saying."

"And I'm always right."

Chapter Five

Monday, just like the week before, I was a jumble of nerves as I did everything in my power to avoid Zac. It wasn't easy. There were a dozen red roses with yet another apology note from him waiting on my desk when I arrived that morning. A week ago, my knees would have buckled at the thought and I would have gone running to his office to accept his apology.

I was a new woman. I would no longer be guided by the immediate needs of my lady parts. I needed to stay the course.

Slow.

Easier said than done, of course.

Moving the flowers off my desk and onto the ledge by the windowsill, I slipped off my new stilettos and distracted myself with spreadsheets and numbers. I was in my glory and didn't notice I'd not only skipped lunch but it was four thirty in the afternoon by the time I stopped to take a break. Reaching in my bottom drawer for a protein bar and a bottle of water, I found, on top of my snacks, a pale blue box complete with a simple white ribbon.

There was no card attached. Needless to say, I ditched the protein bar for a candy bar.

As if it were a bomb, I gingerly placed the box on my desk and studied it. Leaning back in my chair, I stared at the box while I chewed on a pen. It might have been five years since I quit smoking but the oral fixation never fully disappeared.

And was probably the reason I gave such amazing blow jobs.

A knock at my door intruded on my focus. "Come in."

Jenny, my twenty-two-year-old assistant, stood at the door wearing the scarf I'd purchased for her birthday.

"Nice scarf." I glanced up at her before returning my attention to the pale blue alien box on my desk.

"Thanks. I didn't want to bother you earlier. It looked like you were deep in numbers. But I'm leaving a few minutes early today and wanted to give you your messages."

"Great. What are they?"

"You have a noon lunch with the Alonzo account tomorrow, they were just calling to confirm. Berk wanted to let you know he was in the city. Johnson will have the report to you by Wednesday. And Mr. Waterman wanted me to remind you not to forget your promise to stay late and finish the proposal."

"Fine. Thank you. I remember."

"Those flowers are beautiful! Secret admirer?" She rushed over to the window and inhaled the bouquet.

Jenny was one of the most eager assistants I'd ever come across. I handpicked her from a dozen other applicants. When I earned my promotion last year, I was allowed to choose my own assistant and I wanted someone who would make my life easier. She reminded me of me when I was just starting out. She wouldn't be an assistant long and she knew it. After all, I was the one who promised to take her under my wing.

"Yeah. Kind of. Do you know where this"—I the nudged the box with the tip of my chewed-up pen—"came from?"

"No. I don't."

"It was in my drawer." She followed my glance.

"I didn't put it there." She walked back to my desk and sat across from me and eyed the box with interest.

"Then who did?"

"No idea. I only go in your drawer when I restock your protein bars and I haven't done that since last week. Is there a card?" Leaning forward, she inspected the box as well.

"Nope."

"Did you open it?"

"Nope."

"Are you going to?"

"Not sure yet."

"Well, good luck. Do you need anything before I head out? My boyfriend is taking me out to Rocco's for my birthday dinner."

"Yeah?" She had my full attention. Jenny had had the same boyfriend since she was sixteen. My logical brain told me they wouldn't last. My heart didn't say anything. Sometimes I wasn't sure I had one. That isn't true. Zac had mine in his back pocket.

"I think he's going to propose!" she squealed.

I bit my tongue and held my perma-smile in place. I wanted to keep her around and didn't want to rain on her parade. Who was mature enough to get engaged at twenty-two? Hell, I wasn't even mature enough to get my own boyfriend at twenty-nine. I had to borrow one from a married woman.

Almost divorced woman.

I shook the cobwebs away. "Really? Well, if he does, take the day tomorrow. If he doesn't, take the next two."

Her smile was infectious. "You sure?"

"Absolutely. We girls need to stick together."

"You're the best."

"Don't spread that around. I have a reputation," I whispered.

"I won't." She smiled, knowing that the rumors about my being a bitch weren't always true. My favorite was that I walked around sprinkling bitch dust everywhere. As if I had the time.

I did have a reputation. I didn't tolerate bullshit and people who didn't pull their weight. I was a dragon lady to many who worked in the office and I wasn't even thirty yet.

Jenny smoothed out her navy pencil skirt and left me alone with my mystery box.

I picked up the phone and dialed Berk, since I knew he was in the city.

"Hey."

"Hey. You still in the city?"

"Yeah, why? Aren't you working late?"

"I am. I need your expertise for a few."

"I can take a detour. Be there in ten minutes."

I disconnected the call. Rolling my neck to ease the tension, I stood and stretched. I checked the time and figured Zac would expect the team in the conference room around six, so I locked the door, dropped the shades, and contemplated changing into more comfortable clothes. It was really a great perk of working for the company. They didn't expect work attire for late-night meetings and brainstorming. Some people were still more comfortable wearing suits and heels late into the evening. I wasn't one of those people. I mean, I made sure I was constantly put together, but my preference? Naked. Of course, that wouldn't do at the office, so I generally changed into comfortable jeans and a button-down. Besides, I had a point to make. I wasn't dressing up for Zachary Waterman.

I'd decided against changing my clothes when Berk knocked on the door.

"Come in."

He walked over, aviators resting on the bridge of his nose, his hair expertly mussed, and gave me a hug. "Hey there, pretty lady. What was so urgent that you needed me to rush over here at the end of the work day?"

I stepped back and pointed to the box on my desk.

"Who's that from? You look great by the way. Blue really is your color." Picking up the box, he turned it over.

"No idea. No card. I found it in my desk."

Raising his eyebrow, he gave me the look. The look that said I wasn't facing facts. He put the box down and shoved his hands in the pockets of his slim-fit khakis. Tilting his head, he looked at me and sighed. "You know who this is from. Probably from the same person who sent you a dozen red roses."

Taking the card from the bouquet, he read it out loud.

M~ I am so sorry. I was wrong to blow you off. Please accept my apology. ~Z

"Why would he buy me jewelry?" I chewed on my nail until the polish chipped away.

"Wouldn't be the first time." He eyed the watch I wore every day.

I flopped down in the armchair next to the window and looked at the cars below. My fingers reached for the diamond-studded watch I always wore. It was the first gift Zachary had ever given me.

"Did you even open it?"

"No. Not yet."

"What are you waiting for?"

"I don't know. You open it."

"Since when did you become such a pussy?" Berk laughed.

"Every now and then. You should have seen the ridiculous tantrum I pulled for some guitar player named Nick. Care and Sarah call him Nick the Dick."

"Well, I am sure he was an interesting guy. With a nickname like that, how could he not be? Come on, put on your big girl panties and open the damn box."

"I forgot them at home."

"Then you can borrow mine."

"I'd rather go commando."

"Of course you would."

Berk picked the box back up and walked over to be before dropping it in my lap and pulling my thumbnail from my mouth. "You're going to ruin your manicure. It wouldn't do for you to make this messy. Open it. Then return it."

"I guess." I pulled the white ribbon, letting it fall to the floor, and lifted the lid of the box. "Wow."

"What is it?" Berk moved behind me and looked at the necklace over my shoulder. "Holy crap. Either this guy spends money like it's his business—"

"It is his business."

He waved off my interruption. "Or he's got it bad for you, girl!"

I lifted the dainty chain from the box and held the diamond-encrusted musical note in the palm of my hand.

"There's a note!" Berk snatched it and read it out loud. *"For my Melody. ~Z"*

"I can't keep this!"

"Then give it back." He picked up the box and held it out so I could drop the necklace back in.

"I don't want to." Cupping my hands over the pendant, I pulled my hands in close.

"Then keep it." Berk dropped the box back into my lap and walked over to the window and lifted the shades. "You really do have a great view."

"He's married." I chewed my lip and stared at the gift.

"Almost divorced," he said over his shoulder, "as you keep telling us."

"I guess."

"Sweets, I have to run. I get a narb every time I walk in this place." He adjusted his crotch. Very un-Berk-like.

"A narb?" I raised my eyebrows at him.

"A no apparent reason boner."

"You sound like a frat boy."

"Don't tell David." He winked.

"Ahh. Understood. I told you, anytime you want to give notice at Blackwell and Dardston, you have a job here. Even if I have to make one up for you."

"That's because you love me. I'll keep that in mind." He checked his watch. "Really have to go. Meeting David for dinner and I'd rather not walk in with a semi in my pants."

"Yeah? At least your semi is bigger than the hardened disappointment from last guy I banged." I stood and placed the necklace back in the box. "Gonna tell him to shove his superiority up his ass?"

"We'll see. I'm just going to tell him I expect an apology and if he can't take me for who I am, then that's it."

"I hope it works out for you, sweetie." I kissed him on the cheek. "Drinks tomorrow?"

"Yes, it's a must. Murphy's. Seven o'clock. Good luck at your meeting and good luck with the necklace."

Berk left the office and closed the door behind him. Checking the clock I saw I had fifteen minutes before the meeting started. I knew I made the right decision by keeping on my suit. The suit gave me lady balls and I was going to need them if I was going to return Zac's gift.

It was six on the dot when I entered the conference room but there was no one there. Standing at the far end of the large conference table, I was scrolling through the e-mails on my phone to be sure I had the right place and time when Zac walked in.

For a moment, I lost my mind. Wearing dark jeans, he folded up the sleeves of an untucked crisp, white button-down as he approached me with his signature smirk. His dark eyes blazed in the dim light and his hair was damp, which told me he'd just come from the gym shower. The scent of his coconut shampoo wafted toward me as he walked in. It was my favorite smell in the world. A warm heat spread through my center and I thought I'd climax from sheer proximity. I had to take a step back and shake him out of my head.

"Where is everyone?"

"Nice to see you, too. A whole week of avoiding me and all I get is a 'Where is everyone?' That's *not* my usual greeting." Instead of stepping toward me, he sat in one of the leather chairs that surrounded the large oak table and crossed his ankle over his knee. His stare unnerved me. It usually did.

"Well, that's not something we should be discussing on company time." I pulled out my leather portfolio and placed it on the table. Anything to distract me from actually looking at him.

"Oh, right. Company time." I felt like his voice turned to silk and caressed my body. I knew my knees would buckle if I didn't find myself a seat.

I walked around the chair and took up my spot as far from him as I could. I needed space. Distance. I was losing my resolve quickly.

"Did you get the flowers I sent you?"

"Yes. Thank you, they are beautiful. You really didn't have to." I rifled through my briefcase and busied myself with organizing paperwork and legal pads.

"I don't have to do a lot of things. Are you nervous?"

"What?" I sat up straight. He was resting his chin on his hand with his finger curled around his lips. The lips that tasted like cherry lip balm. With the world at his disposal, he relied on something as mundane as drugstore-variety cherry-flavored balm to keep his lips smooth.

Moist.

I was sure if I checked his left pocket, I'd find it.

The sound of my phone hitting the floor echoed in the quiet space.

"Where is everyone else? I thought there was a meeting?"

"There is and by my count, the gang's all here."

"But I thought—"

"Well, my dear Melody, I had to come up with some way to get you to talk to me. You won't take my calls, you won't come to my office when I ask you to. You always send your assistant, Julie—"

"Jenny."

"What?"

"Her name is Jenny."

He waved away my response. "Right. Well, as I was saying, I did what I had to in order to get face time with you. You're lucky I like you. Others may have seen your behavior over the past week as insubordination."

His words hit me like a brick wall. "Insubordination! How dare—"

"Relax. It was a joke."

"You never were very funny." I was losing the battle. I white knuckled the arms of the chair and crossed my ankles to force myself from getting up and walking over to him.

"Maybe not. But you don't really want me for my comedic talent, now do you?"

"You're arrogant." I pretended to be uninterested and examined my chipped manicure, hoping that letting go of the chair wasn't a mistake.

"I am. And you're sexy as hell. Look at you over there. You aren't wearing your usual evening meeting attire. Do you want me to find out what's under that skirt? I'd bet you a thousand bucks that you're having a hard time not touching me right now."

"I'd say you owe me a thousand bucks. And for the record"—I borrowed Berk's line—"I am wearing my big girl panties."

"I'd love to rip those off with my teeth."

"And I'd love it if you gave me that thousand dollars."

"Let's put this to the test, shall we?" Casually, he stood, walked to the other side of the table, and pulled out the seat next to me. "I'm going to touch you and I would like to see if you can resist. Prove to me that you don't want to put your hands all over me."

"Zac—"

"If you can resist, then I'll leave you alone. If you can't, well then, let's hope this table is sturdy." He pushed on the top of the table.

Again with the smirk. Without his even me touching me, my skin tingled and I felt warm. The familiarity of his presence sent my groin into overdrive. I was already wet, an automatic reaction to what I knew he could accomplish with the mouth that held that sexy smirk in place.

As much as I told myself I didn't want him, I knew I did. And I knew what was about to happen. I wouldn't fight it because I didn't want to.

While running his fingers along the top of my hand he asked, "Is this okay?"

I could only nod.

Reaching under the table, he grabbed my leg and lifted my foot into his lap.

"New shoes?"

"No."

"Should we keep them on?"

"You'd like that wouldn't you?"

He took off the shoe and tossed it aside before kneading his thumbs into the ball of my foot.

My head fell back but I quickly righted it and plastered what I hoped was a stoic, uninterested look on my face. In truth, I was about five minutes from my "O" face. With Zac it was only a matter of time. Never an if, always a when.

His hands slowly moved up my calf, slowly kneading the muscles that were suddenly very tense. He bit his lower lip when I let out a small moan. He knew he was getting to me.

Damn him.

Damn me.

Jesus, someone open a window.

Still, I kept my hands to myself. But I was wavering. Zachary Waterman may just very well have been my kryptonite.

"Your skin is so soft. Do you like this? The way I am touching you?" His voice was barely a whisper.

"It's, it's…fine."

"Fine? Fine won't do." He slid his hands up my skirt and massaged my thigh. "Is this *fine*?"

I said nothing but closed my eyes and let out a long breath.

I knew he could feel the moisture between my legs. I knew he knew I was ready and wouldn't be able to hold out much longer. By the strain in the fabric of his pants, he was more than ready. But still he continued along with his game by quickly removing his hands from under my skirt and standing behind me. He wrapped my hair in his hand and gently tugged before whispering in my ear, "Are you still just *fine*?"

"Zachary, we can't do this."

He let go of my hair, spun my chair around, and knelt down to my eye level. "We can."

"But you're marr—"

He placed his fingers on my lips. "Tell me you don't want me and I'll walk away. I won't want to but I'll do it because you want me to. Jesus, Mel. I'm falling in love with you. You can't see that?"

"You're what?" My lips were still pressed on his finger.

"You heard me. Now tell me you don't want this and I'll walk away, no strings." He leaned back on his heels.

My heart beat so hard I could swear it was the only sound I could hear. *He loved me?*

I always said I didn't want to be a relationship girl.

I always said I wasn't girlfriend material.

I always said I didn't want to be bothered.

I always lied.

I couldn't respond with words. Instead, I leaned forward and began unbuttoning his shirt. He didn't make a move to stop me, help me. He just sat back on his heels, eyes locked with mine. He was waiting for me to say the words back. Words I'd never said before. Words that had me running for the hills whenever they were uttered in my direction. Words that scared the living shit out of me. And he wanted me to say them.

Instead, I pushed my hands into his open shirt, feeling the tight muscles of his chest before slowly removing the shirt from his broad shoulders.

"Melody." He grabbed my hands and held them together in my lap, his eyes searching mine.

"Touch me." I finally said before leaning in and nipping his bottom lip between my teeth.

Zac needed no more prodding as his hand moved the back of my head and pulled me in closer, his mouth taking mine. His tongue found its way inside my mouth and I closed my lips around it, sucking until he moaned. He pulled me to his lap, securing my legs on either side of him.

Tugging the sleeves of his shirt until I tossed it to the floor, I paused and took him in. His body never ceased to amaze me. His other hand pushed my skirt up higher on my thigh before slipping between my legs. His fingers trailed along my inner thighs before he slid my panties over. Slowly, he allowed a finger to explore inside me as his thumb rubbed me softly. I closed my eyes, ready for the explosion.

"Look at me. Eyes on me." He pulled my chin until our eyes met. "I love watching your eyes when you come."

He eased in a second finger, dipping in slowly before the muscles in his forearms tightened and he moved faster, harder.

I held on to the arms of the chair, moving my hips to meet his thrusts.

"Now, Melody."

Heat spread and I could feel the nerves firing just beneath my skin, spreading out before contracting in a tight pleasurable ball of release.

"Now."

I let the ball tighten, tighten, until I cried out.

"Zac!" The wave pounded me until I was dizzy, spent.

Shifting his weight, he lifted me off the chair and set me on the table, pushing my skirt up to my waist. He fumbled with the buttons on my blouse as I frantically undid his belt, unzipped his pants, and pushed them down over his ass. He didn't waste time undoing my bra, instead tugging on it until my breasts were freed from the lacy fabric.

"Melody." He breathed into me.

"I want you inside me."

I pulled him out of his boxer briefs, slowly stroking his length. It was beautiful.

"Not yet. I want to see you." He hooked his thumbs inside my panties and eased them off. Widening my legs, he knelt down. "I want to taste you." His tongue flicked my center and I let out a sharp breath.

Using his fingers to open me further, he flattened his tongue and licked me from bottom to top. "Jesus, Mel. You taste amazing."

His tongue pressed hard against me between long, soft licks as his fingers pushed in and his teeth scraped ever so slightly. Heat spread through me lazily, as if in on his secret desire to torture me and make me beg for it. A slow burn began in my belly and spread to my thighs; my nose tingled and my toes curled. A scream formed in my chest but before it could escape, he lifted his head and smiled before standing, leaning over me and biting my bottom lip between his teeth. Shaking from being denied a release, I wrapped my arms around his neck and pulled myself up.

I locked my legs around his waist and pulled him into me. His hand shifted downward and he grabbed his cock and guided it inside me. Dropping his head, he pressed his face into my neck as I gasped at the feeling of him. There was nothing in the world as amazing as that first thrust. He knew it. I knew it. And we held steady for a moment to revel in it before his hands gripped my ass and he pulled me into each frenzied thrust.

Zac dipped his head to my breast and teased each nipple with his teeth. I ran my hands down his back. I could feel my orgasm build slowly throughout my body.

We were fast, hungry, needy. There were no distractions in the conference room. Just me. Just Zac. Us. The way I'd grown to crave. A week spent apart felt like years. Each thrust grew harder and faster, each breath quicker, each moan louder. The slow burn became wild fire that consumed me, consumed him. With one last perfectly timed thrust, everything inside me tightened around him until we both cried out in pleasure and he fell on top of me.

Tangled together in a sweaty mess of lust and satisfaction, neither of us said a word. Instead, Zac pulled me toward him as he sat in the chair. I curled up in his lap as he stroked my hair and I nuzzled into his chest. Neither of us was quick to catch our breath. Closing my eyes to reality, I thought about what life would be like if he were mine. Truly mine. I didn't like sharing and I didn't like being the other woman. I realized that he may have said words out loud that I didn't have the guts to say but, deep down, maybe I felt them.

Maybe.

I felt him lean down as he gripped me tighter. I kept my eyes closed, though I knew he was fiddling with something.

He shifted in his seat and pushed my hair away from my neck. My skin tingled as I felt the necklace drape in front of me. He closed the link and let my hair fall back down. Looking down, I fingered the pendant of the necklace I had intended to give back. His finger tilted my chin toward him and he brushed his lips across mine.

"My Melody."

"Your Melody."

I only wished it were true.

Chapter Six

I strolled into the morning meeting wearing a kick-ass pair of pumps and a smile on my face and snickered when I noticed that Elaine, the resident know-it-all, placed her bagel on the table in the very spot that had supported my naked ass the night before.

Suddenly the memories became very real as Zac walked into the room, ready to start the meeting. A brief flicker of heat passed between us; I had to take a deep breath and remind my lady bits that it was not the time to get worked into a frenzy. He took off his coat and hung it on the back of his chair like he always did before sitting down. Pulling his phone out of his pocket, he typed something before shutting it off and placing it on the table. The rest of us followed suit. As I was shutting down my phone, I noticed a text from him. I looked up and nodded. Starting tomorrow night, I'd be spending the rest of the week at his place. Hopefully in bed. With chocolate sauce and whipped cream.

Since the information he was going over was something I'd already been privy to, I let my mind wander a bit. The way he walked, with his shoulders back, enhanced his powerful presence. I noticed, once again, that the female members of the meeting hung on his every word, watched his every move. They all wanted to be noticed. I could almost see the pheromones wafting toward him.

Every man in the room looked on with awe. They all wanted to be him.

And only I knew what it was like to feel him. Against me. On top of me. Underneath me. Inside me.

Down, girl.

* * *

By six o'clock, I was on the train, coffee in hand, heading home completely fried from the massive amounts of work I'd powered through. I was afraid that if I didn't keep busy, I'd have to start rubbing ice cubes all over my skin. I was still that worked up over Zac. The man was a real and true actual God of Sex.

Lord of the Orgasm.

Sheriff of the Sweet Spot.

General of the G-Spot.

I really needed a new hobby.

My stomach rumbled and the man sitting next to me looked over. I smiled as sweetly as I could while mentally telling him to stop looking at my boobs.

Once again, I'd forgotten to eat and my work clothes were starting to notice. Of course, I loved dropping a few pounds, but not at the expense of my wardrobe, which took me years to collect and refine. I knew I'd have to make a visit to the tailor sooner rather than later if I didn't slow down and take a break once in a while.

Rummaging through my purse, I found my phone and realized I'd totally forgotten to turn it back on since the morning meeting. When I powered it on, text messages poured in. One, from Sarah, just said *call me now.*

She picked up on the first ring.

"Hey."

"Hey. Where have you been? I've been trying to call you. Your assistant said you were busy, your phone went right to voice mail—"

"Slow down. Did you leave a message?" I gulped my coffee.

"No. Just the text. But anyway, what are you doing?"

"Riding the train. I should be home in fifteen. Why? What's up?"

"Cockroaches."

I snickered. "You said cock."

"Nice. I mean I have cockroaches."

"Ew and huh?" I shuddered. Apartment living meant cockroaches and mice. Neither of which I've had the pleasure of dealing with.

"My apartment is infested with them."

"Fucking gross."

"Yeah, tell me about it. Stupid neighbor went away on vacation and left his half-filled garbage sitting in the kitchen like a damned roach motel vacancy sign. Anyway, I am going to stay at Drew's for the next week while the exterminators take care of it but I need a teeny tiny favor."

"Anything."

"I need a place for my brother to crash."

"Jared?"

"Yeah. I need a place for him to stay until we can get back in the apartment."

"My place?"

"Drew has only one bedroom."

"*I* have only one bedroom."

"Right, but I'd rather not have my brother within earshot of me banging Drew."

"Or see any of your sex toys hidden throughout the house."

"Shit. I forgot about those. So what do you think?"

"About him staying at my place?"

"Yeah. Is that okay?"

I couldn't think of one reason why it wouldn't be. Other than the fact that I really didn't want a roommate, even temporarily. "Sure. He can sleep on the couch. And he better not bring any redheads over. I will not listen to him get his bow chicka bow wow on."

"Excellent! Thank you so much! I already gave him the key. He's been there since noon."

"Noon?"

"Yeah. You didn't answer the text and I was stuck. That's okay, right?"

I rolled my shoulders to relieve the tension. "Yeah. Sure. It's just a week, right?" The last thing I really wanted was some unemployed, snarky, know-it-all twenty-six-year-old fresh off the relationship wagon in my apartment. Sarah was really lucky I liked her.

I walked the few blocks from the train station to my apartment and checked my watch. I'd barely taken it off since Zac gave it to me at Christmas. I had just enough time to change and meet everyone at Murphy's.

Kicking off my heels and looking around the apartment I saw there was no noticeable evidence of a squatter. I thought maybe Jared wasn't there.

And then I saw the pyramid of beer cans stacked on the kitchen counter.

You have got to be kidding me.

Fucking frat boy reject.

Remnants of a peanut butter and jelly sandwich stuck to my counter. I didn't even own peanut butter and jelly let alone the starchy white bread it was slathered on.

"Jesus! I didn't know you'd come home." I heard him shout and I screamed, bumping into the aluminum pyramid and knocking the cans to the tiled floor. "What's up blondie?" He smiled.

Goddamn that smile.

"Holy shit! You're naked!" I'd morphed into Captain Obvious as I couldn't help but stare at the obviously grown and well taken care of man in my living room. I knew he wasn't the skinny, annoying boy I last saw eight years ago. I knew he'd become a total hottie. Arrogant and brash but hot nonetheless. But at that moment, standing in front of me, he was all man. His dark hair was wet and messy but his blue eyes looked right through me. And his cock? Half mast. And fabulous.

He looked down and smiled. "I guess I am."

"But you're naked. In my living room." I pointed at him with one hand covering my mouth, attempting to stifle a stutter.

"And you're fully clothed. In the kitchen." He made no move to cover himself and looked to be enjoying the exchange. "No need to point, you know. You'll give me a complex."

"But this is my apartment."

"Thanks, by the way, for letting me stay here. It's a real nice place. Oh, I used your shower. Hope you don't mind. That is one grade A showerhead you have in there." He winked. "And that shampoo you have smells fantastic. What is that? Lavender?"

I nodded and threw him a kitchen towel. Not that I didn't want to look because, God help me, it was a sight to see. But it felt weird looking at my best friend's brother. Even if his naked body gave me lady wood.

He caught the towel and looked at me, one eyebrow cocked, and said, "Not sure this is going to do it." He winked and tossed the towel back to me as he walked away, giving me a full view of his backside. "We're supposed to be at Murphy's by seven."

I caught myself staring at his immaculately sculpted ass before pulling myself back to reality. "You're going?" I was still trying to wrap my head around all the lean lines and perfectly hard abs of *my best friend's brother.*

Breathe, Melody. And tell your vagina to heel.

"Well, yeah. Is that okay?"

"Of course. Why wouldn't it be?" I yelled back.

"I don't know, you just looked a little taken aback."

"I wasn't taken aback. I was a bit disturbed by the beer can pyramid and smear of peanut butter on my counter."

"Then you looked like you'd never seen a naked man before."

I had to remind myself that I'd seen plenty of naked men in my almost thirty years. And I decided to remind him. "I've seen plenty of naked men."

"Have you now?" He sauntered into the room as he pulled a plain white T-shirt over his head. "How many is plenty?"

Jared reached around me, opened the refrigerator door, and pulled out a beer. I stood, my four-inch heels rooted to the floor as contact with him commanded my nipples to attention. A quite noticeable reaction considering I was wearing a thin silk blouse and an even thinner lace bra.

"That is none of your business."

His eyes slowly moved from my chest to my face. "I figure since we're going to be roomies, we could, you know, *share*." I don't know if he injected sexiness into his voice on purpose or if it was part of his makeup.

"Roomies! Really. You'll be gone in a week."

"Then we're going to have to make it fair." He sipped on his beer. "You saw me naked. Now I get to see you."

This wasn't happening. Sarah's brother was not hitting on me. I was not mentally undressing him. I did not have the female version of a throbber pounding in my panties. Sweat slipped between my breasts and I forced a laugh that came out sad and weak before I hurried to my room and slammed the door.

For the first time ever, a man had me tongue-tied and I didn't like it. I dressed quickly and reapplied my lipstick before heading to the door. He was sitting at the counter finishing his beer, no sign of the earlier mess.

"Ready?"

"You think?" I knew I sounded bitchy but I didn't know what else to do.

My tone didn't seem to bother him. "Excellent. Let's go." He held the door open and motioned for me to walk through.

We didn't speak much the few blocks to the bar and that was fine with me. I was preoccupied with the suggestive text messages Zac was sending anyway.

I giggled at one particularly naughty text and Jared said, "Still thinking about me naked?"

I dropped my phone and felt my ears heat up. "You wish."

We both knelt down to grab the phone. I snatched my hand away when he touched me.

"It's okay if you were, you know." He winked.

"I wasn't."

"If you say so." He handed me the phone and I stuffed it in my purse.

"I wasn't." I reiterated as he held the door to the bar open for me.

"I believe you."

"Whatever." I rolled my eyes.

"We can make out if you want. Try to dissolve all this pent-up sexual tension between us."

"There is no sexual tension!" I whispered fiercely and stalked to the back of the bar while Jared made a pit stop to grab a beer.

Berk was sitting at the table staring at his phone.

"Hey." I plopped into the chair next to him and laid my head on his shoulder.

"Hey yourself. Drink this." He handed me a shot glass. I noticed there were four more of the same sitting in front of him.

I tossed it back and licked my lips. "What was that?"

"A Cock-Sucking Cowboy. Good, right?"

"Yes, good. But a cock-sucking cowboy wouldn't do much for me." I crossed my arms over my chest and pouted.

"What's the matter? Things didn't go well with Zac?" He put his phone on the table and patted my head.

"Everything with Zac is fine. It's going to be fine."

"So you didn't give back the necklace." He fingered it out from under my shirt.

"No." I blew a lock of hair out of my eye.

"You kept the necklace and had sex."

"Yep." I buried my face in his neck.

"Sex with Zac usually puts you in a good mood. What's wrong, then?"

Jared walked up and stuck out his hand. "Hey. Berk, right?"

Berk raised his eyebrows and looked at him like he was lunch before giving me the side eye and letting out a slow whistle. "Yeah. Here." He slid a drink across the table. "Have a shot."

"Thanks." He downed the shot and licked his lips. Berk was entirely too entranced but Jared didn't seem to notice. "So where is everyone? My sister said everyone would be here tonight." Jared pulled out a chair next to me and sat down. He smelled like my lavender shampoo. Guaranteed I'll never smell it again without seeing him naked. With a semi.

Damn.

"They'll be here soon." Berk looked at me and tilted his head. "So, I didn't get to talk to you much yet. You moved back here from Georgia?"

"Yeah. I have a job interview coming up on Monday. Thought I'd hang out a bit before then."

"A job interview for what?"

"That was fast," I added.

"Financial. I had a phone interview when I was in Georgia. They called me back this afternoon. Now I get to meet with the big man himself. Something Waterman." He laughed. "I should probably look him up and remind myself of who he is before I show up looking like an ass, right?"

"*Zachary* Waterman?" My stomach dropped.

"Yeah, that's it." He snapped his fingers. "You heard of him?" Jared drained the rest of his beer.

"I have. He's my boss."

"Ain't that something. Small fucking world, huh? Maybe we'll be roomies and work buddies."

"It sure is something." I stared in shock and Berk leaned back to watch him walk away.

"Roomies? Spill." Berk prodded me with his elbow.

"You have got to be fucking kidding me. First I see him naked—"

"Wait, what?"

"Long story."

"What the hell, Melody? You bang the most fuckable man in finance *and* you are rooming with Jared? And a naked Jared, at that."

"Why didn't Sarah tell me?"

"Maybe she didn't know."

"She knew. How could she not know?"

"He said he just found out this afternoon. Whatever." Berk sipped his glass of wine. "He is gorgeous. That hair, how it kind of looks like he just rolled out of bed. Why didn't I know she had a hot brother?"

"No one's seen him in eight years. And those eight years were really, *really* good to him." I leaned back in my chair to get another peek at him across the room.

"How's he look naked?"

"You don't want to know."

"Why not?"

"It's too good to describe."

"I'll tell you one thing, sweetheart, that right there"—he pointed to Jared leaning against the bar, his ass perfectly defined through his jeans—"is just the distraction you need to forget about Zac. And if the interview doesn't work out, I can always find him something at my place." Berk wiggled his eyebrows.

Son of a bitch.

Chapter Seven

I nearly attacked Sarah when she arrived with Drew in tow. Grabbing her arm, I steered her toward the bathroom as Drew diverted and headed toward the bar. On the way, I pulled Caroline away from her kiss with Brian. Kissing could wait. If anyone was going to take my side, it was Caroline.

"Why didn't you tell me your brother had an interview with Zac?"

"Jared has an interview with Zac?" Caroline asked.

"Zac who?" Sarah pushed her sunglasses to the top of her head.

"Zac who do you think?"

"Zac, Zac. Melody's Zac," Caroline explained for me, since I was about to tear out my eyelashes.

"Oh. That Zac," Sarah said slowly, either completely unaware of my issue or playing stupid.

"Yeah, that Zac. Why didn't you tell me?" I felt like we were playing a game of who could say his name more.

"I didn't know. His move back here was pretty sudden and we

didn't get into specifics other than he had some interviews lined up here. Is that a problem?"

"No, it's not a problem. I just felt like I was a bit blindsided."

"Why would it matter?" I thought Caroline was on my side.

I laughed, hoping to brush away any anxiety I felt about it. "It doesn't matter. I just could have, well, you know. I could have helped him is all."

"Well, if he's meeting with your boss, it doesn't look like he needs any help." Caroline, God bless her, really was trying to be helpful.

"What's going on?" Sarah leaned in and tried to read my face.

"Hey sis!" Jared interrupted us before she could read the weirdness that was, without a doubt, etched all over my face. "Roomie." He nodded toward me as he draped his arm around her shoulders.

"Hey you! You all moved in?" She reached up to hug him, since he towered over her by at least a foot.

"Yep." Jared winked at me and I lost the ability to speak. "Melody is very welcoming."

"Is she now?" Sarah pointed the evil eye in my direction. Sweat dripped between my boobs.

"Of course. He's more than welcome to sleep on the couch. And I better not find any rogue strands of red hair on my sofa cushions."

"You got a problem with red?" he asked.

"Of course not, sweetie." I gave him a fake smile. *What the fuck is wrong with me?*

He stared at me a minute before saying, "Anyway, it's a very comfortable couch." Again with the wink. It certainly wasn't helping, since Sarah continued to stare at me with a look that, I'm sure, was intended to melt my face off.

Caroline must've felt the tension and attempted to diffuse it.

"That it is. Of course it will only be for a week, so don't get too comfortable."

"I didn't get a chance to talk to you much the other day. You haven't changed a bit." The traitor returned his hug.

"Come on, let's go have a drink." She grabbed Sarah's arm and pulled her away toward the table. Sarah looked over her shoulder and whispered, "It's my *brother*."

I was left standing awkwardly with Jared. "So, it's pretty obvious my sister thinks something went on between us."

"Wonder why she thinks that, Winky?" I really needed to stop looking at him.

He laughed. "Winky?"

"Yeah, Winky. What the hell is up with that? You have something in your eye?"

"Actually, yeah. My contact lens is all folded up. Be right back."

I felt the weight of his hand pat me on the back before he headed into the men's room.

"Did you just pat me on the back like I'm one of your buddies?"

He stopped in his tracks and turned, smirking. "Yeah. Roommates are buddies right? And, of course, you ass is ten times better than the last buddy I roomed with. Although most of my buddies don't picture me naked every time they close their eyes. "

"I do not—" My protest was cut off by his laugh as he walked away. "Jerk," I whispered to myself.

Caroline snuck up behind me. "Who's a jerk?"

"No one. Come on, let's get a drink."

"Danny's here." She pointed.

"Oh yeah?" I turned around and smiled when I saw his easy brown eyes and stubbled face as he talked to Brian.

We sat at the bar since I really didn't feel all that social.

"Hey babe! Long time no see!" Danny, a close friend of Brian and Berk, stood and pulled me into a hug before turning to Caroline. Danny and I had fooled around once or twice; it never went much further, but he's fun and we have such similar personalities that it's like we've known each other longer than six months.

"Haven't seen you in forever," I said as I climbed onto the stool next to him. Caroline excused herself to go to the bathroom.

"I know. Work has me traveling all over the place." He took a sip of his beer. "So, what's been going on?"

"Not much."

"What's wrong? Come on. Give it to me. " Danny tucked a curl behind my ear and tipped my chin so he could look me in the eye. He was always really good about eye contact during conversations. Too bad neither of us wanted anything more than friendship from each other.

"Let's see. My mom is on my ass about settling down. I had sex with Zac and am staying at his place this week, Sarah's brother is staying at my house for the next week, and I saw him naked."

"Wait, what?" He laughed easily.

"You heard me."

"Okay. Let's break this down. First, your mom. She is always giving you a hard time. Since when does that bother you?"

"I don't know. It's just been grating on my nerves lately." I tore my drink napkin into pieces.

"I think that issue is a lengthier conversation than we have time for. How about dinner on Friday?"

"Can't. Sleeping at Zac's."

"Which brings us to number two. I thought you gave up Zac. I'm not really a fan of how he treats you."

"And how does he treat me?"

"Like a fucking sex toy."

"I guess." I signaled Brian to bring over two shots of whatever.

"Just think about it. He isn't good for you. Now, number three. Sarah's brother."

I moaned and threw my head back as I drank the ounce of whiskey with lime. "Sarah's apartment is full of roaches. Her brother moved back from Georgia. He needed a place to stay. She volunteered my place."

"That doesn't explain how you saw him naked."

"Seems as though he likes to walk around naked after he showers."

"Who doesn't? Can't really fault him for that."

"Right? Anyway, I came home from work, saw his pyramid of beer cans on the counter—"

"No."

"Yes. And he walked into the living room. Naked as a newborn."

"I bet he was surprised." Danny grabbed the bottle Brian left and refilled the shot glasses.

"Smug is more like it. And half hard. He smirked. And he keeps winking at me in front of Sarah."

"Bet she loves that."

"Really. But enough about my shit." I clinked his shot glass with mine. "What's new with you? I mean, gosh, I haven't seen you in like forever! Anything new with what's her name?"

"Allison? Nope. Haven't called her. She's too much of a princess. But I do have other news."

"Yeah? What? You're madly in love with me and you're going

to take me away to an island in the Caribbean?" I laughed at the thought.

"Of course I love you. You're you. But that's not it. I was offered a promotion."

"A promotion? Good for you! Congratulations." I held up my hand to high-five him but he didn't return the gesture.

"Thanks. The thing is, well, it's not in New York."

"Oh no. You're being relocated to Jersey again?" I laughed as Brian set two beers in front of us.

"Not exactly."

"Where?" I couldn't believe he was leaving.

"California. I called Ryan. I'll stay with him while I find a place."

"How is Ryan?"

"He's doing well. Got some part in a movie or something. But anyway, I have to fly out Sunday night. I'm taking the red-eye. That's why I thought we could have dinner Friday. I have a few meetings before I come back here, I'll look for my own place. I officially move out there in two weeks."

"Two weeks? That's like, in fourteen days!" Why did I suddenly feel like everyone else was moving forward in their lives and I was still stuck in park?

"I have to get out there. Heading up a new division."

"That's great, Danny. You are going to take California by storm!"

"Melody, it's a great opportunity. And I'll still fly back and visit. You'll fly out and I'll show you around."

"Honestly, it sounds awesome." I smiled but didn't feel it. I wanted something to be excited about. Something new. The newest, most exciting thing that had happened to me was seeing Jared naked. "Have you told anyone else yet?"

"Not yet."

I watched as Brian made his way down to our end of the bar. "Now's your chance."

I winked and kissed Danny on the cheek before excusing myself. I suddenly needed air.

I stepped out the back into the alley and breathed in deeply. I barely noticed the few small tears that fell and sat down, leaning against the cool brick. I have no idea how long I sat there trying to figure out what was happening in my life that had my panties suddenly in a bunch. Something wasn't clicking. Something wasn't allowing me move out of the tiny box I'd fit myself into. I was barely aware of someone handing me a tissue and sitting on the ground next to me.

"Thanks." I wiped the snot from my upper lip.

"Are you crying because your friend is moving?" Jared spoke softly.

"That would be silly, now wouldn't it? I'm not crying because he's moving. I'm happy for him."

"I kind of think maybe you're not happy for him. Or at least not happy about something."

"You don't know me well enough to kind of think anything." I huffed.

"I kind of think I do, actually."

I kind of thought his voice was sexy.

"What are you, a shrink?"

"Nope. I just call things like I see them."

"Great."

Rifling through my purse, I found my compact and was disheartened to see the mess that was reflected back. I slicked on my favorite lip gloss anyway and stood, hiking my purse over my shoulder.

"You look great, you know. I was too busy busting your chops to tell you earlier."

"Thanks. You're sweet." I half smiled.

"And, uh, thanks for letting me stay at your place."

"You're welcome." I smiled. "Look, I'm going home. Will you tell everyone else I'm fine? I'm just tired and have to get up early for work tomorrow."

"Sure you don't need some company? We could maybe hang out or something. Watch a movie."

I laughed. "Wouldn't want to give your sister the wrong idea."

"Sarah? She knows I'm a grown-up. Besides, my offer of company won't *necessarily* end up with us rolling around naked."

I couldn't tell if he was hitting on me or just being nice.

Then again, rolling around naked with him wouldn't be the worst thing.

Stop. Best friend's brother.

"Won't necessarily, huh?"

"I can't promise you'd be able to keep your hands off me."

"My hands, what?" I rubbed my temples and gathered myself. "Whatever. Forget it. I'm going home. And we can put that rolling around naked under the heading of never. But thanks."

"Well, *I* never say never." The corner of his mouth crooked up into a panty-dropping smirk that yanked the rolling around naked back into the realm of possibility. "Like I'm sure if I asked you out to dinner, you'd probably say no but I'm sure you'd come around eventually."

"Awfully sure of yourself." I tilted my head and took him in.

"I like what I like."

"And you're saying you like me?" I stepped closer to him and smelled my lavender shampoo as a small breeze swirled through the alley.

"Maybe. And maybe you like me."

"Hmm." I stepped back. "Maybe."

"So you'll go out to dinner with me?"

I contemplated him, then contemplated the pit that grew in my stomach whenever I thought about Zac lately. "Maybe."

"Maybe is not no."

I laughed. "Maybe is most definitely not no. See you later."

He reached out and grabbed my hand before letting go quickly. "You sure you don't need me to walk you home?"

"No, you stay here. Have fun." I straightened his collar.

"You going to be okay?"

"I'm good." I plastered the biggest smile I could muster. "I'll be fine. No biggie. You still have your key?"

"Yep." He patted the pocket of his well-fitting jeans.

I turned and started toward my apartment. "Hey," I shouted over my shoulder.

"What?" He stopped.

"No redheads!"

"Wouldn't dream of it. Besides, I'm partial to blondes." He winked and retreated into the bar.

An hour later, there was a knock at my door.

"Did you lose your key?" I opened it dramatically.

"I don't have a key."

Caroline.

"What's going on, doll face?" She stepped into my apartment and walked to the kitchen to grab a couple of beers.

"Nothing. Why?"

"I don't know. You left."

"You left, too." I gestured toward her.

"True. Berk's all annoyed that Danny told you before he told them about the move. He says some sort of man code dictates that he should have told them first." She rolled her eyes.

"Bros before hos?"

"If you say so." She shrugged. "But that's not why I'm here."

"No?"

"No. Something is going on with you." She stated and handed me a bottle of Yuengling.

I flopped onto the couch. "I know. I know."

"Spill."

"I think I'm stuck."

"Stuck?" She eyed me over the top of her beer.

"Stuck. Not moving. Not going anywhere. Not excited about anything." I stood and paced. "I mean, look at you. You and Brian moved in together. Sarah and Drew are doing so great. Berk has a steady boyfriend. Danny is moving up at his job and even Jared moved to another state! New! Exciting! And here I am the same plain old Melody doing her normal, everyday shit. When is it my turn to be excited?"

"Zac doesn't excite you?" She said it as if it were a question but it hit me like a statement.

"Care, he's married." And for the first time, the implications of the scenario dawned on me.

"He *is* married. This is not new information."

"I should tell him that I can't do this anymore unless he gets a divorce."

"I think that's a conversation you should have had a long time ago."

I turned and looked at her. "I think you're right." I drained the last of my beer. "Thanks, Care."

"Anytime. Bitches gotta stick together." She stood and pulled me into a bear hug.

"Truer words, doll face."

"Okay." She finished her beer, too. "I'm going. Make this couch up for Jared before he comes back and has no other choice than to slide into bed next to you."

"He asked me out to dinner."

"What did you say?"

"Maybe."

"Maybe's not no."

"That's what he said. Sarah would kill me."

"Oh, I don't know."

"Not going to happen."

"We'll see." Her laugh followed her down the hall to the elevator.

Chapter Eight

I went to bed before Jared came home and when I woke to get ready for work, he was still snoring on the couch. I packed my gym bag and a small overnight bag and headed out, but not before leaving him a note letting him know I might not be home until Sunday morning. That would all depend on how Zac took my ultimatum.

After my forty-five-minute run, I rushed through my shower and dressed as quickly as I could. I wanted to call Caroline before she left for work to thank her again for the talk. The call went right to voice mail and I ended up leaving a lengthy message detailing ten reasons she was one of the best people on the planet.

The workday went quickly and I could think of nothing other than the fact that I was either going to spend the next few days with Zac or end it all together. Either option didn't sit well in my stomach.

* * *

Zac mentioned, "We're taking Friday off," as he helped me out of the car.

"We are?"

"I put it on both our calendars. I think"—he traced his finger along my cleavage—"we will have more important things to do with our time."

"Why not take off tomorrow, too?" I whispered. His presence was clouding my head and I hadn't yet broached the ultimatum I'd worked out so perfectly in my head the night before.

"Let's see how tired we are in the morning." Zac wiggled his eyebrows and held open the door of the restaurant.

Dinner couldn't end fast enough and he and I were on each other the second we got back in the car. He removed his mouth from my chest long enough to tell the driver to bring us back to his place.

I slipped my hand in his pants, gripped his cock, and rubbed my thumb softly over the head. He unbuttoned my shirt and pushed his hand underneath the fabric of my bra, using his fingers to pinch and twist my nipples before he placed his hand on the back of my head and slowly eased me onto his lap.

As I ran my tongue across his stomach and undid his pants, he cursed softly under his breath and told the driver to hurry.

"I'm going to come." He fisted my hair as my head bobbed up and down in his lap.

I pushed my face into his lap until I was deep enough to feel him in the back of my throat. He came the second his driver pulled up to the apartment building.

"Let's go." His voice was gruff as he zipped his pants and buckled his belt; he all but shoved me out of the car by my ass.

"Thanks, Marco." He two-finger saluted his driver, who was, by that time, used to the damage Zac and I did to each other in the back of that car. What could I say? When it came to Zac I had no shame.

"My bags—" I turned back toward the car.

"Don't worry about the bags. Right now, I want you to focus on nothing but me."

The doorman opened the door in time for Zac to pull me through without slowing down. We didn't have to wait for the elevator, either.

"Excuse us, please," Zac said to the man who worked the elevators after he turned the key and hit the button for the penthouse. By the time the doors slid shut, Zac's hand was at my throat, pinning me against the wall. I gasped at the pressure but didn't fight him. He undid my pants, wedged my legs apart with his knee, and shoved his hand deep inside my panties. He worked furiously at my clit before his fingers found their way inside me.

"Zac!" I called out his name as he crushed his mouth on mine. I could feel the familiar rise of heat begin in my stomach and spread to my thighs; my fingers and toes tingled with anticipation.

"I love to hear you come," he whispered in my ear. "It's my favorite sound."

My knees buckled as he tore at the buttons on my shirt and crashed his mouth on my nipple and bit down. My orgasm hit me in waves and I soaked through my panties. When he retrieved his hand and sucked his fingers, my eyes rolled back in my head and he caught me as I lost my balance. My head spun and the only word I could get out was "More."

"Absofuckinglutely." He nipped my bottom lip.

The doors of the elevator slid open to his foyer and he picked me up, pulling my legs around his waist and carrying me through the apartment and upstairs to his bedroom. He dropped me on the bed. "You're wearing too many clothes." He stood, not taking his eyes off me while he slowly unbuttoned his shirt and let it fall to the floor. Grabbing my legs, he pulled me closer to him, leaned down, and unbuttoned my shirt, licking my chest and stomach as he did. With my shirt splayed open, he tugged off my pants and panties, discarding them in a heap next to his shirt. I unhooked my bra and tossed it across the room.

"Now you're the one wearing too many clothes." I ran my hand down my body and began rubbing myself between my legs.

"I want to watch." He backed up, pulled the chair from the window and placed it at the foot of the bed, and settled in with his legs spread, his elbows on the arms and his hazel eyes on me. His hands tapped the fabric lightly and a small smile spread across his face. "Please proceed."

I placed one foot on each of his knees and teased my nipples before placing a finger in my mouth and sucking hard. A string of saliva followed my hand down my stomach. Spreading my legs wide, I worked myself with my other hand. He began massaging my feet and I could see his pants were straining with excitement. I inserted one finger and moved it slowly in and out while I kept eye contact.

"Faster."

I did as I was told and once again found myself on the edge of insanity. I watched as he gripped himself and joined my pace. Without warning, he grabbed my legs and pulled me off the bed onto his lap.

"Now slow."

With my knees settled in on either side of him, he slid easily inside me. Eyes locked on his, a small moan escaped my mouth before he took my mouth with his. There was nowhere else I wanted to be and when he whispered that he loved me I almost said it back.

I'd all but lost my resolve.

The next morning, I woke up without him next to me. My eyes were barely able to make out the time on his bedside clock that sat right next to a picture of his wife. I groaned and pulled a pillow over my head.

"Problem?" He walked in wearing a pair of tight boxer briefs and holding two cups of coffee.

"Nope." I lied as I took the cup from him and watched as he noticed the offending photo.

"Liar." He settled into the chair that was still fixed at the foot of the bed and tossed me an envelope.

"What's this? Payment for services rendered?" I placed the coffee on the table, picked up the envelope, and looked inside. I pulled out a folded packet of papers and opened them.

"I'm filing those tomorrow."

"Are you serious?" I was holding his divorce papers in my hand.

"Dead serious." He put the coffee down and climbed into bed next to me. "I told you I was going to do it and I'm sorry it wasn't sooner. You deserve better than dinners in dark, out-of-the-way restaurants and shady office sex. And I want to give you what you deserve."

"Which is?" I couldn't look at him. I couldn't believe that everything I'd wished for over the past months was literally being dropped in my lap.

"Which is"—he took the papers, stuffed them back in the envelope, and placed them on the table next to my coffee—"a date with a man in the middle of the afternoon." He kissed my neck. "A bed you don't have to run from at two in the morning." He kissed my collarbone. "A night on the town with all eyes on you and not who you're with." He pulled the blanket I'd been using to cover my breasts down to my waist.

Sun streamed through the window and I leaned back with him resting on top of me. My head swam and blared a warning. A voice in the back of my head attempted to remind me that I shouldn't celebrate until the ring was off the finger. In that moment, kissing him, I didn't listen.

* * *

Friday morning, I rushed out of the building, heels from the night before still in hand, with my shirt barely buttoned enough to cover my boobs. We'd gone out to dinner to celebrate the impending divorce proceedings. After all, we needed fuel. Spending nearly twenty-four hours in bed gave me an appetite. Out of breath from the anxiety of almost being caught—again—I was quite certain my makeup was smeared and my teeth had that sickly film that comes when you forgo brushing your teeth. But that's that happens when your boss's wife comes home from the Hamptons three days early.

Larry, the doorman, already had Marco waiting for me and he smiled knowingly as I rushed past and all but dove into the vehicle. It's like they say: a great pair of shoes will help you conquer the world but what happens when you're in bed with your boss and his wife comes home from the Hamptons three days early? I'll tell you what. Dress faster than you thought humanly possible and exit the apartment via the service elevator like your life depended on it. Sure, his maid gave me a dirty look on the way out but she loved Zac like a son so she wasn't about to spill the beans. Thank God for Larry the doorman and Zachary Waterman's team of look-the-other-ways.

I was only a block away from the apartment on the way to the train station when Zachary called me.

"I'm so sorry about that. Rita wasn't supposed to come back until Sunday."

I pulled my compact out of my purse and tried to make my face presentable as I ignored the dread spreading through me. "No problem. Not the first time I had to rush out in the middle of a blow job. I'm sure it won't be the last."

"It was a very good blow job." I could hear the frustration in his voice. "I'm still feeling the aftereffects of not finishing."

"Tell me something I don't know."

"You left your panties here."

I froze and shoved my hand under my skirt. Sure enough, I was going commando. Again, not the first time. "I left those as a souvenir. I left my bag, too."

"The bag's in the trunk of the car. You know, if you keep leaving trinkets here, my wife may come across one of them someday."

"And that would be bad." I slicked gloss across my lips. I hated that I had to worry about stupid shit like leaving things behind.

"I don't mind bad."

"I know you don't. There are a lot of things you don't mind when it comes to naked, sweaty sex." I fumbled with the buttons on my shirt.

"The best kind. You know, soon enough, we won't have to worry about all this."

"Now that is something I can't wait for. Until then, the ring is still on the finger." My inner snark made herself known.

"That's not fair. For now, we both have to wait, even if somewhat impatiently. Take the rest of the day—"

I interrupted. "I planned on it." I needed to get off the call. I suddenly felt the urge to throw up.

"Of course you did. I'll see you Monday morning."

"It's a date."

"Hey, Mel?"

"Yeah?"

"I love you."

My breath hitched. *No you don't.* "Of course you do."

It was still early when Marco dropped me off at the train station. Checking the time, I figured I'd be able to get home in time to change and spend an hour at the gym. I was sugaring up a coffee I purchased in the terminal when realized I didn't feel like walking the few blocks home from the train station in heels. Of course I could call a cab, but then again, maybe my new roommate would be willing to pick me up.

"Hello?" Hearing the grogginess in his voice made my lady parts stand at attention. "Hey, roomie. Long night?"

"Not really. I stayed in. You?"

"You know me, always doing something."

"Or someone."

"True. Or someone."

"So who was this someone?"

I rolled my eyes. "Oh, no one interesting." I went for vague as I boarded the train.

"Are you kidding me? Two nights out and it's no one interesting?" I heard him yawn.

"I know, I know. Listen, you wanna pick me up at the station? I mean, if you aren't busy fiddling with your dick."

"I have to fiddle with my dick. It's not like you're gonna do it."

"You wish. And seriously, can you pick me up?"

"I mean, I guess I can do that if you tell me who had your interest for the past two nights."

"Why do you want to know?"

"I'm curious by nature."

"Anyone ever tell you curiosity killed the cat?"

"Thank God I'm not a cat. More of a tiger." He growled into the phone.

"A tiger *is* a cat, dumb-dumb. Are you going to pick me up or not?"

"I don't know. Have you decided to go out to dinner with me?"

"If I have to walk, I swear—"

"Fine. What time do you come in?"

"Half hour or so."

"See you then." He clicked off before I could say thank you. Whatever. He was crashing on my couch for a week. He should be thanking me.

I checked my voice mail. No messages. I called Sarah and left a message for her to call me. I needed to talk to her about Zac's decision to file. I needed her to tell me it was true and real and I shouldn't worry about the dreadful feeling crawling over my skin. I threw my phone in my bag and downed the last dregs of my burned coffee and gathered my bags. By the time I hit my station, I was collected enough to enjoy the summer morning as I sat on the concrete bench waiting for Jared. Thankfully I didn't have to wait too long.

"You bring high class to the walk of shame." Jared walked up in a pair of low-slung cargo shorts and a tight white tank showing off the muscular arms I hadn't taken the time to notice before, let alone appreciate. My eyes were, at the time, focused elsewhere.

"And you're dressed like a member of the Jersey Shore cast."

"Beggars can't be choosers. Remember, I got out of bed on a Friday morning to pick your ass up. You're lucky I'm wearing shoes. Get in."

"You know, most people work during the week."

"Give me a break. I've been in New Jersey barely two weeks. And if all goes well on Monday, then I will be back to making the bacon." He looked over at me as I settled into the passenger seat of his pickup truck. "Your buttons are messed up."

"What?" I looked down. He was right. I'd buttoned the shirt wrong. Smiling, I unbuttoned completely, shook out the shirt, and began the process of buttoning it correctly. I glanced at him out of the corner of my eye. "Perv. Keep your eyes on the road."

"Hard to do that when you're half naked in the front seat of my truck."

"Would you rather me be half naked in the backseat?" I countered.

"So"—he cleared his throat—"want to tell me where you were last night?"

I rolled my eyes. "Why do you want to know so badly?"

"'Cause by the looks of it, whoever he was had a way better time than I did watching reruns of *Seinfeld*. And"—he pulled in front of the building—"methinks you made a mad dash to get out of there this morning. Your skirt's on backward, too."

He hopped out of the truck, went to the back, and pulled my bags out of the bed.

"Hey! You don't get to judge me!" I leaned against the car as I tried to put my shoes back on while spinning my skirt. "You don't know me!"

He held up his hands. "I'm not judging. Hey, I told you, I call 'em like I see 'em. Here." He tossed my bags on the ground and walked into the building.

Unbelievable. Who the hell did he think he was? I picked up my bags and followed him in. When I finally caught up, he was unlocking the door.

"If you must know I was out with my boss. Yes, my boss. The one you're interviewing with on Monday. And it was wonderful and it was sexy and it was—"

"Cut short?" he pushed the door open, threw his keys on the table, and walked to the kitchen.

I tossed my bags on the couch. "Yes. Yes, it was. His wife came home from the Hamptons early." I reached around him to retrieve a bottle of water.

"You're fucking your *married* boss? Jesus, who knew you'd be hard up?"

"I am not hard up! What Zac and I have is special." I was finally beginning to actually hear myself and I didn't like what I heard.

"And he's leaving his wife for you."

"As a matter of fact he is. He is filing the papers today. I saw them with my own eyes."

He laughed, leaned in unbearably close, and whispered in my ear, "It ain't over, sweetie, till the ring is off the finger."

I froze. The exact words I was thinking earlier sounded more ominous when I heard them spoken out loud. "What do you know?" I pushed him away.

"Nothing." He spread his arms out wide. "I'm new here. But I can tell you what I think. I think you're lost, little girl. I think you use sex as a defense mechanism so you don't have to get close to people."

"Fuck you." I pushed him harder.

"Harsh. Don't be mad at me because your boss's wife almost caught the two of you doing the horizontal mambo. I'm just saying, it isn't smart to allow the company pen to be dipped in your ink."

"Why not, when his name's on the pen?" I shot back. I raised my hands to push him again and he grabbed my wrists.

"You certainly are testy this morning. Fine. You do what you want but when it all blows up in your face, don't forget who told you so."

"You sound like your sister."

"She's a wise woman."

"Both of you should mind your own business." I cringed, knowing I'd just called her for her advice not thirty minutes prior.

"You love him?"

"What? Why does that matter?" I finished my water and tossed the bottle into the recycle bag.

He stepped close enough that my back was pressed against the refrigerator and placed a hand on either side of my head. "Do you love him?"

"He told me he loves me." I looked down at the floor and he used his finger to tilt my chin back up.

"That's not what I asked. Do *you* love *him*?" His voice was barely a whisper.

I couldn't think of anything to say. His lips were close, too close. His tongue slipped out and ran across his bottom lip. I felt a familiar throb between my legs and a not so familiar skip in my heartbeat. It was hot, too hot. I leaned in, close enough to kiss him, and he tilted his head. I closed my eyes and waited.

Instead, Jared stepped back and laughed. "You mean to tell me the guy has told you he loves you and you won't say it back and you're okay with him leaving his wife for you? You're something."

"It's not that I won't say it. It's just not something I've ever said. I don't know if I ever will. And you know what? That's okay." I kicked off my shoes.

He was too close again. "Oh, you'll say it, sweetheart. You just don't know it yet." His finger tapped my chin and I growled in frustration. I turned and stormed to my bedroom, slamming the door for emphasis.

Chapter Nine

After I sulked for a sufficient amount of time, long enough to realize I didn't want to be confined to my bedroom for the rest of the day, I walked out to the living room, executing the most nonchalant swagger I could muster. Jared was sprawled out on the couch with his nose in his phone, his thumbs jabbing furiously. By the sound of the music, he was playing some game on his phone.

I saw him peer over the top of his screen and regard my presence. I raised an eyebrow and plopped down in the armchair that used to belong to my dad. Grabbing the newest tabloid, I flipped through the pages stiffly, not really reading any of the words. After a few minutes—I assume he ran out of lives—Jared placed the phone on the coffee table and leaned back, arms stretched across the back of the sofa. I noticed his blanket, sheets, and pillow neatly stacked at the far end.

"What's up?" That sexy smirk played at the corners of his mouth. It wasn't until he snapped his fingers that I stopped staring.

"Nothing. Why?" I resumed flipping through the magazine.

"Seems like something's up."

"Nope. Nothing."

"Okay then." He picked up his phone off the table, walked over to his suitcase, and pulled out clothes.

"Where are you going?"

"The gym. Not going to sit here all day and stare at your ass, though I wouldn't mind."

"*I* was going to go to the gym." I launched out of my chair. I wasn't actually.

"Then go."

"So what are we, roomies *and* running buddies?"

"No one said we had to work out together but, yes, I am going to run. You are welcome to join me."

"Well, I guess"—I stood and dropped the magazine on the table—"there is nothing else to do."

He laughed as he closed the bathroom door behind him.

He was waiting by the front door when I emerged from my bedroom.

"Damn."

"What?" I asked innocently and bent over at the waist to pretend to tie my shoe.

"Nothing." He shook his head. "So, I was wondering if you could do me a favor," he said as he handed me a bottle of water.

"What?"

"Leave the bitch face at home. I mean, really, I don't want it making a sudden appearance and ruining my workout. Or at least the part of my workout where I stare at your ass, watch sweat slide from your neck and down your chest into your sports bra, or ogle your breasts as they bounce when you're running. You know, normal stuff I look forward to when I'm at the gym."

I couldn't think of anything clever to say, which was so not like me, so I stood staring at him with my mouth hanging open. Finally, after what seemed like an eternity, I managed to say, "Bitch face?"

"Yeah. You know, that look you get when it looks like you've been sucking lemons?" He demonstrated what I could only assume was his interpretation. "Bitch face."

"You're an ass."

"That right there!" He pointed at my face. "Leave that here. Let's go have fun."

I slapped his hand out of the way and walked out of the apartment.

I popped in my ear buds and turned up the music, making sure there was no miscommunication. I didn't want to talk. Who the hell did he think he was? Of course, I had to double-time my stride just to keep up with him and it made me feel like I was chasing after him. He didn't seem to notice, of course. He was busy checking out every student who decided to stay for the summer, and he made no move to hide it.

It took a minute but I shook out the cobwebs. He was doing nothing more than what I did every day as I walked to the gym. He was a good-looking—scratch that, great-looking—single guy. Why should I be mad if he was checking out some coed? He was closer to their age than I was, a fact that grew ever more real the closer I got to my birthday.

By the time we got to the gym, I opened the door and waited while he exchanged numbers with some chick he met half a block away. Was I losing my way? Was I out of touch with my reality? That was my shtick.

Tapping my foot, I checked the time on my phone and cleared

my throat. He looked over, winked, and said goodbye to the cute brunette with the waist-length hair I could never achieve because of my annoying curls.

"Didn't mean to make you wait, princess."

"I'd like to think I'm past the princess stage. I'm more of a queen."

"Well, a queen needs a throne. My face is available if you ever need one."

"What makes you think I'd want to sit on your face? It's all scruffy. Like a dog. Or a hobo." I walked in, leaving him holding the door. Smiling to myself, I felt a bit more normal. Trading jabs with Jared was fun, even if I didn't want to admit it. Not to mention, the scruff was actually very sexy. It didn't take much to imagine his five o'clock shadow rubbing against my thighs. Truth be told, I loved the beard. I believed in all things bearded.

"Hobo, huh? That's a new one. Sex god. That's what I'm usually referred to as." He headed toward the nearest set of open treadmills.

"I bet you are," I said, not quite loud enough for him to hear.

There was no escaping the fact that Jared Myers threw me off my game. For the first time in a long time, I'd finally met someone who knocked me off balance. Zac and I were different. There was something entirely too intense about Zac and me. I welcomed the ease of being with Jared.

With Zac, I always felt like I was reaching for something. As a rule, I didn't chase men. But I chased the hell out of him. And I felt like I'd never reach the finish line. But Jared. Jared called me on my bullshit, called me on my drama. Only the girls did that. Well, the girls and Berk. But this was different. The snarky bravado, the I-don't-give-a-shit attitude, seemed less about asserting dominance and more about something I couldn't quite put my finger on.

Everything else in my life was all about immediate gratification. With Jared, it was more of a slow simmer.

We spent the next hour in silence, each running at a pace to challenge the other. By the time we got to the cool down, I felt like my legs were going to fall off.

"Where are you going?"

I turned to him. "Showers."

"You aren't going to stretch?"

"Stretch? I stretched back at the apartment before we came."

"If you don't stretch after, you'll cramp. Basic rule of working out. Come on. We'll do it together, it will take less time."

I watched him drop to a mat in the corner and crook his finger toward me, motioning for me to follow. Sighing, I threw my towel around my neck and kneeled down in front of him.

"Help me stretch my hammies." He lifted his leg in the air and I pushed it gently toward his head. As he switched legs, his shorts gapped and I sucked in hard. He wasn't wearing any underwear and by the look of it, he had a lot to offer a girl. He noticed my slight hesitation as I admired the view.

"What's the matter? You look like you've never seen a dick before." He lifted the other leg and I averted my eyes just enough that I could still peek out of the corner of my eye if I wanted to.

I rolled my eyes. "I've seen plenty of dicks before."

"So you keep telling me." He sat up. "Your turn."

We switched places and I lifted my leg for him. Unlike Jared, though, my leg easily stretched back toward my head until I was nearly in a split. It was my turn to notice his hesitation.

"What's the matter? Never seen a girl spread like this before?"

He laughed. "Like I said, if you need a throne…"

"As if." I switched legs and stretched before I stood and touched my toes. It was hard not to notice him standing behind me noticing me. "See something you like?"

I jumped as he snapped my ass with his towel. "Time to go. I forgot to tell you, we have people coming over for dinner."

"Who? Redhead?" I crossed my arms and tapped my foot. And then I realized my arms were crossed as I tapped my foot. And then I realized he noticed. "I mean, what? Like you have a date?"

"No. But it wouldn't be the first time I've had two women for dinner."

"Cute." I bitch-faced him. "Who's coming?"

"Well, I was hoping both of us could—"

I shoved him. "Would you stop?"

"You're awfully handsy. What's with you and all the touching?"

"I like touching." I winked at him.

He leaned in close enough that I could smell the faded mint of the gum he'd popped into his mouth just before we left the apartment. "I like touching, too." His fingers grazed my cheek and I closed my eyes, nuzzling into his touch.

"I'd like to kiss you," he whispered.

"Then why don't you?"

"Not yet." He stepped back and shook out his arms.

I took a shaky breath and noticed my stomach was knotted. "So"—I attempted to diffuse the almost kiss—"who is coming to dinner again?"

"Sorry." His laugh told me that he was not, in fact, sorry. "My sister, Drew." He took a long swig of water. "Berk, Caroline, and Brian. I'm cooking."

"You're cooking? How very domestic of you. Are we playing house?"

"I could think of a few other things we could play."

Since my lady balls were back to being appropriately sized, I stepped close enough so that my breasts we barely touching him. Putting on my best seductive face, I said, "I like to play."

"You are something," he whispered as he tucked a stray tendril of hair behind my ear before patting my shoulder and heading out the door. "By the way, you're helping me cook!"

Completely satisfied with myself, I followed him out.

* * *

At the grocery store, I was the driver of the cart. I wasn't terribly amused at the idea of following him around the store. Until I followed him around the store.

Perfect ass.

I was lost in a daydream of ass perfection when he must've stopped short and I rammed the cart into the backs of his legs.

"Still thinking about me naked?" He winced and rubbed the backs of his thighs.

I scoffed, "You wish," and was glad he couldn't read minds.

"That's gonna bruise, you know."

"Poor baby. We'll grab a bag of frozen peas on the way out."

Shaking his head and smiling, he picked up a rubber-banded bunch of asparagus and lectured me on the dos and don'ts of such a vegetable.

Jared Myers's cooking tip number one: yellow and loose tips are not good.

He tossed lemons and garlic into the basket followed by a container of spring greens, a few bunches of herbs, and a handful of shallots. Considering I'd never seen a shallot that wasn't cooked in my food, I thought it was a weird-looking onion. I really needed to buy a cookbook.

"Do you have olive oil?"

"What?"

"Olive oil. You have some?"

"I do."

"Okay." Without another word, he dove back into his mental checklist and I followed him to the fish department.

"So are we going to have to crack open crabs to make these crab cakes you've been talking about?"

"Well, that would be tedious. No, we're going to buy lump. Already cooked, already shelled."

"Ahh. Okay."

I watched as he conversed with the fish guy and ordered a pound and a half. Daydreams about his ass aside, I was actually a bit fascinated by the whole process. After a few more minutes of plucking items off the shelves, he was ready to go.

"I think I have everything."

I took out my wallet when we got to the registers.

"What are you doing?" He placed his hand over my wallet.

"Paying."

"Why?"

"If you're going to cook, I can pay."

"You don't need to do that." He shook his head and took out a credit card.

"I want to. Let me."

I think he could tell I wasn't going to back down. Shaking his head, he said, "You really are something."

"So you keep telling me."

Bags in hand, we walked back to the apartment.

"You go shower, I'll put everything away." He unpacked the bags and began filling the fridge. I watched him move easily through my kitchen before turning on music and heading to the shower.

"Leave me some hot water!" I heard him yell through the closed door.

"Can't guarantee that. You might have to hop in here with me." I laughed.

Silence.

"Jared?"

"Yeah?" He replied softly.

"I was kidding."

"I know. Tease."

He laughed and I continued to shampoo the sweat out of my hair. Of course, whenever I smelled the floral scent, I thought of him and the first day he was in my apartment. Freshly cleaned from a shower. Smelling of lavender. Naked and amazing.

The familiar tingle of want spread between my thighs. With nothing better to do, I decided to take my orgasm into my own hands.

I had no idea how long I was in there until I heard banging on the bathroom door, effectively pulling me away from the cliff I was so close to falling off.

"You know," Jared yelled, "ten minutes is a shower. Any longer than that and you're playing with yourself."

Struck dumb by his words, I couldn't think of a snappy retort. So I slipped on the bar of soap I dropped instead. And screamed as my elbow met the side of the tub with a loud thump.

"Mel! You okay?" I could hear him fiddling with the door lock.

"I fell. It hurts." Tears stung my eyes and I bit back a yelp.

"Hold on."

"No, don't come in! I'm naked!" As I said it, he shouldered the door open and rushed to the tub, pulling the shower curtain open.

"You okay?"

"Fine. It just hurts." I winced and tried to stand up. "What?"

"Nothing. Just lookin' atcha naked is all." His wiggling eyebrows ticked me off.

"Seriously? Get out. I can do this by myself." I attempted, again, to get out of the tub.

He leaned down and placed his hands under my arms and lifted me up and out before wrapping a towel around me and sitting me on the toilet seat.

"Don't move."

He walked out of the bathroom before returning with the frozen bag of peas. Kneeling down in front of me he said, "Put this on it."

"Thanks." I mumbled.

"What was that?" He brought his hand to his ear.

"Thanks."

"Wow. You're welcome."

"Did you really see me naked?" I don't know why it mattered, but I'd rather him not have seen me naked for the first time crumpled in a heap at the bottom of my bathtub.

"Eh, didn't see much. You were kind of curled into a ball. But I saw enough to imagine." He winked.

"So you can close your eyes any time you want and imagine me naked?"

"Yep." He closed his eyes. "Doin' it right now."

I leaned in and brushed my lips on his. He tasted sweaty from the gym. It was delicious.

His eyes snapped open. "What was that for?"

I stood, handing him the bag of peas. "Whatever you were just imagining, it's wrong. I'm much hotter."

With that, I walked to my bedroom, dropped the towel just inside the door, and tossed it into the hallway.

"Not fair! Now I'm going to have to take a long, cold shower."

"You're a big boy," I yelled through my door. "I'm sure you can *hand*le yourself."

"Such a tease," I heard him say under his breath.

"What was that?"

"Nothing. Get dressed!" He yelled back.

* * *

He met me in the kitchen thirty minutes later.

"Want a sandwich?"

"Sure." He leaned against the counter and watched me.

I handed him his plate and a bottle of water before grabbing my own and sitting down next to him at the table.

"So, you're gonna cook for us tonight?"

"Yep." He took a large bite of his sandwich. "You really don't cook?"

"Not really. Unless you count cereal, sandwiches, takeout, and the random microwaveable thing."

"I'll teach you."

"Teach me, huh? So this isn't a one-time thing?"

"I wish it were an all-the-time thing," he said and I choked on my water.

"Huh?"

"I wish I could cook all the time. I love being in the kitchen. I love making all kinds of food. Crab cakes? They're easy."

So he *wasn't* professing his desire to be my personal chef. "Then why don't you?"

"I don't know." He took a sip of water. "Finance is the thing I majored in, the thing that will pay the bills. I've never had any formal chef training, so it's not like I could get a job anywhere other than as a fry cook. It's just a dream."

"Tell me about this dream."

He laughed easily. "Tell you, huh? You really want to know? My desire to spend time in the kitchen doesn't make you want me any less, does it?"

"Depends on what you think less actually is," I retorted, smiling.

"Yeah, well. I don't know. I'd love to one day open my own place. Something small. Like a bistro or something and serve just a few items, have a changing menu, just so, you know, I could experiment."

"And you're good with experimentation?" I raised my eyebrows and saw immediately he latched on to the innuendo.

"Very good." His eyes locked with mine and I had to look away.

"So why don't you do it? Open a place, I mean?"

"Money, mostly. I don't have the funds to open a place on my own."

"What about a partner?" I took his plate and placed it with mine in the sink.

"Who do I know that would front the money for something like that? Take a chance on me? No, maybe one day, but now I'll run numbers and put myself to sleep with spreadsheets until I can retire and do something with it." As he leaned back and stretched, his shirt lifted slightly and I peeked at the hint of a happy trail. I closed my eyes for a minute, remembering where that trail led.

"You won't know until you try. You know, Berk does real estate. He could help you find a place. And I'm in finance. I am sure I could find someone to back you."

"Thanks, but it's really not a thing. It will happen when it happens. Right now, I'll stick to a nine-to-five and figure it out later." He stood and grabbed his wallet.

"Where are you going?"

"To the liquor store. Need anything?"

"Wine."

"What kind?"

"Surprise me."

"I will." He winked and headed out the door.

* * *

By nine o'clock that night, we were all sufficiently stuffed from the homemade crab cakes and roasted asparagus dinner. I was quite impressed. When he said he was making dinner, I originally thought he meant what I usually mean—ordering takeout. But he demanded I help him prepare dinner and it was kind of nice. A definite step away from my normal Friday night of either trolling the bar scene or curling up with a pint of Chinese and my television.

I'd been directed to pick through the crab for any rogue shells and I'd whisked lemon juice and olive oil for the asparagus.

It was nice to catch up with everyone and the fact that Jared was flirting with me all night didn't escape me. Of course, it didn't escape Sarah either, and when I went to grab another bottle of Pinot Grigio from the fridge, she cornered me in my small kitchen.

"What's up with you and my brother?"

"Nothing, why?"

"I see the way he looks at you. You look at him the same way."

"It's true." Caroline hopped up on the counter. "I think you'd make a cute couple."

"Cute couple?" Sarah looked at Caroline like she had lost her marbles before returning her focus to me. "Did you bang my brother?" Sarah wasn't angry, she was nosy, and I felt Caroline lean in, waiting for my answer.

I looked between the two of them and laughed. "Look at you two. A lady never talks."

"Then tell me where I can find one." Sarah laughed. "Spill."

"Look, I haven't banged your brother." I looked toward Caroline. "I am not looking to be part of the cute couple club. He's just staying here until he can move back to your apartment."

"Look, I'm just saying, you could do worse."

"And you have," Caroline piped in.

"Oh, so now you want me involved with your brother? The other day you were shooting daggers at me."

"I've had some time to think about it and I think the two of you would be good for each other. It's almost as if you and he are the same, you know?"

"Well, for your information, I am not looking to get involved with your brother. Have I checked out the goods? Yes. Am I impressed with said goods? Immensely. But that's not where I am right now."

"Zac again? You know that won't end well," Caroline whispered.

"You know I am a grown woman and can decide for myself what will and what won't end well, right?" I pulled out the cork and filled my glass.

"Of course we know that. But you can't keep doing this, you know. It isn't right."

"Not everyone can live the dream above a bar with a boyfriend and a dog," I said to Caroline with a bit too much snark.

"Ouch," Sarah interjected before I could continue. "We're just saying. You're going to be thirty. Not saying you need to be in a relationship, but one with a married man isn't the best option."

"How can I forget that when I have the both of you yapping about morals in my ear every damn day? Did you forget how Caroline actually met Brian? Pretty sure she threw away her morals for a bit before she landed him."

"No need to be a bitch." Caroline hopped down from the counter.

"I'm sorry. Look. I'm not saying you two are wrong. I'm just not there yet. I get what you're saying, I really do. Maybe Zac *isn't* right for me."

"Finally." Sarah threw up her hands.

"I'm not making any promises. But I will think more about what you're saying. Deal?"

"Deal." Caroline and I hugged it out. Sarah jumped in.

"Hey!" Drew called out. "Don't keep that shit under wraps. We wanna see."

"Speak for yourself," Berk offered.

Laughing, I grabbed Caroline's boob as Sarah squeezed my ass.

The girls and I were clearing the table and loading up the dishwasher when the buzzer sounded. Jared hopped up. "Yeah?" he spoke into the intercom.

"Um, I'm looking for Melody. Melody Ashford."

I stiffened. I knew exactly who it was. The voice sent shivers through me.

"Who's this?"

"Zachary Waterman."

Everyone in the apartment turned and stared. The silence was uncomfortable.

"What is he doing here?" Berk asked.

"No idea," I whispered. "Let him up."

"Come on up." Jared stiffened and pressed the button to unlock the door. No one moved for what seemed like an eternity. The knock at the door startled me.

Smoothing down my pants and fluffing my hair, I walked through the sea of eyes and felt every single one of them. I opened the door to find Zac, disheveled and drunk, a far cry from the boxer shorts of earlier that morning.

"What are you doing here?"

"Melody, I need to speak to you." He rushed in before noticing everyone looking at him. "Can we talk in private?" His words slurred and he gripped my arm a little too tightly. Jared stepped forward and I waved him off. Zac's other hand gripped a paper bag with contents that would have burst into flames if someone lit a match.

"Yeah, sure." I ushered him into the hallway. "Be right back." I closed the door behind us. "What's going on?"

"Ah, Melody." He leaned into me.

I crinkled my nose when he breathed out. "You've been drinking. A lot. This isn't like you. What's wrong?"

He slouched against the wall, his wrinkled shirt untucked, unusual for the well-put-together man who told me he loved me for the first time only days ago.

"I don't know how to say this."

My stomach dropped. "Say what, Zac?"

"I love you. You know that, right?" He placed his hand on my cheek.

"I do know that. What's going on? You're scaring me. This isn't like you."

"Tell me you love me back."

"You're drunk. I will not say it back to someone who is drunk."

"Then I'll just say it—"

"Say what?"

"Rita is pregnant." The words punched me in the chest and I thought my heart would stop.

"What?"

"I told her I was going to leave her. I told her I was in love with someone else. She told me she was pregnant. I thought she was lying, trying to get me to stay. But she took a test. We went to the doctor's. She is pregnant. Eight weeks to be exact."

"Rita is pregnant? What does this mean?"

"It means I am not leaving her. I can't leave her."

I stepped back. I didn't know whether to laugh, cry, or beat the shit out of him.

"Are you fucking kidding me? After all this? After I run out of your apartment like a bat out of fucking hell this morning, after everything you said, you're ending this?"

"No, no. Of course not. I still want you. We're just not going to be able to do this out in the open."

"You son of a bitch. You never intended to leave her. You strung me along like a fucking puppet. You made promises you never intended to keep—"

"No, no. I still want you!"

"Look, sleeping with a married man is one thing. Sleeping with a married man who is expecting a baby is a line even I won't cross. I could handle it if you were still divorcing her." I put up my hands and shook my head. "No. You know what? My friends were right about you. You and I were never going to end well." I put my hand on the doorknob. "You need to leave, Zac. Go home, sober up, decorate your nursery. I don't care. Just go."

He grabbed me and pulled me close. "No, Melody. You and I have something—"

I straightened up, pulled away from him, and erased all emotion from my face. "We had orgasms. That's it. Nothing more, nothing less." I fisted the pendant he gave me and yanked off the necklace. "Take this. I don't need it anymore."

"Melody—"

"No. I'll see you on Monday. And don't you dare make this any more awkward than it has to be. Or I will take my clients with me when I give notice. Go home. Go back to your wife and leave me alone. I'm done."

I left him standing in the hall. Slamming the door, I hurried through the living room, knowing the walls were thinner than a private conversation could handle. Taking an opened bottle from the fridge, I went to my room, locked the door, and let the tears fall.

Hours later, I heard the lock to my door being picked, but I didn't have the strength or care to roll over and see who was coming in. I could smell Jared's cologne as he walked through my room, covered me with a blanket, and took the empty wine bottle that I was still clutching. I kept my eyes closed as I felt him brush away the hair from my face, kiss me on my forehead, and close the door quietly behind him.

Chapter Ten

I spent most of Saturday in bed mourning what was left of my dignity and nursing the hangover that still lingered even after I drank two bottles of Gatorade, ate a protein bar, and took the aspirin Jared left on my nightstand. It wasn't until Sarah and Caroline came in at five that evening that I even thought about getting out of bed.

"Get up. We aren't doing this again." Sarah ripped the comforter off my bed. "And you didn't even put on pajamas. Is it really that comfortable sleeping in skinny jeans?"

"God," Caroline said, "be careful. You'll get a yeast infection with those things so tight against your hooha."

"We aren't doing what again?" I flipped over and buried my head under my pillow. "And hooha? What are we, twelve?"

"Look, I was in a funk for six weeks when Steven broke up with me. Let's not revisit that shit again."

"Zac didn't break up with me. He got his wife pregnant." The situation sounded more ridiculous when I said the words out loud. Shouldn't a baby be cause for celebration? Apparently, not if it's your boss who you are sleeping with that is having the baby with his wife.

Fuck.

"Exactly. That is why we need you to give Operation Foreplay another try," Caroline mentioned casually.

"No." I raised my hand over my head and gave her the finger.

"Look, we're not saying you need to go out and sleep with the next person you meet."

"We're just saying," Sarah continued, "maybe you could meet someone nice. Take it slow. Abstain from sex for a while. Enjoy the slow simmer."

"*Abstain* from sex for a while? Who put *that* back on the table? I don't recall leaving that topic open for discussion."

"We just thought, after what happened last night, you'd be more open to such a topic."

I shot up. "Are you fucking joking? There is no fucking way I am going without sex for any amount of time. Jesus. After two or three days, I'm climbing walls looking for my next orgasm."

"Use this then." Caroline tossed my vibrator at me.

"And these." Sarah handed me a bag full of batteries and two porn DVDs.

"And if you get stuck"—Caroline pulled a magazine out of her bag—"use these guys."

She tossed me a dirty mag filled with large dicks and hard asses.

"Really? Porn, movies, and a battery-operated boyfriend? Thanks, but I'd rather stick with a real cock." Instead of handing the gifts back, I tucked them away in my nightstand drawer. Who knew when I'd need a good porn flick?

"Listen." Caroline started riffling through my closet. "We just want what's best for you." She tossed a clean pair of jeans at me.

"And Zac, sorry to say, babe, is not what is best. You need to get out there. Have fun without the night necessarily ending with the horizontal mambo. Go on vacation. Go visit your mom for a few days. You know?" She tossed a slinky silver tank top at me. "Now get dressed. We love you too much to watch you drown in a sea of spooge."

"What the hell is wrong with sex?" I asked as I finally crawled out of bed and grabbed my bathrobe. "Sex. I like that shit."

"Me too!" I looked up and saw Jared standing in the doorway.

"Who asked you?" I grimaced.

"Looks like someone ate their bitch flakes today. Nice to see you up and about. How's the elbow?"

"Fine." I turned it over to see the lovely purple bruise had spread wider.

He turned to Sarah. "We still heading out?"

"Yeah," she answered with a smile on her face.

"Cool. Just let me shower first."

"Oh no! I'm showering first."

"Pretty sure I'll get there before you but you are more than welcome to join me. It would be nice not to have to wash my own balls for once." The challenge twinkled in his eye. Any other day and I probably would have called him on his bullshit.

"Ew, Jared. I don't need the visual!" Sarah closed her eyes.

"Whatever. Go take your fucking shower. I need to eat something anyway."

"Your loss." He pinched my cheek and headed toward the bathroom.

I yelled toward him, "Don't use all the fucking hot water or your ass is mine."

"Promises, promises," he yelled back.

"So"—Sarah pointed between where Jared stood a moment ago and me while Caroline stifled a laugh—"there *is* a thing between you and my brother."

"You're crazy," I said over my shoulder as I walked to kitchen to make a sandwich.

"Um, I don't think I am." Sarah followed me.

"You know who says they aren't crazy? Crazy people."

"Maybe Jared can be your foreplay," Caroline offered.

"Maybe not." I tilted my head and gave her a shut-the-fuck-up face.

"Just do me a favor." Sarah put her hand on my shoulder. "When something happens, please don't tell me about it. The last thing I need is to know the ins and outs of my brother's sex life."

"So you don't want to know if I end up showing him the ins and outs of my vagina?" I giggled.

"Oh, shut up." Sarah glared at me as she popped a grape in her mouth.

"You know, for what it's worth, I really am sorry things didn't work out with Zac."

I considered my words before I spoke. Caroline was being honest and I appreciated that. I just wasn't ready to discuss my failed attempt at stealing a married man from his wife. "Thanks. I'm not ready to talk about it."

Jared walked into the kitchen with a bright blue towel wrapped around his waist.

"The shower is ready for you, my queen." He bowed. And nearly lost his towel.

"Come on, Jared! No one wants to see that! Get out of here!"

Sarah shrieked, shielding her eyes with the dishtowel that had covered his junk just the other day. I kept that little tidbit to myself and stifled a laugh.

"Speak for yourself," Caroline said quietly as she and I leaned across the counter to watch him walk away. "What the hell! When did he get that body?"

"You know that's my brother, right?"

"I don't care if he's a celibate priest. A body like that should be illegal."

"For real," I added with a sigh.

My cell phone blared Justin Timberlake's latest and pulled me out of my daydream.

"Who's that?" Sarah asked.

"Blocked number."

"Do you think it's Zac?"

"No idea."

"Aren't you going to answer it?"

The second round of the chorus began and I hit ignore before tossing the phone into my utensil drawer. "Nope. Leaving it here for tonight. Be back. Shower."

I never did make that sandwich.

Opening the door to my room, I stopped short. Jared was lounging on my bed wearing nothing but a loose pair of khaki shorts.

"What are you doing in here?"

"I figured you'd be in the shower so I got dressed in here. I figured my sister wouldn't appreciate me getting dressed out there." He nodded toward the living room. "That okay?"

"Um, yeah. I guess." I rummaged through my underwear drawer to find something matchy. "No biggie."

"You okay? I mean after last night. Him showing up like that was kind of douchey."

"I'm fine. I don't really want to talk about it, you know."

He slid over to the side of the bed and let his feet fall to the floor and tugged at my shirt. "You do know you deserve better than that, right? You don't deserve all that sneaking around and shit. You're better than that."

"Ha!" I slammed the drawer shut. "Thanks, but I got just what I deserved with that whole scene. And if I don't move past it, I'll sink."

"You're too strong to sink. Besides, I won't let you."

"You don't even know me." I laughed.

"I know enough."

"Enough from three whole days of living with me? Two of which I wasn't even here?"

"Hey, when you know something, you just know it."

"Look, I'd love to stand here and wax philosophical with you all night but I really need to take a shower and you really need to put on a shirt."

"You don't like?" He spread his arms as if to say, *Look at this*.

"Not that I don't like it. I just don't need the distraction." My hand flew to my mouth as soon as I said the *D* word.

"Distraction, huh?" He stood and pulled me in close. He lifted my free hand and held it tight against his chest. His heart was beating fast; it matched the rhythm of mine. I could feel his hot breath against my ear when he said, "Maybe you're about due for a little *distraction*."

He walked out of the room and closed the door. "That's what everyone keeps telling me."

I showered quickly and settled for towel-drying my hair. I slicked on gloss and mascara. Thankfully I was able to get away without much makeup and still look somewhat presentable. I slipped on the jeans and slinky tank Caroline had chosen and checked myself out in the mirror. It was odd going out and not being all made up. My usual red lips were nowhere to be found. The eyeliner was taking the night off. And, for a change, so were the shoes. I settled for a cute pair of black flip-flops, popped a fedora on my head, and headed to the living room.

"Ready?"

"You're ready?"

"Already?"

Caroline and Sarah spoke in unison while Jared let out a long whistle.

"What?"

"You just look—"

"I mean—"

"*Wow* is the word I think they are looking for." Jared handed me my purse and I looked at him, wondering.

"It's like you've never seen me without makeup before."

"No, it's just we either see you with or without. Never in between. And the flip-flops? Weren't you the one who said flip-flops belong at the beach?" Caroline walked around me. "And you didn't dry your air! It's going to curl up!"

"So—"

"Something"—Sarah waved her finger at me—"is going on here. Where is Melody and what have you done with her?"

"She's taking the night off. Can we just go?"

"What the queen wants—" Jared held out his arm and I slipped my hand through.

"Why the fuck do you keep calling her queen?" Sarah called after us as we walked out of the apartment. Jared and I just laughed.

"Where are we going?" I asked once we hit the sidewalk.

"Italian place in the city. Brian has the night off so we're all meeting there."

"So that's why we're heading out for dinner at"—I reached for my phone but remembered I'd left it at home so I dug into Jared's pocket and retrieved his—"six thirty."

I slipped the phone back into his pocket. He didn't flinch, whereas Sarah and Caroline stopped in their tracks.

"What was that?" Caroline asked with her eyes all squinty, as if that would help her see something that clearly wasn't there.

"What?" Jared asked.

"Nothing." Sarah looked between us as we headed toward Jared's truck.

"No train?" I asked, hopping into the front seat. "Oh, so you're like our driver." I winked.

"Something like that." He winked back. "I like the shirt you wore yesterday better, though."

I looked down before remembering my brazen display of lingerie when he picked me up yesterday morning. Was it only yesterday morning? Jesus. I was going to need a calendar to keep track of all the craziness. "Do you now? I'll have to remember that."

"What shirt were you wearing?" Caroline peeked her head between the seats.

"It was a button-up. Cute. Had a whole suit thing going on when he picked me up from the station."

My watch caught the light from the passing streetlights and I stopped for a minute. The gift from Zac suddenly felt heavy and awkward.

"Fuck this." I unstrapped the watch and rolled down the window.

"What are you doing?" Sarah asked.

"Letting go." I held up the watch for her to see before tossing it out the window.

"Mel, that was a really expensive watch," Caroline said.

"So, maybe I need to get rid of some stuff before I can move on." I glanced at Jared, noticed his smile, and knew I did the right thing.

"We need some music," I said, changing the subject. I played with the dials on his radio before landing on my new summer song. I turned it up. The girls and I rolled down the windows and sang at the tops of our lungs all the way to the restaurant. We were laughing and out of breath by the time we parked; Jared placed his hand on mine and squeezed before he hopped out of the truck. The touch didn't go unnoticed and I felt a weird flutter in my chest. I wondered for a moment if I was having a mini heart attack but brushed it off as hunger. I was starving.

We were the first to arrive. The waiter walked us to our table, set for nine.

"Who else is coming?" I asked as the chair was pulled out for me.

"Everyone, I think," Jared said as he took a seat next to me.

"I know the rest of your party has yet to arrive. Can I start you off with some drinks?"

"Want to go for something fun?" I wiggled my eyebrows at the girls.

"What am I missing?"

"You'll see, little brother. What were you thinking Mel?"

"I'll be right back. Let me go talk to the bartender. See how stocked his bar is."

"Sure, it's his bar you're interested in checking out."

"Hey! It's the new me. Maybe you girls are right. Maybe giving up sex is just what I need right now."

Jared spit out his water and began choking on an errant ice cube. "No, no. That's not a good idea," he choked out as I patted him on the back.

"No?" I could feel a weight lift off my shoulders. "I think it's just the right thing for me right now."

"Nope. Not a good idea."

"Why not?" Sarah teased. "I say just until your thirtieth birthday."

"That's a thought."

"Wait, wait, wait." Jared held his hands up.

"What?" I smiled.

"Just, well, what if—"

"What if?" Caroline asked, her arms crossed over her chest.

"Nothing." He looked away.

I laughed and walked to the bar. The waiter followed me back ten minutes later with a tray of pink drinks, a maraschino cherry at the bottom of each glass.

"Ooh! Pink! What's this?" Caroline asked as the waiter handed her the concoction.

"I'll let your friend tell you." He blushed, deposited the rest of the drinks on the table, and left.

I sat, picked up my drink, and raised the glass. "To friends!"

"To friends!" The other three followed suit and drank deeply.

"This is so good! What is it?" Sarah asked, taking another sip.

"Bend Over Shirley."

"What?" Jared's eyes widened.

"Welcome to the club, sweets. Are you sure you're ready to drink with us? I mean really drink with us? I can assure you, we can get quite fucked up. And I need to get quite fucked up." I ditched the straw and took a big gulp.

"Oh, I'm more than ready. Bring it on!" We clinked glasses.

"That's what I like to hear."

"You started without me?" Berk walked in, letting go of David's hand long enough to give me a hug. "What are you having?"

"Bend Over Shirleys."

"Well, Shirley isn't usually my type but I'll make an exception for tonight."

"Waiter!" I clapped. "Please, bring us more Shirleys!"

"No problem. How many?"

"The others are outside," Berk offered.

"So"—I did the calculation in my head—"please bring us five more."

"Six," Caroline squeaked through a hiccup.

"Six it is." The waiter disappeared to round up our drinks.

Berk and David took up seats across the table. It was sweet, I thought, when Berk leaned in and whispered in David's ear.

"David. You remember Melody. This is Sarah, Caroline, and Sarah's brother, Jared."

"Nice to meet you all. Nice to see you again Melody."

Jared stood, walked around the table, and shook David's hand. "Nice to meet you."

I'm pretty sure David licked his lips, and not because they were dry. I couldn't blame him really. Jared's dark hair fell just above his eyes and had a natural wave that I envied. His blue eyes were set off nicely by his baby blue dress shirt, rolled up to expose his forearms. Add in the khaki shorts, boat shoes, and a confident, relaxed demeanor and he was swoon-worthy. Not that I swooned. I'd get a lady boner, sure. But never had I ever swooned.

"So what's new?" Berk asked.

"Melody is abstaining from sex until she turns thirty."

Jared groaned and dropped his head and Berk spit out his Shirley. "We are going to need more drinks for this story."

The rest of our party arrived and we played musical chairs to get everyone sitting next to who they were supposed to. I ended up with Danny on my left, Jared on my right.

Berk raised a glass and stood. "I'd like to congratulate a few people here. First, David for closing on that huge penthouse by the park. I knew you could do it." He paused a moment to plant a juicy kiss on David's lips. "Next, to Danny. May you find out that Malibu Barbie is real, your new job is as sweet as we all think it is, and we wish you a safe journey to California."

"Thanks." Danny stood and bowed.

"Sit down!" Brian yelled and we all laughed.

Berk kept his glass raised. "To Melody. I hope that abstaining from sex doesn't shrivel up your, um, taco. No one likes shriveled-up tacos. At least that's what I'm told."

"No chance. Gotta keep it nice and moist." I winked.

"Ew. Seriously, ew." Berk crinkled his face before continuing. "And to the newest member of our group. Jared. Welcome to New Jersey. And good luck tomorrow on your interview with your guaranteed new employer Blackwell and Dardston. Cheers!"

I was shocked. "Blackwell and Dardston?" I whispered. "I thought you were meeting with Waterman tomorrow."

"I canceled it. We'll talk about it later." He reached down and squeezed my knee and I shifted in my seat, suddenly very aware of a minor throb that began between my legs. I told myself to knock it off. I was supposed to be off sex. At least for the night.

I smiled and sipped my drink even though questions swirled in my head. What the hell happened to the other interview? I had gotten used to the fact that I'd probably be working with him and now he wasn't even going to the interview.

I brushed it off and filed it away. He and I were definitely going to talk about it later. That moment, I reminded myself, was not about me and my quest for answers. It was about my friends. Their wins. Not mine. Not that I had any to brag about.

"Are you ready to order?" Our waiter returned.

"Absofuckinglutely," Brian said. "I'm starving."

My stomach growled as soon as food was mentioned.

"So is she." Both Jared and Sarah said at the same time.

"I'd like to start with the mussels. Fra Diablo. And for dinner"—I flipped through the menu one more time—"I'll have the grilled vegetables and pasta. Light on the oil, please." I handed the waiter the menu and sat back as the rest of the table ordered, then I felt a foot hook my ankle. Jared pulled my leg toward him before he unhooked himself and smiled.

The conversation flowed smoothly even though most of us had seen one another the night before. The night Zac dropped his fucking nuke.

Ignoring that particular train of thought, I asked Jared, "How's your calamari?"

"Not bad. A little chewy."

"You could do better?" I raised my eyebrow.

"I could. I'll make it for you."

"I'd like that," I said.

By the time we were done, David picked up the bill despite our protests and we all made plans to bar hop for the rest of the night. My stomach hurt and I headed toward the bathroom after promising to meet everyone outside.

A sudden cold sweat hit me and I felt like I was going to throw up. I turned on the faucet and splashed cold water on my face. When I could finally stand without my stomach cramping, I walked out to meet everyone.

"Someone take me home."

"You okay?" Caroline asked.

"My stomach hurts. I feel like I'm going to hurl."

"I'll do it," Jared offered.

"You sure? I can do it." Danny said. "The train's only a few blocks from here."

"Nah. It's okay. I've got my truck here. We're going to the same place and I'm not really feeling the bar scene tonight."

"Do you want us to come, too?" Caroline asked me.

"No, you guys go. Have fun. You know what? Jared, you can stay here. I'll take the train."

"It's okay. I'll take you." He placed his hand on the small of my back.

I heard Sarah say "thank you" as he steered me toward his truck.

Chapter Eleven

The ride home was silent. Between the stomach cramps and the cold sweats, I curled up in the seat. I didn't notice we were home until Jared opened my door.

"Thanks," I said as he helped me hop out of his truck.

"Anytime," he replied as he walked up the steps to the building entrance. "Want me to run to the store and get you some ginger ale or something?"

I rubbed my arms. It was summer but the breeze dropped the temperature. "No, I'm good. But thanks. You can go back if—"

"Nope. I'm good. Wouldn't be good if I bar hopped anyway." He jingled his keys. "Designated driver."

"Oh, right." I said as he unlocked the door and held it open for me. I made it to the apartment before him so it was my turn to unlock and hold the door.

"So, what do you need me to do? Make you soup?"

"I just want to put on my jammies and curl up in bed and watch a movie. My stomach is calming down a little."

"Oh, well"—he tossed his keys on the table—"good night, I guess."

I turned. "You can come watch with me, if you want."

"In your room? Your bed?"

"Yeah, I guess. We're adults. I'm sure we can figure out a way to keep our hands to ourselves."

"You sure?"

"Yeah. Just no funny business."

"Who, me?" He feigned shock. "I'm an innocent party."

"Yeah, my grandma always said you're only as innocent as the horns holding up your halo."

"Your grandma was a smart lady. Do you mind if I make popcorn?"

"As long as you don't mind if I don't eat it."

I went to my room, riffled through DVDs, and settled on a testosterone-filled movie full of awkward moments. I had just finished putting on my favorite summer pajamas when Jared walked in wearing low-slung gray sweatpants.

"Do you ever wear a shirt?" I laughed.

"What?" he asked as he shoved a handful of popcorn in his mouth. I watched some of the pieces fall and glance off his stomach. Lucky popcorn.

"Get over here." I patted the bed next to me. "No funny business." I warned.

"Got it. No funny business."

* * *

I woke up with a weird feeling. With my head snuggled against his shoulder, his arm tight around me, and a smile on my face.

For the first time in forever, sleeping with a man took on a new definition. There was no funny business. There was no expectant touching, no furious attempt at ripping clothing to shreds, no jackhammer to my nether region, and, I am happy to report, no unsightly bodily fluids were hardened to my hair.

I'd fallen asleep sometime halfway through the movie and other than a few stray popcorn kernels my sheets were still fresh from the dry cleaner. I listened to Jared breathe steadily, watched as his long eyelashes fluttered, and, as I placed my hand gently on his chest, felt his heart beat calmly. His dark hair fell over his eyes. He was in desperate need of a haircut, at least according to him. A small dusting of chest hair populated his defined chest. And for the first time I noticed a small Chinese character tattoo on his rib cage. I made a mental note to ask him what it meant.

I had to admit, I liked being with him more than I imagined I would. I looked forward to spending time with him. It was new. I liked the feeling.

I had to shimmy my way out from under Jared's arm. He barely moved, let out a light snore, then rolled over and hugged my pillow. It was nice watching him sleep for a few minutes before I padded barefoot to the kitchen to make coffee. While waiting for it to brew, I pulled my phone out of the drawer. I had a bunch of texts from Sarah, Caroline, Berk, and Danny, all making sure I was okay.

I shot off responses to everyone letting them know I was alive and well, assured Caroline and Sarah that I'd be at the noon spin class, confirmed dinner plans with Danny, and sent Berk a picture of my boobs. At least he'd get a laugh out of it.

Checking the clock, I saw that it was only a little past six, so I decided to pour my coffee in a to-go cup and head to the bakery for some fresh bagels. Hopefully spin class would melt away the carbs later.

Sneaking into my room, I quickly grabbed a pair of shorts, a tank, and my flip-flops. As I was making my way out the door, I froze when I heard Jared talking in his sleep.

"No good. No good."

I giggled and stepped closer.

"Mels. No good. Don't go."

Mels? Was he talking about me?

"Melody wait."

He was talking about me. Feeling awkward about intruding on his subconscious, I backed out of the room but not before he rolled onto his back, complete with a saluting soldier, and mumbled, "See you naked."

* * *

I met the girls a little before noon in the locker room at the gym. I was last to arrive, as usual.

"Hey. How are you doing?" Caroline asked.

"I'm fine." I shoved my bag in a locker. "I'm good, really. I don't know what the hell I ate or drank but my stomach was rough last night. It calmed down mostly by the time we got home." As I leaned down to tie my shoe, I noticed Sarah's tapping foot. "What?"

"We?" Sarah asked.

"Yeah, we. You placed your brother in my apartment when you were infested with rodents and roaches."

She held her hands up. "Just clarifying."

"No clarification needed," I snapped and then realized I'd become protective of the times Jared and I spent together.

"Well," Caroline began, "how are you doing with the whole Zac thing?"

"Look, you guys were right. Zac and I aren't meant to be together, no matter how badly I wanted it. And to be honest, looking at it from this side of the glass, being with him kept me stagnant. It's surreal."

"Good for you," Caroline said, but she didn't sound convinced.

"No, really. From now on, I'm going to start looking at things differently. Not saying I want to look for a relationship but I think"—I took off my shirt and reapplied my deodorant—"I'm not going to actively hide from one either."

"Really?" Sarah shut the locker door and eyed me.

The two of them stared at me, so I continued, "I just think that maybe I should finally try out your foreplay idea. Maybe go out on some dates that don't end in sex. Maybe hold off, you know, slow simmer and all. I can save that for the second date, if there is one."

"You honestly can't hold off until you turn thirty?" Sarah asked. "It's less than a month away."

"Of course I *can*—"

"Then do it," Caroline piped up.

"Why would I?"

"Because we don't think you can."

"Are you double dog daring me to abstain from sex?"

"Triple dog dare. Berk doesn't think you can do it either." Caroline showed me her phone. She'd been text messaging with Berk during the conversation, giving him the blow by blow.

"A month?" I asked.

"About that," Sarah answered.

"What do I get if I do this?"

"A libido recharge?"

I chewed my lip for a moment. "Eh. I'll take it."

I winked and skipped—yes skipped—out of the locker room, but not before I heard Sarah whisper to Caroline, "I think she hit her head."

"Which one?" Caroline replied.

Warden Suzy was our spin class instructor and was in rare form that afternoon.

"Remember, ladies, good things come to those who get their asses on a bike and fucking earn them. I'm going to make you ride so hard you'll be dizzy by the time I'm done with you."

"Sounds like last night with Drew," I heard Sarah snicker.

"Still playing tie me up, tie me down with your boy toy?" I asked during the warm-up.

"Of course. But"—she began to breathe harder—"he keeps mentioning how much more convenient it would be if we shared a space."

"Shared a space?" Caroline asked.

"His words, not mine."

"So." I changed gears as the Warden yelled. "He wants you two to live together?"

"It's too soon. Right? Too soon?" Sarah looked between Caroline and me.

"If you have time to talk you have time to kick it up a notch!" Suzy screamed over the bumping bass. I swear, if she turned the music up any louder, I was going to need earplugs.

"Brian and I moved in together and we've been together less time that you and Drew."

"But Drew and I really aren't serious."

"Does he know that?" I asked. My legs were starting to burn.

"Probably not."

"I say go for it. Then give your brother the apartment so he can get the hell out of mine."

"I don't think it's as bad as you want us to think it is." Caroline giggled as the class amped up.

"He's been there for what? Five days? What's another couple? Not saying I'd throw him out of bed for eating crackers"—*or popcorn*, I thought—"but I'm not used to sharing space."

"About that," Sarah began, then took a long swig of water, "it might be a little longer. Seems there's a bigger infestation in the building."

"How much longer?"

"No idea."

My response was cut off by Warden Suzy. "Ladies, if you want to chat, go make a lunch date. If you want to melt away your fat asses, shut the hell up and fucking spin!"

* * *

Later that night I called my parents while Jared was in the shower.

"Hey, Dad." I grabbed a slice of pizza from the fridge and poured a glass of red.

"Melly! How you doing kiddo?"

"I'm good, Dad. How's the beach?" I said with a mouthful of sausage and cheese.

"Perfect as usual. When are you coming to visit?"

"I have to work, Dad."

"Right. Well, okay. We'd love to see you."

"I know. I'm just so busy." I gave my usual excuse but felt a pit in my stomach that hadn't been there before.

"You're a successful woman, Mel. I get it." I could hear the disappointment in his voice. "Well, your mom wants to talk to you. Take care of yourself and don't work too hard, sweetie."

"Thanks, Dad. I love you."

"Love you, too Here's your mom."

"Melly! It's been so long since I've talked to you."

"We talked last week, Mom."

"When are you coming down here?"

"Mom, I'm—"

"Busy. Yes, I know. I'm busy, too. Just yesterday I had lunch with Martha and tonight I have a meeting with my book club. See, busy. But *I* make time."

"Lunch with your friends is hardly—"

"Mel! Where's the shaving cream?" Jared interrupted.

"Who was that?" I cursed my mom's excellent hearing.

"No one."

"Mel! Seriously." I heard cabinets slamming. "Did you use all my shaving cream?"

"Is that a man?"

"Yes, Mom, it's a man."

Jared walked in with a towel wrapped around his waist. "Mel." He stood close and I could smell how clean he was and it clouded my head. I hated that he knew how he affected me.

I placed my hand over my phone and said, "My mom is on the phone and she can hear you."

"So?" he whispered back.

"So she's going to think you're my boyfriend."

"God forbid." He rolled his eyes. "Where's the shaving cream?"

"In the bag." I pointed to the bag hanging on the closest doorknob.

"Thanks." He leaned down and kissed my cheek.

"Sorry, Mom."

"Melody, who is that man in your apartment?"

"Jared? Sarah's brother. He's just staying here for a bit."

"I taught you better than that, Melody. When are you going to grow up and realize you can't have random—"

"Jared isn't random." I cringed as Jared looked over at me.

"Then what is he? Your boyfriend?"

I took a deep breath. "Yes, Mom, he's my boyfriend." I held the phone away from my ear as my mom yelled her hallelujahs. Jared crossed his arms over his chest and smiled.

"What are you smiling at?" I asked. He really did have pretty eyes. And long lashes. And a tiny dimple that appeared only when he smirked. I wanted to lick that dimple.

"Nothing."

"Yes, Mom. He's a nice guy. Tell Dad he is nice. We can't, Mom. We are busy, he has to work, I have to work. I can't just forget everything and come down." I dropped my head to the counter and banged it a few times. "Come on, Mom. Yes, I promise you'll meet him. No, I wasn't keeping him a secret."

Jared walked over and took the phone from me. "Hi, Mrs. Ashford. Yes, this is Jared. Nice to finally speak to you, too. I've heard so much about you." He tweaked my nose. "Of course! Melly and I would *love* to come down and see you. I would love to meet you. Sounds perfect. Yes. I can't wait either. I'll tell her. Thank you so much. See you Wednesday. Bye."

He handed my phone back to me and I stared at him, open-mouthed.

"Wednesday?" I asked.

"We're going to see your parents on Wednesday and will stay for a few days."

"So you're offering to pretend you're my boyfriend so I don't have to deal with my mother nagging me all week?"

"That depends. Do I get to hold your hand?" He clasped my hand in his.

"Well, yeah. I guess."

"Do I get to grab your ass?" His hand slipped around me as he patted my behind.

"In front of my parents?"

"You're right. Um"—he looked like he was enjoying the idea entirely too much—"do we get to kiss?" He pulled me in close. He smelled like my lavender shampoo and peppermint gum. Our lips were barely an inch apart. My heart felt like it would pound out of my chest.

"I, uh, I really hadn't—"

"Well, think about it now." His voice was deeper than I'd heard it before. The kind of deep that sent a woman's stomach into a flurry, turned her knees to jelly, and made her brain go fuzzy. The kind of voice that dropped panties, commanded attention, and induced orgasms. And it made me want to hand over control.

"I guess a boyfriend and girlfriend would kiss." I couldn't breathe.

"Good. Looking forward to it." He released me and clapped his hand over my shoulder before he walked back to the bathroom to shave.

Jerk.

"You're welcome." He yelled from down the hall.

I guess we were going to visit my parents.

Chapter Twelve

I woke up Monday morning ready to face the day. I needed to find myself, who I wanted to be. The self-confidence I owned was no façade. It was something I held in spades. But as thirty approached, I thought a new outlook was necessary. And it pained me to realize Sarah and Caroline were right. I needed a new hobby. Life as a bed-hopping bunny was probably not going to be a good look forever. And besides, I needed to get my head straight for the impromptu mini trip to the beach Jared had planned with my mother.

I arrived at my office earlier than usual since I skipped my morning workout. Of course, my ass would revolt but sometimes a girl needs a day off. Jenny was filling my drawer with protein bars and water when I arrived.

"Morning. You're back."

"I'm back."

"So what happened with the boyfriend? I notice you're not screaming for me to look at your ring. Things not go as planned?" I eyed her as I placed my bags on the chair.

Jenny plopped in the chair across from my desk. "No. No ring. No nothing."

"I'm sorry to hear that."

"I broke up with him."

"Because he didn't propose?" I settled into my chair and leaned back.

"That and a lot of things. He thinks we grew apart. I feel like he's being unfair."

I rummaged around my drawer and pulled out my stash of French chocolate. Handing her a piece, I said, "I'm really sorry to hear that. Is there anything I can do?"

"You can put in a good word for me with Waterman."

"For?"

"There's an opportunity to start working with my own clients and I requested to be interviewed. I was hoping with your recommendation and possibly your willingness to mentor me, I'd have a better chance."

I considered her for a moment. I knew she had the stuff necessary to move up. I worried about her lack of experience, though. She and I hadn't had the opportunity to get her groomed for such a position. On the other hand, I had been green when I was given the opportunity to start with the company and the need to pay it forward ranked high on my list of priorities. "When's the interview?"

"Noon."

"I'll make the call."

"Thank you so much!" Jenny jumped from her chair and ran around the desk to give me a hug. "You are so amazing! I know with you helping me out, I can do this job."

"You'll do fine. Now, hop out of here so I can call Mr. Waterman."

Jenny closed the office door behind her and I dropped my head to my desk and pounded it a few times on the hard oak. Calling Zac was not what I wanted to do first thing in the morning. I hadn't had enough cups of coffee to prepare me for such an early-morning intrusion. But a promise was a promise and I didn't make those often.

"Jenny?" I buzzed her.

"Yes?"

"Can you get me a large chai latte and some aspirin? And clear my schedule from Wednesday on. I'm going to be out of the office from then until next Tuesday. And then again next Friday." The headache was already making its way to the back of my head and I rolled my shoulders with hopes to derail it.

"Absolutely. Be back in twenty."

I took a deep breath, counted backward from twenty, and reminded myself that regardless of the relationship Zac and I had, he was still my boss and I still worked for him. It wouldn't do to allow what transpired to turn into awkward daily confrontations.

Just as I was about to pick up the phone, it buzzed.

"Ms. Ashford? Mr. Waterman would like to see you in his office."

"Now?"

"Now. He has a busy schedule today."

"Be right there."

I guess Jenny's recommendation would occur face-to-face.

Standing, I smoothed out my skirt and buttoned my blazer. I was dressed more conservatively than usual and I hoped he'd get the message.

His secretary waved me into the office and I stopped short when she closed the door behind me. Zac barely looked up from his paperwork and waved me to the seat across from him.

His navy blazer was hung in the corner of his office like usual. The pale blue dress shirt that was tailored to fit him was rolled to his elbows. His hair was mussed just enough to pass for acceptable in the work place. Sitting across from him, I could see his brow was furrowed, like he was trying to work something out. I couldn't tell if he was truly focused on whatever he was doing or if it was some sort of power play game. It was minutes before he turned his attention to me.

"Melody. Thanks for coming in on such short notice." The lack of familiarity in his tone was disconcerting and the hard edge to his stare gave me goose bumps.

"Well, when the boss calls..." I tried to keep my tone light but I knew it wasn't.

"I'm booked solid all week but I made time to interview your assistant later on today. What's your recommendation?"

"I was actually going to call you about that. I'd stand behind the decision to move her forward for sure. She's competent, eager, and smart. She'd make a good addition to the group." Without thinking, I fidgeted with my ears, playing with the diamond earrings Zac had given me. I needed to remember to take them off.

"Good to know. Well, thanks." Without another word, he resumed whatever it was he was doing when I came in and I was effectively, and coldly, dismissed. I know I shouldn't have let it bother me but tears stung the backs of my eyes. I stood, staring at him. Willing the past to erase itself, wanting him to look at me, to show me that I mattered.

"Yes?" He dropped his pen and clasped his arms behind his head. A small smirk played at the corners of his mouth. I knew what he was doing. He was waiting for me to cave. He was fucking playing games.

"One more thing." I forced my voice to remain even. "Something has come up and I am going to need to take Wednesday through Friday off. I'll be visiting my parents."

It was clear he wasn't expecting that. I knew he was expecting me to change my mind, beg for him to stay.

"Your parents?" He kept his eyes on me as he stood and walked around to the front of the desk. He leaned back, arms crossed over his chest as he studied me, like he was daring me to look away first.

"Yes. I had Jenny clear my schedule. I will, of course, bring anything with me that needs to be addressed. I'll be on e-mail if you need to get in touch with me."

"E-mail? So this is how it's going to go?" He stepped toward me, reaching out before thinking better of it and dropping his arm to his side.

I breathed out, thankful he was the one who had addressed the elephant in the room.

"Zac, listen. You need to be with your wife and I need to not be sleeping with a married man."

"Mel—"

"No, Zac. Please don't make this weirder than it has to be. I'll be back next Tuesday. We'll figure out how to be in a room with each other without the need to strip naked."

His laugh was soft. "I just wanted to apologize for showing up at your apartment like that. To apologize for, honestly, not treating you the way you deserve. You're one of the brightest, most beautiful women I've ever met, and it hurts me to know I might have been holding you back from being happy." He leaned against his desk. "I fell in love with you so fast and so hard that I didn't stop to see that I might be hurting you."

"Zac—"

"You crave reciprocation, Mel. You want something you can shout from the rooftops and let everyone know about. You deserve that. I want that for you."

"I don't know what to say." I was honestly shocked to hear those words come from him. To know he saw things I hadn't noticed about myself.

"Let yourself be free, Mel. Let yourself be happy."

I squared my shoulders and lifted my head. "I will."

He waved me off. "Go. Be with your parents. Take the week. It's okay. And don't bring work with you. I'm sure there is nothing that can't wait."

"Thanks, Zac." Warmth replaced the cold stare I'd received when I first arrived and I thought maybe working with him wouldn't be so bad after all. "I also had Jenny clear my schedule for next Friday."

Zac looked at me a moment. "Your birthday."

"Yes," I replied and smiled before leaving him behind.

Jenny arrived at my office, latte in hand, just as I did.

"Thank you. Mr. Waterman gave me the week off. I'm starting my vacation today." I took the drink. "E-mail me if you need anything while I'm gone."

"Everything okay?"

"Yep. Just a much-deserved getaway. You're all set with Mr. Waterman. Text me if you find out before I get back."

"Deal. And thanks."

I smiled and headed into my office. Checking the time, I packed my bag, set up my voice mail and e-mail auto-reply to let people know the dates I'd be out of the office, shut down my computer, and headed out. If I hurried, I'd be able to make it.

I was sitting in the lobby of Blackwell and Dardston when I saw Jared step off the elevator. A short crop replaced his usual floppy hair. Instead of shorts, jeans, or those teasingly low sweatpants he liked to lounge in, he was wearing a perfectly tailored blue suit. He walked in my direction with his head down, looking at his phone as he loosened his tie. I thought the receptionist was going to lose her shit as she stared at him walking past.

Hell, I was about to lose *my* shit. He was so fucking delicious.

"Hey you."

He looked up and smiled broadly when he saw me. "Hey. What are you doing here?"

I tilted my head toward the exit and he nodded as we walked. "I took off a little early after I took care of some things. Figured I'd meet up with you here. That okay?"

"I guess. I mean, I don't know how I feel about you coming to my work and stalking me—"

"Stalking you?"

"What would you call it?"

"I would call it a friend coming to congratulate you on getting a new job."

"How'd you know I got the job?"

"I know things."

"You know things, huh?"

"Yes. And I think this calls for a celebration."

He stepped toward me and draped his arm around my shoulder. Though he was wearing cologne, I could still smell subtle hints of lavender. Jared became that smell. I couldn't get enough. "Celebration? Like that dinner you promised me?"

"I never promised." I smiled. "I said maybe."

Jared stepped in front of me and ran his hand along my cheek. He leaned close and said, "Maybe if I ask you again you'll say yes."

"Maybe," I breathed and closed my eyes.

"Will you go out to dinner with me?" His mouth was so close I could feel the warmth of his breath on my lips and I ached with want.

"Yes."

"Good." He tugged my bottom lip between his fingers. "Let's go home. And let's grab a sandwich on the way. I'm hungry."

He walked away and I was left adjusting my lady boner.

Chapter Thirteen

S o where do you want to go for dinner?" Jared asked me after I emerged from the shower.

"I don't know. What are you in the mood for?" I took the towel off my head and let my curls fall free around my shoulders.

"Did you cut your hair?" he asked.

"No, why?"

"It looks shorter."

"Just because the curls make it shorter. When I blow it out and straighten it, it looks longer."

He reached out and softly tugged a strand and watched it bounce back. "I like it."

"Thanks." I adjusted my towel as I realized I was pretty close to naked. "So." I blew out a breath. "Dinner?"

"Up to you. I'm easy."

"Nice to know."

"Not that easy."

"Too bad." I stuck out my bottom lip. "Cheeseburgers?"

"You want cheeseburgers? I figured our first date—"

"Our first what?" I raised an eyebrow at him. "Who said anything about a date?"

"No, no." He backpedaled. "I meant for the first time you and I"—he cleared his throat—"when I ate you out—"

I drummed my fingers on the counter. "When you what now?" I enjoyed watching him get flustered.

"When I took you out—"

"That's not what you said."

"You know what I meant!"

"I must say, Jared, I don't know the kind of kinky things that go through your mind but I'm pretty sure I would have remembered being eaten out, as you say."

Exasperated, he dropped his head and pointed toward my room. "Go get ready so we can get you some cheeseburgers."

Laughing, I padded off to my room. After I blow-dried my hair and added a few touches of makeup, I stared at my closet as I tried to figure out what to wear.

"Hey, Jared!" I yelled.

"Yeah?"

"What should I wear?"

"Whatever you want to wear."

"Well, I can't figure out if this is a date or if I'm getting eaten out. They require totally different outfits."

"Shut up and get dressed."

Laughing, I grabbed a kelly green strapless sundress. Not too dressy but dressy enough to pass as date attire. Plus, it was a dress, just in case, well, just in case.

Chapter Fourteen

Two days later, we were driving down the Garden State Parkway.

"Why are we listening to this?" I groaned. Jared had a habit of finding the twangiest sad sap of a country song and singing it at the top of his lungs. Every time I attempted to change the station, he slapped my hand away.

"Country music is real music. It has meaning. Listen to the words." He proceeded to sing his way through a very whiny chorus.

"Other music is real music. I mean, the song doesn't have to be about your favorite girl leaving you alone with your dilapidated pickup after she stole your hound dog and ran off with the tax man."

"What are you talking about? I have never heard a country song about a girl running off with the tax man." He downed the last of his energy drink.

"Well, I am sure there is one. You just haven't heard it yet." I huffed, crossed my arms over my chest, and looked out the window.

Sand in the front lawns. We were getting close.

"Are you pouting?"

"No."

"You are totally pouting! How old are you going to be? Five?"

"Oh, shut up! You move to Georgia for like six years—"

"Eight years."

"Eight years and suddenly you turn into a cowboy."

"There weren't many cowboys in Georgia. And besides, what's wrong with a cowboy? I thoughts chicks totally dug cowboys? I mean, I don't have the hat or boots or anything but if you're into that kind of thing I'm sure I could find—"

"Stop right there buddy." I held up my hands.

"Buddy?"

"Yeah, *buddy*. Let's get something straight. You're here *pretending* to be my boyfriend so my mom gets off my back and if you think there's going to be any hanky-panky this week—"

"Who says I *want* hanky-panky with you? That's awfully presumptuous. I barely even know you." He stared straight ahead and turned up the music, a small dimple forming at the corner of his mouth.

"You'd be lucky to hanky-panky with me." I thought about it. He and I really didn't know each other at all.

"I don't believe in luck."

"Interesting. I mean, your being Irish and all I figured you'd be looking for a little lady luck."

"Nah. She's bat-shit crazy. I'd rather make things happen for myself."

"Do you always get what you want?"

"Nope. But then again, slow and steady wins the race."

"Who are you in a race with?"

"Myself. I work hard. I play hard. When I want something, I go after it. I don't always get it, but I try to make sure the effort is memorable."

"Memorable?"

"Educational."

"Educational?"

"Are you going to repeat everything I say as a question?"

"No." I looked out the window. "So what are you after now?"

"You."

"Me?" I whipped my head around and shifted in my seat.

"Is that a problem?" He looked at me and raised an eyebrow.

"What do you want from me?"

He stared straight ahead and I chewed on a fingernail.

He finally answered, "I just want to know you better."

I thought for a minute and decided to ask one of the questions I wanted to know the answer to. "Why did you and your girlfriend break up?"

"Pulling out the big guns, huh?" His smile didn't quite reach his eyes. I figured he knew I was looking when he pulled his sunglasses off the top of his head and shoved them on his face. "Didn't work out."

"That's not vague at all." I played with the strap of my favorite navy blue sundress.

"Yeah, well." He changed the radio station from country favorites to eighties hair bands. "Honestly, there's not much to tell other than that. We grew apart. Wanted different things. I don't know. I mean, am I sad about it? Yeah kind of, but not how I thought I would be. She's a great girl, just not great for me nor I for her."

"That sounds very grown-up."

He shrugged, "Grown-ups do grown-up things."

And the second question that was burning in my brain? "Why'd you cancel the interview with Zac?"

"Didn't really want to work for a guy like that." I noticed his knuckles whiten as he gripped the steering wheel.

"A guy like what?" I almost bit my tongue as I asked. I knew the answer. It was written all over his face.

"He's a douche."

"He's not a douche. He's just—"

"Sorry. A douche *bag*. What the hell do you see in that guy anyway? Is it because he's loaded?" He sounded annoyed, angry even.

I felt a sharp pain in my chest. "*That* is insulting." For the first time in my life, I actually was ashamed of myself. Sure, Gabe the Fart Machine grossed me out, but I hadn't felt ashamed. Just resigned to the fact that a girl can't always expect a guy to make her come.

"Oh, right. I forgot. It's because he's great in the sack *and* he's loaded."

"For your information"—I shifted in my seat so my back was against the door and I was looking straight at him—"I don't *see* anything in Zachary Waterman. Not anymore anyway. I made a mistake. That's it. End of story. Is he loaded? Yeah. Could he fuck like a champ? Every fucking day. But neither of those things mean anything. Sex doesn't always have to *mean* something. And if you knew me, you'd know that."

"Well, I don't know you." He looked out the window and muttered, "And it drives me nuts."

"And why would it drive you nuts?" The sharp retort had me cringing.

"I don't know, Melody. Like I said, I want to know you. I want to see what it is you're hiding behind all that snark. You wear a mask, Mel. And you aren't fooling me. God, you are so blind."

"Blind to what exactly?"

"Me. Everyone around you. Blind to how fucking great you are. Blind to the fact that I have been trying to get to know you, figure you out. I want to figure out why you keep telling yourself you don't want a relationship when I kinda think you do. I want to know how you take your coffee in the morning. I want to know where your favorite vacation spot is." He paused and blew out a breath. "I want to know what it feels like to kiss you."

I looked down at my hands. "I don't know what to say about that."

"Then don't say anything." He turned up the radio again. "Don't say anything at all."

With an hour to go, the rest of the drive was full of awkward silence. And eighties power ballads. I'm surprised I didn't burst into tears.

* * *

We arrived at my parents' Second Avenue condo in North Wildwood by three in the afternoon. The breeze was light and warm. A perfect afternoon at the beach.

Jared parked his pickup across the street from the building. "Leave the bags. I'll get them later."

"We're talking now?"

"Gotta start the charade sometime." He sighed and opened the door.

"Let's go look at the beach first." I jumped out, wondering if I'd made a mistake in asking him to pretend for me.

We walked down the ramp to the beach and walked toward the water. I closed my eyes and let the sea air hit me. Just like my grandma used to do, I lifted my hand and rubbed my fingers together.

"What are you doing?" he asked.

"My grandma would always stick her hand out the window and do this whenever we came down here. When we were close enough, she would say she could feel the salt in the air. That's how she knew her vacation had started."

He leaned his elbows on the railing and dropped his head. "I like that."

"Me, too."

We spent a few more minutes watching the waves break along the shoreline before heading to the condo.

We hadn't always stayed in the condo. For years we stayed on the other side of the boardwalk in the Towers. I loved driving into Wildwood and seeing the large beach ball in front of the conference center, the view from the Towers, the pool, the easy walk to the hotel next door to get banana pancakes in the morning. I think Grandma was sad when we first stayed in North Wildwood. She missed the long walk from the boardwalk to the water, dragging coolers and chairs and towels, listening to the conductor remind us, "Watch the tram car, please."

As a kid, I always loved the lights and sounds of the boardwalk at night. But the older I got, the more I wanted to just relax without having sand kicked in my face, without funnel cake being shoved down my throat. I was twenty when my parents finally stopped renting and finally purchased the condo. They just started living there full time last summer, after Dad retired.

Still, every summer since I can remember, Wildwood was my home.

"Mom? Dad?"

As usual, my parents were sitting out on the deck, Mom reading a book in the lounge chair and Dad with his binoculars and three fingers of scotch that he'd nurse until dinner. I was a near replica of my mother, but whereas she was stick thin, I had curves. We both had naturally brown hair, though I dyed mine blond. My eyes were my dad's: big, hazel, and evenly spaced—a trait my mother thought was worth noting.

"Melly!" My dad pulled me into a huge bear hug. "I saw you looking out at the water. Thought about calling out to you but it looked like you and he were sharing a moment." His laugh echoed, even in open space.

"Dad, we weren't *sharing a moment.*"

"Felt like a moment to me." Jared piped up and stretched out his hand. "Hi, I'm Jared. Nice to meet you, Mr. Ashford."

"Please, call me Bill. Handshake schmandshake! We hug around here." My dad pulled him in and clapped him on the back as my mom kissed me before turning to Jared.

"It's so nice to meet you. Truth be told, Melody hasn't told us much about you—"

"Mom—" I rolled my eyes.

"Hush now, Melody. You must be thirsty." My mom linked her arm in his as she steered him toward the kitchen. "So, Jared. How did you and my Melody meet?"

"I'm Sarah's brother. Moved here from Georgia not too long ago. Melody and I just kind of hit it off, I guess you'd say."

My mom poured Jared her summer drink that my dad affectionately called the Too Fruity—a mixture of lime and coconut rums, pineapple juice, cranberry juice, and a healthy squeeze of fresh lime.

"Here you go, dear. Where are your bags?"

Jared took a healthy sip of the drink and said, "Thank you, Mrs. Ashford. In the car. I was going to get them later."

"You can call me Nora. And don't be silly. You've driven a long way. Melody and Bill can get them."

My mom gave me *the look* that told me I was traipsing downstairs and dragging the bags up to the third floor. "Sure, Mom."

"You two can have your room. I've redecorated. Wait till you see!" She nearly shoved Jared onto the back deck.

"Come on, Melly. Let's get those bags."

After we schlepped the bags upstairs, I dragged my large suitcase down the hall, following my dad. I stopped in the doorway and stared at the freshly made queen-size bed in the middle of my room.

"Dad? Where are the twin beds?"

"Oh, we got rid of them. Isn't a bigger bed more comfortable?"

"Where is Jared going to sleep?"

"Well, I assume your mother has him staying here with you. Is that not okay?" He looked alarmed and placed his hands on my arms. "You know, you can say no. It's your body. You should never let a man have his way with you—"

"Oh my God, Dad. Stop. It's fine." The conversation took me back to eighth grade, when I was getting ready for my first boy-girl dance and Dad thought it would be a good idea to have "the talk" with me. I'm surprised I wasn't scared off penises for the rest of my life.

"As a man I can say that men have only one thing on their minds. I remember when I met your mother—"

"Dad! I am almost thirty years old. I think I know a little more than I did when I was a kid."

"What's all the yelling?" My mom rushed in. "Do you like the room?" She ran her hand over the brightly colored comforter, looking at me expectantly.

"It's great, Mom." I almost smiled.

Jared peeked around the doorway and said, "Nice bed."

I looked at him, mortified, hoping the innuendo that dripped from his words were lost on my parents. "It's fine, Mom. Thanks."

"Well, you're a little too old to be sleeping in a twin bed with princess sheets. I just figured you'd like something more grown-up. And now that you have a man in your life, I thought—"

"Princess sheets?" Jared mouthed the words silently.

"It's fine, Mom. Really." I hugged her as I gave Jared the finger.

"Good. Come on. I have some shrimp cocktail for everyone. It's a special day, we can start happy hour early."

"Be right there. I'm going to unpack so I don't have to do it later."

"I'll help her." Jared's offer made my mom's smile unnaturally wide and unsettling. I felt like I was Alice and she was the Cheshire Cat.

"You two take your time. We'll be out here getting the snacks ready." She winked at me and smiled at Jared before walking out of the room.

"Still like your wine, Melly?"

"Yep. Thanks, Dad."

He closed the door behind him and Jared fell onto the bed.

"Comfy."

"*You* are sleeping on the floor!" I ripped the pillow out of his hands.

"What would your mom think if you made me sleep on the floor? I mean, you are my girlfriend, right?"

He was right. At least partially. Partially being only for the week, only in front of my parents.

"Fine. You sleep over there. I'll sleep here." I dramatically slammed the pillow in the middle of the bed, highlighting our sleeping arrangements. "No funny business."

"I wouldn't dream of it."

He sat on the bed, having finished his unpacking in a matter of minutes, and watched as I unpacked my bag, shoving items haphazardly into drawers.

"You're going to wrinkle your clothes." He pulled a hanger out of the closet, picked a dress from the top of the pile, and hung it up.

When he reached in to grab another dress, the top of my blue bikini fell to the floor. Bending over, he picked up the small swath of fabric and held it in front of him. "What's this?" he asked, cocking his eyebrow.

I snatched it out of his hands, balled it up, and stuffed it in a drawer. "My bathing suit top."

"That thing"—he pointed at the drawer—"covers those?" He pointed at my chest and I knocked his hand away.

"As a matter of fact, it does."

"That's something I have to see. Where is the bottom?" He ransacked my suitcase.

"Stop that!" I tried to close the lid and ended up tangled in his arms and we both fell to the floor with a thud, him lying on top of me.

Covered in a pile of my summer clothes, Jared and I froze. I could smell that he'd used my shampoo again and lavender had never smelled sexier.

I stared at his lips and my stomach flip-flopped. His hands

brushed the hair away from my face and he leaned closer. My breath hitched and my voice caught in my throat as he brushed his lips against mine.

"God, you're beautiful." He dropped his forehead to mine and shifted his body. I gasped as a jolt of heat shot through me.

His mouth crashed on mine and his hands slid down my sides as mine pushed under his shirt. I lifted my hips as he pressed into me.

I bit my tongue as he scraped his teeth along my jaw and ran his tongue down my neck to my shoulder. The need to cry out only intensified the feeling. His hands cupped my breasts before he moved to grab my leg and hitched it up alongside him, his hand sliding to my ass. He pulled me toward him as our mouths met once again.

"Jared," I whispered, knowing my parents were only steps away in the other room.

I felt his hand slide between my legs, his thumb rubbing against me though my panties.

"God, you're wet," he mumbled between kisses.

"Oh my God." I bit my lip, afraid to make too much noise. I rocked my hips in rhythm with his thumb and it wasn't long before the buildup rose through me. I pressed my mouth to his as I came quick and furious. I was still shaking when he removed his hand.

"You okay?" he whispered.

"Better than. You?"

"I'm good." And there was that smirk.

"I can tell." I shifted my eyes down as he adjusted himself.

"Uncomfortable?" His hips settled between my legs.

"Not really. You?"

"Naw. It's neat how we fit this way. Like a puzzle."

He was right. Our bodies fit together in such a way that even though he had at least seventy pounds on me, I couldn't feel the weight. Just his heartbeat. And the warmth of his breath.

"Well, I guess we better not keep your parents waiting." He stood, never breaking eye contact, and held out his hand.

I grabbed it and let him pull me up.

"Your eyes," he started, "aren't totally blue. They're kind of green, too."

"Hazel." Was I actually blushing?

"Interesting. That they change, I mean."

"Change isn't always a bad thing." It struck me that I was only beginning to understand the true definition of change. And changing fuck buddies didn't count.

"No, it's not." he responded. "I think I'm going to like pretending to be your boyfriend this week."

Chapter Fifteen

Wow, Nora. Dinner was excellent. Thank you." Jared patted his stomach.

"It was good. Thanks, Mom." I finished the last of my wine and my dad was quick to refill my glass.

"Anytime, sweetie. I love cooking for you. Just wish I could do it more often—"

"Mom." I rolled my eyes and stretched.

"Don't 'Mom' me. You know we don't see each other nearly enough. I mean, you're just a drive down the highway. What's a couple hours out of your weekend to come and see us?"

"Dad, tell Mom to stop making me feel bad."

"Hey, I have no control over her, you know that. And besides, she has a point. The last time we saw you was when? Christmastime? You're always so busy. What are you doing that's keeping you so busy all the time?"

"I mean, if you had a family, we'd understand. But it's just you! There is no excuse to go six months without seeing your parents."

"Mom!" I groaned and began clearing the table.

"I'll do that. You should sit, hang with your parents." Jared took the dish from me.

"You're killing me," I whispered.

"I know. But look at it this way, you'll be here all week. Get this guilt trip stuff they love so much out of the way so you can show me around this place." He quickly kissed my cheek and brought our plates to the sink. I felt the burn from his lips down to my toes.

"Dad, I work. I put in very long hours."

"You're too young and too pretty to be wasting your life sitting behind a desk. When do you get out? Meet people? When do you have time to date?" My mother waggled her finger at me.

"What does pretty have to do with it? Besides, I date."

"Who? Who do you date? Jared's the first boy you've brought home since high school."

"Look, I just haven't found the right person for me. I don't have time for relationships." I slouched back into my chair before getting up and helping to clear the table.

"You mean you didn't have time? I mean, you have time now, for Jared." Jared smiled at my mom as she mentioned his name. "And seems like a perfectly lovely young man."

"Thank you Mrs.— I mean Nora."

My dad eased out of his chair and walked to the kitchen. He clapped Jared on the back and said, "I always knew my Melly was picky. And if you're good enough for her, then you're okay in my book. And if you need any pointers on how to keep an Ashford woman happy"—my dad actually winked—"I've got thirty-five years of experience." He leaned in and whispered not so quietly, "It's all in the foreplay."

If I didn't know any better, I would have thought Jared was blushing. I banged my head a few times on the cabinet door.

"Oh, Bill." My mom walked over and kissed my dad, the kind of kiss no kid wants to see, even at almost thirty years old. Yeah, it was endearing but there was something not quite natural about my parents sucking face.

I gagged and my mom giggled as she pulled away. "Oh honey, like you've never kissed anyone before. I bet you and Jared kiss all the time."

I realized I was standing awfully close to Jared when I felt his back stiffen. The hairs on my arm stood on end and my face heated. "Yeah, sure. Of course we do. Right, sweetie?"

Jared kept washing dishes. I elbowed him. "Right, sweetie?" I asked through clenched teeth.

"Right. Kiss. All the time. Love to kiss your daughter." I nearly burst out laughing as his words rambled into a nearly incoherent string of syllables and his dish rinsing took on an intensity normally reserved for war.

"You two are so cute!" My mom pinched both of our cheeks. "Have you ever been to Wildwood, dear?"

"Ah, no. I've never been. Seems like a fun place."

"Oh, Melly! You have to take him to the boardwalk. He'll just love it!" My mom ran to her room. "Wait here. I have a card that has some credits left on it you can use for rides."

"We don't need your card, Mom," I yelled after her before turning to my dad. "Dad, you have to tell Mom to lay off."

"She just loves you, sweetie. And she's so excited to meet Jared. When you were unpacking she told me she could tell it was true love. You two are going to end up together for a long time. I can feel it."

All I could think was *Maybe*.

* * *

After a pair of wiggly eyebrows sent us on our merry way, Jared and I headed toward the famed Wildwood boardwalk.

"So what's all the fuss with the boardwalk?"

"Everything. It really is amazing. You'll see the lights, but wait until night falls completely. You've never seen anything like it."

Sure enough, as soon as we turned off Second Avenue and started walking toward the boardwalk, Jared's eyes grew wide.

"Wow," he said after a long whistle of appreciation.

"What did I tell you? Awesome, right?" I grabbed his hand and pulled him toward the crowd.

Once we hit the first pier, he looked around and tightened the grip on my hand. "How the hell have I never been here?"

"Yeah, Sarah said you guys never came here. I've been coming since I was a kid." I signaled with two fingers to the guy at the lemonade stand. Reaching into my pocket I pulled out a twenty. Jared stepped ahead and paid the man instead. He handed me my lemonade as I shoved my money back into the front pocket of my kelly green twill shorts. He still hadn't let go of my hand.

"Thank you." I took a sip and closed my eyes for a moment to savor the sweet and sour goodness. "You're still holding my hand," I mentioned, attempting to inject nonchalance into my voice when in reality, he could probably feel the cold clamminess of my palms.

He lifted our clasped hands and said, "Huh. I guess I am." He dropped our hands down, sipped his lemonade, and walked through a crowd of people. "Probably better to hold hands. Wouldn't want to get lost in a crowd this big."

"I just didn't want you to get the wrong idea." I couldn't hide my smile.

"Are you trying to tell me you think I'm going to get all girly about holding your hand?" He batted his lashes. How had I never noticed how ridiculously long they were?

"Girly? Who said anything about girly?" I focused on drinking my lemonade.

"Relax. I know what the deal is. We're pretending so Mommy doesn't give you a hard time. Who knows, maybe they'll magically appear out here and wonder why we aren't making out or something. At least we can tell them we're holding hands." He squeezed my hand. "We can make out later."

"If you're lucky."

"I told you, I don't believe in luck."

We weaved our way through throngs of summer beachgoers, stopping occasionally to grab a hot dog, fried Oreos, or cotton candy. God only knew how he could eat so much.

"You sure you don't want anything?" he mumbled through a greasy mouthful of funnel cake.

"Thanks. I'm good." I licked my thumb, reached up, and wiped a smudge of powdered sugar from the corner of his mouth.

He laughed and powdered sugar puffed from his lips. There really was no clean way to eat a funnel cake. "Did you just lick your thumb and clean me? Like my mom did when I was a kid?"

I stared at my thumb. "I guess I did. You had sugar on your mouth."

"Thanks." He leaned down and kissed me on the lips like it was the most natural thing in the world.

I licked my lips and tasted sugar. Jared's eyes remained on me and threw me off balance. I quickly changed the subject. "Are you going to eat your way down the boardwalk? Pretty sure there's a French fry stand you missed."

"We'll make sure to work it off this week." He winked and squeezed my hand before using it to shove fried dough in his mouth.

His sexy, smirky, powdered-sugar-covered mouth.

Was it sad that I thought the way he ate funnel cake was sexy? How long had it been since I'd had sex? Four days? It was beginning to feel like four months. Something had to give.

"Glad to hear you say that. I was hoping for a workout buddy this week. It's no fun doing it alone." I handed him a napkin, afraid to wipe the rest of the sugar from his mouth. I figured if I touched him again I'd rip his clothes off in the middle of the boardwalk.

His eyes were trained on mine when he said, "Alone's not so bad if you know what you're doing, but it is *always* better with a partner."

I forced myself to take a step back. The innuendo was slight, almost invisible, but I needed to remove myself from his personal space. "Be ready at six."

He got the hint and resumed eating. "In the morning?"

"Can't handle it?" I teased.

"I can handle anything you throw at me."

"We'll just have to see about that."

The next few hours were spent riding roller coasters—something Jared probably shouldn't have done after eating all that food—and playing games. By eleven o'clock we were headed back to the condo, each with giant stuffed animals under our arms. I'd won Jared a giant monkey and he'd returned the favor by winning me a large, stuffed banana. Dr. Ruth would've had a field day with all the dirty banana thoughts running through my head.

My parents had turned in for the night and I secretly thanked my lucky stars. There was no way I wanted to deal with them, especially when I had wondered to myself about the sleeping arrangements the entire walk home.

Jared made his way to the kitchen. I watched as he poured a huge glass of water from the sink, downed it, and poured another. This went on through four glasses before I abandoned my post at the counter and made my way to my bedroom.

I hadn't brought much in the way of pajamas. Tiny shorts and a tank top sufficed, especially since my mom kept the thermometer at seventy-six degrees year-round. I liked to sleep cold. And seventy-six wasn't cutting it.

I coiled my hair into a messy bun, grabbed my toothbrush, and made my way to the bathroom Jared and I would be sharing. He walked in as I finished brushing my teeth.

Wearing nothing but boxer shorts.

And a six-pack of tight abs.

And a happy trail that begged for my tongue to take a trip.

I shook my head and sprayed toothpaste all over him and the mirror.

"Really?" He wiped the foam from his cheek. "I walk in wearing boxers and you lose your mind."

"What? I didn't…You can't…" He was kind enough to give me the heads-up that I was caught looking by the large shit-eating grin plastered across his face. I decided to rise above it and be the mature one. I stomped my foot, growled—yes growled—and stormed quietly back to my room. I didn't want to wake my parents, after all.

I felt the bed sink when he climbed in. My back was to him. I didn't want to give him the satisfaction of my eyes popping out of my head when I checked out his body. So I kept my eyes away.

"Mel?"

"Yeah?"

"I ate too much."

"I told you that you were going to have a stomachache."

He shifted in the bed and I could feel him lift the covers off himself and toss them to my side of the bed. The pillow that separated us followed.

"Mel?"

"Yeah?"

"Will you rub my belly?"

"Seriously?"

He rolled over, big spooning my little spoon, and nuzzled his face into my neck. Maybe it should have been awkward but it wasn't. It felt—I don't know. Felt like something. Something *simmer-y*.

"It really hurts," he whispered into my hair.

"Hold on." I went to the bathroom, took the Pepto from the medicine cabinet, and filled a glass with water, then took them to Jared.

"Drink this."

He took the bottle and downed about half of it.

"Do you need water?" I asked.

"No, thanks." He groaned.

I placed the water on the side table and slid back into bed. I nestled my head into the crook of his arm and lightly rubbed his stomach.

"Use your nails," he mumbled.

"Awfully bossy for someone whose stomach is about to revolt."

"Lower."

"What?"

"You know you want to."

I rubbed his belly in silence, thinking about what Zac had said about my being free and what Jared had said about wanting to get to know me and I had to admit that from the moment he helped me carry the bags up to his sister's apartment, I had been intrigued. Something about him threw me into a tizzy. He was refreshing, unpretentious. He made me feel good, feel safe. I wanted him and not just for sex. For something I wasn't sure I could admit. And because of that feeling, I knew I needed to keep sex off the table for now. Especially after what happened earlier.

God, this is gonna be hard.

Pun intended.

Propping myself up on my elbow, I leaned my face close to his. I spent an awful lot of time admiring the high cheekbones, perfect eyebrows, and day-old stubble that I wanted to feel rubbing between my thighs. My stomach flopped at the thought and I had to reach under the covers and adjust my shorts.

"Did you just adjust yourself?" He opened one eye and looked at me.

I yelped and jolted back, nearly falling off the bed. "You're awake?"

"You didn't answer my question." Both eyes were closed.

"For your information, men are not the only ones who have to adjust themselves on occasion."

"Yeah, but when we do it it's because we have a boner. Do you have a lady boner that needed adjusting?"

"I do not have a lady boner!" I totally had a lady boner.

"I'm just sayin'. You stare at me, an inch from my face, for like a minute then you reach under the covers and adjust yourself. Were your panties shifted over or something? Did your lady boner push them aside? Are your panties all wet now?" He rolled over and propped himself up on his elbow and stared directly at me. "I am suddenly interested in the size and scope of your lady boner."

"For your information, I am not wearing panties." What sounded like a great comeback to prove he was wrong turned out to come across as nothing more than a cheap come-on.

He rolled over on his back, looked at the ceiling, and blew out a long breath.

"Is your stomach bothering you?" I asked, suddenly worried.

"No. The Pepto worked. Thank you."

"Then what's wrong?"

"I need to adjust my shorts."

"You're an ass." I hit him with my pillow and he rolled over and tackled me.

"Mel?" He lay on top of me, his lips close to mine.

"Yeah?"

"Will you rub my belly again?"

"No!" I pushed him off me, laughing.

"Well, the least you can do is adjust my shorts."

I smacked him in the face again with the pillow. "Jared?"

"Yeah?"

"Go to sleep."

"Only if you're little spoon."

"Fine." I rolled so my back was to him and he wrapped his arms around me and kissed my hair.

He whispered, "Definitely going to have to adjust my shorts."

I elbowed him in the stomach, smiled, and closed my eyes.

Chapter Sixteen

Wake up!" I hit Jared with a pillow. "We have yoga on the beach in…"—I checked my phone for the time—"fifteen minutes."

"I don't want to." He stretched, tightening his back muscles as his arms reached above his head, and disappeared under the pillow.

"You promised. Let's go. Up. Up. Up." I ripped the blanket off him and tossed it on the floor. Taking a moment to admire the way his boxers sat just below his tan line, I chewed the inside of my cheek, wishing it were his ass I was biting. "Come on." I took a chance and slapped his ass.

"Did you just slap and grab?"

"I slapped. There was no grab."

"I distinctly felt a bit of cuppage. You grabbed." He turned his ass toward me. "Do it again."

"If I grab your ass will you get up and go do yoga with me?"

"Yes."

"Fine." I saw him tense as he waited for me to take a handful. Laughing, I kicked a leg over and straddled the backs of his thighs.

With my hands hovering over each of his cheeks, I heard him inhale right before I performed the ultimate smack, grab, and lift on his perfect ass. His tiny groan caused my lady parts to throb a bit. "Now can we go? As it is we'll have to run to get there on time."

He shifted under me so I was straddling the most important part of his boxer shorts and placed a hand on each of my thighs, his fingertips grazing just underneath the hem of my running shorts. "I like your shorts." He squeezed my thighs.

"Thank you." Just to tease him, I squeezed my thighs against him and shifted.

Reaching up, he ran his finger across the bottom of my bright orange sports bra. "I like your sports bra shirt thing."

"Again, thank you." I pushed his hands down.

He sat up quickly, pinned my arm behind my back, and pulled me closer to him. I could feel him between my legs and I inhaled sharply. Nuzzling against me for a moment Jared finally whispered, "Do I have time to pee?"

"You have time to pee," I was barely able to squeak out. I thought my tongue would jump out of my mouth and lick him all on its own.

"Great." He let go of my arm, grabbed me by my ass, and lifted me off, tossing me to the side of the bed. He pulled on the sleeveless shirt I threw at him, and stepped into a pair of running shorts.

I pulled two water bottles from the fridge and tossed him one when he walked in the kitchen, still groggy from a night of gorging himself on fried everything.

"We gotta go." I handed him a towel as we headed out the door.

We jogged easily to the yoga class that was already in progress and joined in after tossing our shoes in a pile and laying out our towels. Thankfully, they were still in seated meditation, so we didn't miss

much. I found a spot at the end of a row and Jared fit himself in behind me.

At five minutes after six in the morning, I was sitting on the
beach clearing my head of extraneous gunk. The salty breeze felt
good against my skin and the soft flow of the waves calmed me. Yoga
had always been a favorite of mine. A simple retreat into meditation
helped my often hectic life.

We moved from our sitting mediation, stood, and stretched our
arms upward before moving to downward dog. I could feel my body
stretch, the sun fall on my exposed skin. I could hear Jared's low
whistle behind me. I giggled and gave him the tiniest shake of my ass
before we moved to plank and back to downward dog. For the next
forty minutes we went through leg raises, knee circles, and cobra
planks before finishing up with a forward fold and stretch upward.

I shook out my towel and took a swig of water as I looked out to
the ocean. Jared handed me my sneakers.

"Thanks. You hungry?" I asked, my eyes still on the rolling waves.

"I could eat."

I turned to look at him and smiled. "We'd have to run for it."

"Run for what?"

"Breakfast. Banana pancakes to be specific. The best in the world.
All the way down the boardwalk to the hotel past the Towers. You
up for it?"

"So I get to run with the most limber girl I've met in a long
time—nice downward dog, by the way—"

"Thanks."

"All the way down the boardwalk to some random hotel to eat
the best banana pancakes in the world?" He pursed his lips, tied his
sneakers, and said, "Wouldn't miss it."

He smacked my ass and took off toward breakfast. I had to dodge a large number of bicyclers before I caught up.

"No fair." I settled into his rhythm.

"All's fair," he responded.

"In love and war," I finished.

"So which is it?" He glanced toward me.

"Which is what?" I tried to keep my eyes ahead, knowing full well what he was asking.

"Love or war?"

I fell back, running behind him as he clarified.

"Today?" I smiled. "War." I pantsed him and took off as fast as I could, knowing he'd catch up soon.

When he didn't immediately run up behind me and exact his revenge, I turned and trotted backward, looking for him. I didn't see him. I stopped running and walked back toward the spot where I'd dropped his pants. I chewed my fingernail, worried that maybe I'd gone a bit too far and pissed him off. Well, pop a point on my tally sheet for being an asshole.

"Jared?" I yelled.

Turning around, I couldn't figure out where he'd gone, though I could probably guess he was back at my parents' condo packing up his shit so he could get the hell out of here. I was beginning to panic when a weird feeling washed over me; anxiety mixed with something not quite familiar. It was almost like, maybe I—my stomach almost revolted at the thought—missed his being around or something.

I'd spent almost five minutes looking for him on the boardwalk, finally given up, and started walking back to the condo when out of nowhere I was lifted off the ground and thrown over a muscular shoulder.

"What the fuck! Put me down!" I yelled and hit the back of my attacker. Until I noticed the ass that was attached to the body of the muscular shoulders belonged to Jared.

"You ass! I thought you left."

"Nope." He continued to carry me, stepping off the boardwalk onto the sand.

"I was looking for you."

"I know." He laughed and quickened his pace.

I turned my head to see that we were headed straight for the water. "Don't you dare!"

"You asked for it." He reached the water and ran in, hopping over the small waves that rolled in.

I gripped his shirt in a frantic attempt to remain dry and the fabric tore away as he pulled me by my hips and tossed me in the ocean. We were only in waist deep but for a moment it felt much deeper. The water was colder than I thought it would be and my laughter was momentarily stifled by the shock of the temperature. Jared was doubled over laughing so hard he didn't notice that I'd caught my breath and wrapped my arms around his leg. I yanked it out from under him and he splashed in next to me.

"How's it feel?" I laughed.

"I had to do something. You pulled my pants down in the middle of the boardwalk! Good one, by the way. You got me. Wasn't expecting that. You're lucky I was wearing underwear." He ducked his head under a small wave.

"For what it's worth"—I let a wave push me a bit closer to him—"you have a great ass. I am sure patrons of the boardwalk were honored to be in its presence."

He cocked his head and smirked. "I think you just wanted to see my ass."

"Oh you do, do you? Hardly." I rolled my eyes but the picture of his perfect ass walking away from me back at my apartment stomped through my brain.

He wiped water from his face. "If you wanted to see my ass, you could've just asked."

"I've already seen it and maybe I don't want to have to ask to see it again." I pushed my hair away from my face.

"Then I guess if you really want something"—he swam closer—"you should just damn the consequences and go after it." He licked his lips as his eyes drifted toward my mouth. He was smiling but it wasn't his usual sexy smirk or the teasing grin I'd come to look forward to staring at over the past week. It was something else I couldn't place.

Another wave pushed me up against him. "Jared?"

"Yeah?" His voice deepened.

"I can't kiss you again."

"Why not?"

"Not until I explain something."

"Explain what? That you don't want to kiss me?"

"No. No. I *want* to kiss you. Dear lord, I would kiss you all fucking day. But, see, I made this kind of bet with the girls—"

"The no sex till your birthday thing? That's a real thing?"

"Yeah."

He blew out a long breath. "So you want to kiss me, but you're afraid kiss me because you think it will lead to sex." He dunked his head under the water for a second.

"In a nutshell."

"So"—he waved between us—"you and I have something here? I'm not imagining it?"

"You aren't imagining it. And to be honest"—I swam closer to him—"I've really had a great time with you and getting to know you has been kind of eye opening."

"How so?"

"The fact that I like you enough *not* to jump your bones? Huge."

"So the fact that sex is off the table is a good thing?"

"I think so."

"So we can kiss and other kinds of things but we can't have sex." It wasn't a question. It was as if he was explaining it to himself. "This is going to be a rough couple of weeks."

He smiled, wrapped his arms around my waist, and pulled me in tight. My arms reached up around his neck as we settled against each other. My heart felt like it was going to beat out of my chest until I realized I could feel his speed up, too. For a moment I felt the two beats struggling to get in sync but it wasn't long before they were marching in unison.

His hands fell from my back and settled on my ass. He squeezed tightly and I let out a tiny moan before his lifted me out of the water and I wrapped my legs around his waist. His lips pressed against mine and I opened my mouth slightly as his tongue begged for entrance. The kiss deepened and I could feel warmth spread through my stomach, down my legs, and curl my toes.

I'd never been kissed so slowly, so completely. There was no pretense, no expectation of it leading to anything else. It was a kiss. A kiss that muddled my brain and stole my breath.

He was right. It was going to be a rough couple of weeks.

Chapter Seventeen

I really need to work on my tan." I rolled over on my towel and turned my head to look at Jared. We'd all but forgotten about breakfast and when we finally pulled ourselves from the ocean, our lips were sore from making out. Thank God for tropical-flavored lip balm. And Jared's full, suckable lips.

I hadn't had sore lips from making out since middle school. Hell, I don't think I'd actually made out with anyone since I was sixteen for longer than a few minutes before it led to either a hand job, blow job, or sex.

Seriously.

And honestly? I'd put that oceanic make-out session with Jared on a pedestal above the most mind-blowing sex I'd ever had. Even Zac, with his dexterous hands, magical lips, and ever-ready cock, was no match for what had gone down in the waves earlier. It was that fucking amazing. Not to mention I could feel his excitement every time the waves rocked us together. Maybe I should've been embarrassed that I had a very slow, simmering mini orgasm from the kissing and what, I guess, would be considered dry humping, courtesy of Mother Nature. The way his hands felt on my ass, the way his arms felt holding me, the way his chest felt against mine, the way his tongue explored my mouth, and the way he pulled back, smiled, and watched with intensity and interest when he realized he didn't have to be inside me to make me come. And the look on his face when he realized how surprised I was at the fact was sexy as hell.

"Don't tan too much. You'll end up looking like a wrinkly leather bag." He sat up and rubbed suntan lotion all over my back.

"Better than looking like an Oompa Loompa. Nothing says stereotypical New Jersey than orange skin and high hair."

"Don't remind me." He smacked my ass. "There. All covered. Do me." He held out the lotion.

"Here? In public?" I snatched the lotion from him and smiled. "What are you, a freak?"

He rushed forward and pushed me on my back as he settled in on top of me. His knee wedged between my legs, he said, "You weren't complaining earlier. And that"—he sprinkled kisses on my neck—"was a pretty public display."

Hooking my legs around him, I pivoted and rolled over until I was lying on top of him. "So you're into public displays?" I reached down between my legs to feel him. My hand gripped him through his shorts and he sucked in a breath. I gave him a squeeze, leaned over, and bit his bottom lip. "Maybe another time."

I rolled off him and resumed my position in my towel. "I need to at least get some color. Pasty white just won't do."

"Tease." Laughing, he rolled over on his stomach, too. But not for the tan; he needed to stifle his growing excitement.

"So tell me about this dream of yours to become a chef," I said after a while.

"I don't know." He rolled to his back and popped on his aviators. "I just like to cook. I hate to bake. Baking is not my thing."

"There's a difference?"

"Yes, there's a difference!" He shook his head. "Baking requires precision, measuring, following directions."

"That's funny because your *job* requires precision and following directions."

"Not the same thing," he said quickly.

"Good to know." I moved so I could place my head on his stomach. I covered my eyes with my arm since I had left my sunglasses back at the condo.

"With cooking, I get to be more creative. Experiment more."

"So you're into experimentation." I smiled.

"Absolutely." The sexy smirk made its obligatory appearance and were I not already lying down, I might have swooned.

Those swoony thoughts clouded my head, so I cleared my throat and said, "Please continue."

"I have a few recipes locked in my head. A few go-to items that always come out good. But my favorite is when I get stuck with a few ingredients and have to figure out what to do with them. Which herb goes with what. What flavors meld. You know?"

"I do. Kinda like flying by the seat of your pants."

"Exactly."

"So why don't you do it? Why don't you get a place and live the dream?"

"I wouldn't know where to start."

"Well"—I sat up—"you're a numbers guy. I'm a numbers girl.

Berk is a real estate guy. I am sure together we can find something. I mean, even Brian owns his bar. He could help, too. Maybe give you some advice. You should totally do it."

"Nah. It's not realistic. Look, this job I got with Berk is great. I'll make great money, add to my portfolio of investments—"

"You have a portfolio of investments?"

"Yeah. Don't you? We do *work* in that industry. I thought it was a given."

"No, I do. But I'm almost thirty and have been doing this eight years. You're twenty-six—"

He cocked his head and looked at me strangely. "What does age have to do with anything?"

"It doesn't. Forget it. I didn't mean anything by it, honest. Sometimes I feel like I've been doing this for a million years. I'm great at my job but I get tired of it. I forget what it's like to slow down and look around sometimes. You know, smell the flowers? I've been so busy moving up the ladder, I forget to see where I'm going or to check out the view."

"And how's the view?"

"Right now? Perfect." I leaned down and kissed him softly.

"Well"—he sat up across from me—"what are your dreams? I am sure you didn't always want to do math for a living."

I laughed. "I don't ever remember having a particular dream. I worked hard at whatever I did. Took a math class in college, loved it, and the rest is history."

"But no dream job? No bucket list?"

"Nope. I can't even remember wanting to be a princess as a kid. I guess I was pretty okay with who I was. Still am. For the most part. Is that awful?"

He smiled. "Not awful at all. Surprising with how driven you are, but not awful."

"Well"—I leaned my face into his hand as he caressed my cheek—"maybe I can help you with your dream."

"Oh, yeah? Right now my dream is to go take a nap, wake up next to you, take a shower, and drink a really cold beer. Oh, and maybe sneak off for another marathon make-out session. In no particular order, of course." He cocked his eyebrow and smirked.

"I think I can manage to help with that." I stood and held out my hand. He grabbed it and I pulled him up. "Let's go get that nap."

"What day is today?" He draped his arm around my shoulder as we made the short trek back to the condo.

"Thursday."

"I feel like I've been back in New Jersey forever but it's only been like, what? A month?"

I nodded. "And in that time, you've been shuffled from your sister's place to mine, got a new job, and escaped to the beach to pretend you're my boyfriend."

"Yeah, that's the part that sucks. All that kissing and ass grabbing. Terrible." He made a face and stuck out his tongue.

"Awful. Just awful." I shook my head.

"Maybe"—he pulled his arm from my neck and opened the door to the condo entrance—"we just need more practice. I mean, just for authenticity."

"You're right. I don't think my parents are buying it. More practice might be good." I walked up the steps with him behind me. I tossed a glance over my shoulder and noticed his gaze was focused on my ass. "So you're an ass man?" I laughed.

"I guess I am." He reached up and smacked it.

When we reached the third-floor landing he quickly pulled me aside and pushed my back up against the wall, pressing himself close. "I'm also a neck man." He nipped at my throat. "And a boob man." He tweaked my nipples between his fingers and I inhaled sharply. "And a lip man." He lightly pulled at my bottom lip with his teeth before abruptly stepping away and taking a deep breath.

His eyes never left my face.

"Now who's the tease?" I whispered, unable to raise the volume of my voice.

"This isn't teasing," he whispered back and opened the door to my parents' place, motioning for me to enter, "it's foreplay."

And just like that, I knew Berk was right. Jared was my slow down, slow burn.

"What's the matter, sweetie?" My mom all but jumped off the couch and made her way over to me. "You look flushed. You feeling okay?" She placed the back of her hand against my forehead and I looked at Jared, knowing full well why I was flushed. He tried to stifle a laugh.

"I'm okay, Mom. Just probably need a cold shower after all that heat."

I could feel Jared's eyes on me. I'd always been very good at knowing when I caught someone's attention but with Jared, I could feel his gaze follow me, take me all in. I became hyperaware of my every movement. It was almost unnerving, and I suddenly realized I'd felt this way around him since the first time I saw him in my apartment, like I was being watched. It was sexy as hell to feel like I was wanted every time I walked in the room, like I was noticed and appreciated. It was no wonder I'd been walking around the past week with a constant lady semi and ready to fire electricity buzzing between my legs.

He was right. Just being in the same room with him was foreplay. Every time he looked at me was a silent promise of what could be between us, not only in the bedroom, but in life.

My best friend's brother. The guy who wanted nothing more than to spend time with me. He liked kissing me, he didn't push, he called me on my bullshit, and he wasn't always in my face. He was a good guy.

I excused myself and headed to the bedroom. I hadn't realized how tired I was and figured I needed a nap.

I'm not sure how long I was out; when I heard the door to my bedroom open I was barely awake and then I felt the bed sink down as Jared climbed in. He ran his fingers through my hair, carefully smoothing out the knots, and I tensed at his touch.

"I know you aren't sleeping. But I'd prefer it if you pretended that you are, just for a minute." I heard him chuckle. "It will make what I have to say easier, since you won't talk back and I'll be able to say what I want to say without your smart mouth interrupting me."

He took a breath. "There's a thing or two I need to get off my chest. And, I guess, better now than never. You see, Melody, when you and I first met at my high school graduation party, I thought you were the most beautiful thing I'd ever seen. And since then, I've compared everyone else I've met to who I thought you were. You'd recently graduated college and you were obviously way out of my league—older, beautiful, confident, and best friends with my sister. There was no way in hell you were ever going to look at me. But I promised myself, if I ever had that feeling again, that funny pit in my stomach over a girl, I would never let her go.

"Here I am eight years later, you're even more beautiful than I remember, your smile is brighter, your boobs are bigger, and that funny pit in my stomach is still there." He paused and laughed softly. "I never thought in a million years I'd see you again other than in passing and here I am lying in bed next to you as you pretend to sleep. I watched you in the kitchen. I watched you pull away the moment you realized there might be something more than pretend between us. I'm okay if you want to run, for now. I've seen you open and free and happy. I've seen the cracks in your confidence, the peeling paint on your façade."

He pulled his hand away from my hair and shifted his weight. "Do you think I wanted to come here and get involved with someone? Hell no. Never in a million years did I think you could live up to how I built you up in my head. But here we are.

"Christ, Mel." He stood. "It's not like I'm asking you to run off and spend the rest of your life with me. Just enjoy it for what it is. We could have a lot of fun, you and me. We're more alike than I think you'd care to admit."

He rummaged through his drawers and quietly left. I heard the shower turn on before I opened my eyes.

Chapter Eighteen

When she wakes up, just let her know we went out to dinner with Nick and Mia. She's knows who they are. You sure you don't need anything?"

"No, I'm good, Nora. You two have fun. I'll make sure she eats something."

"You're a nice young man, Jared. I have a good feeling about what the two of you have." My dad, always the voice of reason.

I heard the door close as my mom and dad left to have dinner with their friends. I listened as the ice maker dropped ice into a glass. The slider to the back deck opened, then closed. I took a quick shower and changed into a pair of tiny white running shorts and a gray tank. The sun had done a bit of a number on my shoulders earlier, so for the moment I was sans bra and the air-conditioned temperature in the condo made the fact quite apparent. Rubbing my nipples to warm them up did nothing more than harden them further. Sighing, I realized there was nothing I could do about it, so I pulled on Jared's blue hoodie, stuffed my hair into his baseball cap, and slicked on my sheer lip gloss.

I opened the door to my bedroom and stepped out into the hall. I could see Jared on the bright orange lounge chair, a glass with three fingers of my dad's Black Label whiskey next to him on the teak table. Sunglasses perched on his face, Jared was soaking up what was left of the late afternoon sun. His shirtless form always drew my attention. I swear that boy has an aversion to shirts. Not that I minded.

Good Lord. I needed to stop thinking with my vagina.

I grabbed my sunglasses off the kitchen counter and made my way to the deck. Opening the door, I slipped outside. Jared didn't stir but I knew he wasn't asleep by the way the corner of his mouth lifted. Picking up his glass, I took a deep swallow of the whiskey and curled up in the gravity chair my dad loved so much. Taking in a deep breath, I filled my lungs with fresh sea air and my nose with Jared's scent—coconut sunscreen, my lavender shampoo, and salty sweat. I swallowed as I began salivating like a hungry puppy.

"There's this thing about you," I began, taking another sip. "There's this quality you have that I can't quite pinpoint. It's more of a feeling that I have when I am around you. It's like the most amazing thing takes over and I can see what it would be like to be with you. And when I finally opened my eyes, I realized the thought makes me happy."

I paused and held my breath. Jared didn't respond and the silence made me jittery.

"The past eight years have been good to you. I remember you from when you were in high school. A skinny kid. Cute. Young.

Great smile. Now that same smirk takes on a whole new level of panty-dropping sexiness. And you're fun. And you're nice. And you're, I don't know, just something different from what I've ever experienced."

The other corner of his mouth lifted.

"However"—I downed the whiskey and paced the deck—"I don't really know how to do relationships. I don't really know how to be in one. At least not a romantic relationship. I move quickly, I don't take the time to smell the roses, I find what I want, take it, and move on. Generally I live by the sex only rule. No phone calls. No texts. No clinginess. It's less messy that way, you know?

"But something weird has been happening to me. More and more lately, I haven't been able to brush off my feelings as easily, I haven't been able to dismiss them as quickly as I once did. Which is fine, I've been able to deal, kind of, with all that. But then Zac told me he loved me." I blew out a breath. "And he lied. And I hate that I believed him. And I hate that he lied. But what I hate the most is that I am so angry about his lie but I fail to recognize that there is no reason for me to be angry with him. Because I don't feel the same way. I don't love Zachary Waterman. Never have."

I threw open the sliding glass door and stalked to the kitchen and filled the empty tumbler with more whiskey. I drank deeply before Jared came up behind me, took the glass from me, and placed it on the counter.

"Damn it, Jared. I've always said I don't believe in *love*." I put the word in air quotes. "But that's a lie, too. I just wouldn't even know where to begin."

"Who says"—he lifted my chin—"that you have to love anyone

but yourself right now? All I'm asking for is the opportunity to get to know you better. Don't label it. Just let it be what it is."

"Which is what?"

"I don't know. Maybe for now we just hang out. Take everything slow." He lifted me up and placed me on the counter.

"Slow?" I snickered. "Like foreplay."

He laughed quietly. "Yeah. I guess it kind of is."

"I told you. I don't know how to do slow."

"Slow *I* can do. We can go slow together." His fingers traced shapes on my thighs.

"Can we still make out?" I asked softly.

"Sure. I don't see why not." He picked up the drink and looked at me over the rim of the glass as he took a sip. "We'll call it part of the get-to-know-you process."

"Can we make out slowly?" My finger slid across the indents between his abs, and his stomach tensed as goose bumps covered his skin. I slowly traced the top of his shorts, pausing along the little trail of hair that led from his belly button and disappeared under the elastic waistband.

He nuzzled his face against my chest and let out a small growl. "Don't make me regret all this slow business."

I placed a hand on either side of his face. "As long as you don't make me regret slowing down."

There was a tiny pause between us, a small hitch in our heartbeats. We were steady but the anticipation sizzled between us. I could live in that feeling. That butterfly, tingle-inducing feeling that arose right before we kissed. The butterfly, tingle-inducing feeling I hadn't felt since my first kiss ever in the seventh grade with Mark Turner.

My lips parted slightly as our mouths met. The kiss was urgent and slow. Soft and commanding. I let him dictate the pace; I was tired of always leading, taking charge. Jared convinced me with his touch to be moldable, bendable, and the feeling was freeing, amazing, and sexy as hell.

My hands slid slowly from his face down his arms and I paused along the taut muscles in his biceps, his forearms. His kiss grew more intense as his arms tightened around me. I reached back up and wrapped my arms around his neck, pulling myself in closer. I suddenly couldn't get close enough. The kiss, the skin-on-skin contact—my senses were in overload.

"Melody." He whispered my name and I pulled him in tighter and he bit my bottom lip and pulled.

He lifted me up quickly and I wrapped my legs tighter around him. His hand fisted the hair on the back of my head as he walked to the living room couch and deposited me on the cushions. He leaned above me for a moment, his eyes taking me in. His gaze swept every inch of me from my head to my toes and back. A slow gaze, a hungry and patient gaze. The act sent my nether region into a tizzy and within seconds of his eyes sweeping me, I had a full-on throbber. I honestly felt like if I didn't get his dick inside me, I would pass out from the anticipation. He must've sensed the urgency because his body dropped onto mine and his lips found my lips, his tongue tangled with my tongue, his moans matched my moans.

I spread my legs wider apart and he settled in. Holding my hands above my head, he pushed his hips forward, pressed against my center, and I gasped. My eyes flew open and I saw he was watching my face, biting his bottom lip. Gazes locked, I felt him push against me again, slowly and with more lingering pressure than before. My mouth dropped open but no sound came out as he pushed against me over and over again, watching me. Holding me still as he pressed himself between my legs.

"I want you inside me." I breathed out, ready for the most intense orgasm known to man. I knew the minute he pushed inside me, I'd sing like a bird and explode like fireworks on the Fourth of July.

He smiled and kissed me, pressing up against me again. I was being dry humped to within an inch of my life. And it wasn't enough.

"Jared. Now. Please." I pulled my hands away from his grip, found the waistband of his shorts, and tugged. I was never going to be able to hold out.

He pulled away quickly, stood, and adjusted himself. His eyes were glassy but focused and he looked like he was trying to maintain his balance. He was breathing as heavily as I was but more even, like he was fighting for control, whereas I was ready to jump off a cliff and fall into orgasm heaven. "Nope. Slow, remember?"

"Wait! What?" There was no way I'd heard him right. My orgasm was standing in the on deck circle practicing her swing when the game was called.

"Slow. We agreed to take things slowly." He leaned down and kissed the tip of my nose. My orgasm grabbed a bucket of balls and threatened to start throwing bean balls at the referee.

"I've changed my mind." My clit was so swollen and throbbing so much, I thought my entire lady area would revolt and remove itself from my body.

"You've changed your mind?" He ran his thumb across his mouth.

"I reserve the right to change my mind. It's one thing to *say* you're going to give up sex, it's quite another to go through with it. I give up." I realized my voice was bordering on hysterical but there was nothing I could do about it. "You can't just stop." The throbbing was seriously intense and I cried out a little as my hands flew to my crotch. "This is fucking insane."

Jared said nothing, just stood looking at me with that sexy smirk on his face. I wanted to lick it off and keep it for myself.

"When we said slow, I meant relationship type stuff not sex slow." I tried to reason with him.

Seriously.

The throbbing.

I knew this is what death felt like.

He went to sit in the chair across from the couch and fisted his hands tightly. It was good to know I wasn't the only one affected, especially since I noticed how he adjusted his junk more than once. As he adjusted, I watched with laser focus as if his were the last penis in the world. The thought pushed a small moan from my lips. I closed my eyes tight and cupped my crotch, trying not to touch the throbber because each time I did, a jolt would surge down my legs and into my stomach.

"Here's the deal, Mel. You've been pretty…how do I say this? *Active* in your sex life." Was I about to be slut shamed? I was dying inside and he was going to discuss how active my sex life has been?

"And your friends have mentioned how it would be good for you to gain some, um, *vertical* perspective when it comes to men, yes?"

"Yes but—"

"Let me finish." He blew out a long breath. Son of a bitch was gaining control as I was lying on the couch with my hands shoved between my quivering legs, wondering if I would die from blue balls. "I recently—well, a couple months ago—got out of a long-term relationship." He winked and I throbbed. "I am thinking, with all this slow business, it would give us each time to detox our prospective parts. Give us each a clear head."

"Detox? Jesus Christ, we aren't radioactive." I pulled my knees to my chest and curled up into the fetal position, my hands still shoved between my legs.

His laugh sent electricity shooting down my legs. Seriously? How long did blue balls last? Would there be permanent damage? Could Jared's climactic detour be considered physical abuse? Was there a number I could call?

He was cock-blocking himself and when his balls turned purple, shriveled up, and died he would have no one to blame but himself.

"No, that isn't what I meant. I am thinking of this as more of a challenge. Our pants stay on for a while as we discussed before. I like the idea of getting to know each other without sex getting in the way. We'll just need to figure out a way to distract each other."

That fucking word again.

Distraction.

Fuck distraction.

I needed dick.

"So you're content with handing me some blue balls and sending me on my way?"

Again with the laugh. "No. Believe me, I'm not immune either. But this"—he pointed at the couch—"is where we will live. With a condition."

If dry-humping and heavy kissing was where I was going to live for a while, we were going to break the couch. "What's the condition?" The pulsating was finally beginning to subside. It wasn't a painful process, per se, but instead felt kind of like my vagina was shriveling up and dying in protest. I'd always been very good to her. Now the bitch was giving me attitude. Couldn't say I blamed her.

"Neither of us can come."

"What?" I jumped up and almost lost my balance when my knees threatened to give out. "No dick *and* no orgasm? What are you, a fucking sadist? Who the fuck withholds dick, let alone orgasms? You are out of your fucking mind. No way. I'll take care of this shit myself." I held up my hands in protest and started toward my bedroom to take care of business. Fuck that shit.

"Wait. Hear me out." He grabbed my wrist and turned me to face him. "I'm not saying we do this forever. I'm just saying we'll take it slow and when you decide you can take off your running shoes, we'll put orgasms and dicks and vaginas back on the table. Look, I'm not totally ready for anything serious either. I don't even know if I really want anything serious. Amber and I dated for five years. When we broke up, I went on a bender and fucked everything that had tits and a pussy. I don't want that now. Let's just get it out of our system and start thinking about what we really want." He pulled me into a hug and I felt his soldier wake up and look around, which sent all the blood in my body rushing back between my legs. "You and I have been thinking with the wrong heads."

"So we are going to hold hands and get to know each other?"

He kissed the top of my head. "Yep." His body tensed up as his sleepy soldier started to rise.

"And make out and dry hump like teenagers?" It wouldn't be all bad.

He breathed out a shaky breath. "Yep."

"But we are not allowed to have orgasms. Even self-induced?" Yeah. It was bad.

"Right." He shifted his weight from leg to leg.

"How long?" My fists opened and closed as I tried to ease the tension and frustration.

"You turn thirty on—"

"July thirty-first."

"How many days is that?"

I counted on my fingers. "Fifteen days."

"Fifteen days?"

"You think we can do this?"

"I don't know, never gave up sex before." He rolled his neck.

"Why would you ever do that? Two weeks is a long time." I marched in place.

"Never had a reason to before. And two weeks is not so long." He tapped the tip of my nose and hugged me tighter.

"Jared?" My lady boner was climbing my walls.

"Yeah?"

"I don't think I can do this."

"Honestly?" He pulled back and held me at arm's length. "Not sure I can either."

He stepped away and started jumping up and down.

"What are you doing?"

"Controlling my boner."

"By jumping?"

"Yeah and saying 'stinky pussy' over and over in my head."

"Stinky pussy?" I crossed my arms over my chest, not amused by his display.

"Yeah." He continued to jump up and down. "Once when I was in high school, I went out with this girl. We were about to do the deed but when I pulled her pants off, she had the stinkiest pussy you could ever imagine. Needless to say, my dick went soft faster than the speed of sound. Now, when I need to control the boner, I jump up and down and think of stinky pussy. You should try it."

"I don't want to try it." I was pouting. And I didn't care. I was about to have a full-on toddler tantrum and I could not give less of a fuck than I did in that moment.

"You mean to tell me that you've got that"—he pointed at my crotch—"under control?" He stopped jumping and moved so he was standing in front of me, our bodies almost touching. My orgasm wanted to claw itself out of the top of my head. "You'd be okay if I knelt down in front of you"—he dropped to his knees—"and did this." He blew a long slow breath between my legs. My knees buckled again and I cried out, grabbing his shoulders so my fingernails pressed into his skin.

He jumped up quickly and began jumping again.

"Fuck you." I was holding myself like I had to pee.

"Soon enough. But for now, we think of stinky pussies."

"Blister dick." I jumped up and down with him.

"What?" His face looked like he'd bitten into a lemon.

"When I was in college, I dated a landscaper." I would have thought the jumping would only exacerbate the swelling and throbbing, but no, it was quite the opposite. "And he fell into some poison ivy, sumac, or whatever. That doesn't matter. What matters is that *somehow* he got it on his dick. And when we went to fuck one night, I yanked off his underwear and he had poison whatever blisters on his dick. So, yeah, blister dick, might just help control *my* boner."

"Excellent! Blister dick it is."

Like fools, we continued jumping around the living room attempting to control our boners. I'd gone five days without sex at that point. I could hold off a bit longer. For him, I could hold off. I hoped.

What the fuck had I gotten myself into?

Chapter Nineteen

I shot out of bed at half past six the next morning.

"Whatsa matter?" Jared asked, sleep still heavy in his voice.

"It's Friday." I chewed on my thumbnail.

"I know. Stop biting your nails and go back to sleep." He wrapped his arm around me and pulled me into little spoon position. His fingers grazed my stomach and if I were a cat, I would've clawed the ceiling.

He giggled. "Sorry."

"Do you know what this means?"

"We go home tomorrow?"

"My birthday isn't for two more weeks." I whispered the fact because I thought if I said the words too loudly, hell would open up and swallow me whole. Either that or my very angry vagina would seek revenge and eat Jared.

"Congratulations. It's been like two months since I've had sex, if you don't count the hand job I gave myself after you walked in on me naked, so two more weeks won't kill me. By the way, I pictured you the entire time. It was a good hand job." He smiled with his eyes still closed. "Now go back to sleep." He pulled a pillow over his head.

"I can't. What if I can't do this? I don't think I can." Panic washed through me.

"Blister dick."

"Right. Blister dick. Blister dick." I tried to snuggle in but was too antsy. "Blister dick," I continued to whisper, to no avail.

Jared could tell I was about to crawl out of my skin. He tore the blanket off, hopped out of bed, and threw on a T-shirt and sneakers. "Fuck. Let's go."

"Where?" *Blister dick, blister dick.*

"For a run. Your anxiety is fucking with my Zen. And honestly, it's too early for me to start thinking about stinky pussies. So we will run it off. Let's go."

I fumbled around for something to wear and settled on a fluorescent yellow sports bra and a pair of tiny black spandex shorts. I was stretching my arms when I walked into the living room to meet him.

"What the fuck, Mel?" His shoulders slumped.

"What?"

"You have to wear that?" Looked like Mr. Let's Take It Slow had a bug up his butt.

"What's wrong with this?" I looked down at myself. The tiny abs I'd been working on for the past few months were slowly making an appearance. "Hey, look at that!"

He opened the door. "Nothing." As I walked past, I swear I heard him mumble *stinky pussy* at least a few times.

Served him right.

* * *

"Mom, what time is our reservation?"

"Four thirty, sweetie," she answered from her bedroom.

I rolled my eyes. "Who eats dinner at four thirty in the afternoon?" I yelled back.

"Your father and I like eating early."

I looked at my dad, who shook his head and shrugged. "You aren't geriatric patients, you know."

"Relax." Jared rubbed my shoulders. "You and I can go out for drinks or something after."

"I guess." I pushed up on my toes and gave him a quick kiss on the cheek.

"Look at our little Melly, Bill! All grown-up with a boyfriend." My mom flitted into the kitchen to pour herself a glass of wine.

"Mom, serious—" I choked on the rest of the syllables and Jared patted me on the back.

"Repeat after me: 'two days.'" He laughed as I punched him in the arm. "You know"—he leaned down and whispered—"I kind of like when she refers to me as your boyfriend."

"As if!" I looked at him. "Wait, you aren't. Are you?"

"No way! I could never be the boyfriend of a woman so obsessed with blister dicks." He rolled his eyes dramatically. "Besides, we're still in the get-to-know-ya phase."

"What phase comes next?"

"Not sure. I'll let you know when we get there." He squeezed my shoulder before pulling me into a tight hug.

* * *

"What are you having for dinner, sweetie?" My dad asked, somewhat impatiently. He'd skipped lunch, knowing Mom was dragging us out for the pre–early bird special, and he was starving, as evidenced by the consistent low rumble in his tummy.

"I don't know. You guys order first."

"Excellent. I'll have the veal special." Dad snapped his menu shut and handed it to the waiter.

"Fettuccini Alfredo." Mom handed the waiter her menu and poured another glass of wine. At least I knew where my love of fermented grapes came from. At any given time, I was sure one of us had it flowing through our veins.

"Grilled chicken with eggplant and roasted red peppers, please. And can we get another bottle of wine for the table?" I was glad Jared had noticed that Mom and I would probably finish the bottle on the table before dinner was served.

I stared at the menu a beat longer. "I'll have the—" I bit my bottom lip and Jared inhaled quickly. I glanced over at him and saw he was regulating his breathing. Son of a bitch was controlling his boner and dinner hadn't even been served.

Boner.

Jared's boner.

Jesus Christ.

Blister dick.

"Ma'am?" The waiter snapped me out of my trance.

"I'll just have the penis points with steamed vegetables."

The waiter snickered and my mom gasped. Dad chuckled and Jared squeezed my thigh.

"I'm sorry?" The waiter asked.

"Pencil points," Jared answered.

"I'll be right back with your wine and other drinks."

"What?" I looked around at my parents and Jared.

"Penis points, Mel? Really?" My mom clucked.

"Mom!"

I glared at my mother, waiting for an explanation.

"Who orders penis points? Really?" My mom shrugged.

"I don't know Mom, who?"

"Um, you did," Jared whispered in my ear.

"No." My eyes widened and my hand flew to my mouth.

"Yes." His eyes were wide.

"Fuck. Save yourself. I'm going down with the ship." I sank in my chair.

"No worries." Jared leaned back and whispered, "You bite that bottom lip one more time and I'm going to blow a load in my pants."

It was then I spit my wine out all over the table.

"No one likes a spitter, Mel. Am I right, Jared?" My dad laughed like he'd told the world's funniest joke.

"Oh, honey"—my mom dipped her napkin into her water and wiped the corner of my dad's mouth—"you have a little spooge here on your face."

My head hit the table and I banged it a few more times for luck.

"Holy shit," Jared whispered as he adjusted his pants.

* * *

We bolted out of the restaurant the minute the check was paid. I thanked my parents, kissed my dad on the top of his balding head, and led Jared out the door.

"Sorry about that."

"What?"

"My parents. Awkward."

"Nah. They're good. It's nice to see two people so in love after so long."

"True." I tightened my grip on his hand. "Mini golf?" I pointed to the miniature golf place across the street.

"Sure."

"Grab your clubs and select your balls." The old lady at the window appeared bored.

"I want blue!" I snagged a blue ball from the basket.

"You can't have all the fun." He selected a pink ball.

"Whatever. You go first. Knock the ball in the hole." I choked on my gum and putted the blue ball too hard and it jumped the barrier.

"You need to adjust your grip on the shaft."

I turned and stared at him before picking my ball back up and placing it at the beginning of the course. I did as he said and lightly tapped the ball.

Jared squared up and missed the put when I said, "It bends a little to the left."

"What?" I asked when he narrowed his eyes at me and took the shot again.

Seven holes later, I'd lost count and asked, "How many strokes?"

"With *your* hands, no more than a dozen." He winked.

"Is it us or is golf really perverted?" I licked my melting ice cream cone. Three holes ago, Jared had abandoned the course and ran inside for two cones. He finished his quickly. I was taking my time.

"It's us. And would you finish that ice cream already? You're killing me."

"Oh you mean you don't like it when I do this?" I licked the melting ice cream from the bottom of the cone to the top, swirling my tongue around the sweet white cream.

"Stop."

"No." I continued licking the cone, my tongue wide and flat. I bit the bottom of the cone and sucked the ice cream through the hole.

"Mel." He warned.

"Jared." I didn't care. I kept licking and sucking my ice cream cone like a porn star. I bit the bottom of the cone and sucked the ice cream from the bottom.

He picked up the balls and walked us to the last hole. "We bang this in together."

Once again I spit out the contents of my mouth.

"You know what your dad said. No one likes a spitter."

"You've got spooge on your cheek, dear." I pulled his head down and licked the ice cream off his face.

He started jumping. "Ball. Club. Now."

"I spread my legs like this?" I widened my stance and stuck out my ass, gripping the club tightly. Jared ignored me and took up the spot behind me.

"On three. One. Two. Three."

We both putted out balls and the second the balls entered the hole, a fountain of water spurted from the ground. He shook his head, rubbed his hand down his face, and said, "I can't take it. Drinks?"

I knew exactly what was going through his head. "Yeah. Drinks."

* * *

"To sexless relationships!" Jared raised his glass and laughed.

"Who needs sex? Not us!" I clinked my glass to his.

"Think your parents are upset we left right after dinner?"

We'd walked around the boardwalk for an hour before stopping at the bar. As the sun went down the boardwalk got more crowded. After mini golf, we ended up at a small local bar a few blocks inland.

"Nah. I think my mom is trying to give us more alone time." I took a sip of my beer.

"Alone time. A week ago I would have killed for alone time with you. Now it makes me feel like I'm going to vomit." He half laughed.

"Thanks!" I punched his arm.

"You know what I mean. Do you have any idea how bad blue balls hurt?"

"As a matter of fact, I do. Girls get lady blue balls. Kind of like a swollen clit with no stimulation for release."

"Too much clit talk. More drinking." The last half of his pint slid down his throat. His Adam's apple bobbed slightly.

Bobbed.

Head bobbing.

Blow jobs.

The palms of my hands tried to rub the vision away from my eyes.

"Ahh! How come when we take sex completely off the table, that's all we can think about?"

"Are you kidding? That's all I could think about before I took it off the table. Removing it made it worse."

"I swear to God my clitoris is going to pack her bags and take a trip to fuck-off land."

"And my dick is going to join her."

We sat in silence, drinking our beers and staring at the television. But watching baseball didn't help. I started thinking of running through first.

Rounding bases.

Sliding into home.

Home run.

Sex.

Sex.

Penis in my vagina.

And I woke up the shriveled old lady that was once my best friend. I crossed my legs to stifle the spread of heat but to no avail. I downed my beer.

"Wanna get hammered?"

As soon as I looked at Jared, I knew he was having as hard a time as I was. "Yep." He drained the last of his beer and slammed the bottle on the table, motioning for the bartender.

I thought back to the night of Caroline's one night stand. "Wanna get hammered on sex?"

"What? Sex is off the table, remember?"

I proceeded to explain the night of Caroline's infamous one night stand when she and Ryan wooed each other with explicitly named cocktails that ended with an ice pack for her lady parts in the morning.

"But Caroline is with Brian."

"Right."

"So who is Ryan?"

"The one night stand."

"What?"

"Forget it. Do you want to get fucked up with dirty cocktails or not?"

"Let's do it." He slapped the bar top.

"Do you know how to make a Sex on My Face?" I asked the bartender, who smiled and nodded.

"Yes, I do."

"Make it two and make them shots." I turned to Jared. "Good?"

"Sex on My Face?" His face was screwed up; he looked to be in pain. I was in the same kind of pain.

I mentally counted backward from ten. "Yeah." I thought a minute. "Since you're all into stupid challenges and shit, here's one for you. Whoever gets a boner first loses."

"So what do I win?" He smiled and I sighed at the sight of his dimples.

"Who says you'll win?"

"I'm ten times better at controlling my boner than you are." He spread his arms and plastered a shit-eating grin across his face.

"You think so?"

"I know so. A hundred times." He picked up the drink the bartender handed him.

"We'll see about that." I downed my shot before he did. "Your turn."

"Two shots of Blue Balls."

"Coming right up." The bartender was suddenly more interested in our end of the bar than he was before we decided to drink fuck each other under the table.

"Blue Balls?"

"I'm a glutton for punishment, what can I say?"

"You don't have to say anything. But you *can* kiss me."

He leaned over and barely touched his lips to mine, appearing uninterested.

"Was that a kiss?" I asked the bartender as he delivered our Blue Balls.

"No, ma'am."

"That was me controlling my boner. I have more self-control than you do." He picked up his shot glass, winked, and said, "Drink up, loser."

"Hell, you have more self-control than I do." The bartender placed both palms flat on the bar and ducked his head.

"Whatever." I threw my head back and let the alcohol pour down my throat. I grabbed the bartender's hand. "Suck Bang Blow. Make it two and make it snappy." I snapped my fingers. Hours of steady drinking followed by our insane who-has-more-control-over-their-boner challenge was clouding my head and I was getting feisty.

"What did you order?"

"Why? Can't handle a little," I leaned in and whispered in his ear, "Suck Bang Blow?"

Jared cleared his throat and tugged on the bottom of my strapless white-and-navy striped tunic that was doubling as a dress and was entirely too short to begin with. I gave him the side eye and he coughed. "It was, uh, riding up."

"You don't like that?" I tugged the hemline back where it was. "I'm so sorry." I pouted, then bit my bottom lip.

"Don't do that." He growled.

"Don't do what?"

He tugged on my bottom lip before leaning in and biting it himself.

"Here you go." The bartender dropped the drinks in front of us. "So what is all this for?"

"It's a bet," Jared said without taking his eyes off me.

"Trying to see who gets a boner first." I finished the explanation.

"Looks like I win then!" The bartender laughed and said, "What's next?"

Jared handed me my drink and said, "Leg Spreaders."

"Fuck." The bartender shook his head and walked away.

"He wins, huh?" I asked.

"Hardly." Jared ran his hand up my thigh, his fingers toying with my hemline.

"Be careful," I cautioned and placed my empty glass on the bar top as the bartender deposited our next drink. "I'm not wearing any panties."

"Shit," the bartender whispered and walked away.

"Fuck *me*! Goddamn it, Mel!" Jared groaned, threw back the last shot, tossed money on the bar, grabbed my hand, and all but yanked me out the door.

"Where are we going?"

He dragged me toward the back of the building before spinning me so my back flew against the wall. His lips attacked mine. The second his mouth took mine, my entire body sang out in a chorus of *'bout fucking time.*

His hands cupped my breasts and his fingers pinched my nipples through the fabric of my dress.

"Yes." The word slipped out of my mouth. I no longer had control of my vocal chords. Gutteral sounds, moans, sharp, high-pitched squeals, and a slew of *oh fuck*s escaped from my mouth any time he concentrated on any other part of my body.

"Melody." His hands snaked around my back and one hand fisted my dress and lifted it up as the other felt my bare ass and squeezed before he lifted my leg and hitched it around his waist.

My eyes crossed as my insides pulsated every time he shoved his tongue in my mouth. I grabbed a hold of it and held it in place with my teeth before sucking it hard.

"Fuck." He breathed and unbuckled his belt before I came to my senses.

"Blister dick!" I pushed him away.

"What?"

"Stinky pussy!"

"No, no. Not now." He dove back inside my mouth.

I shoved him away again and started doing jumping jacks, muttering *blister dick* over and over.

"Are you fucking kidding me right now?" He leaned over with his hands on his knees, panting and dropping his head.

"Blister dick, bitch. I win, motherfucker! A ha ha ha ha!" I circled him while doing my jumping jacks.

"Fuck." He started doing jumping jacks in time with mine while repeating *stinky pussy* over and over.

"We are two fucking peas," I said between jumps.

"Come again?"

"Well, look at us. Two people who go through life looking for our next orgasm doing jumping jacks in the back alley of a bar because we are too horny."

"Real stellar moment." He sounded out of breath.

"I don't know." I smiled and stopped circling him. "I can't think of another pea I'd like to share this particular pod with."

Chapter Twenty

Thank you for inviting me. I had a great time this week." Jared kissed my hand after I hugged my parents and hopped into the truck.

"I did too."

"You still okay with our little agreement?" He pulled out onto the street and headed home.

"Sure. Why not? I can do—or not do—anything for another fourteen days."

"Thirteen."

"Thirteen what?"

"Days. Today is thirteen days. Yesterday was fourteen days."

"That"—I glanced over at him—"may be the sexiest thing any-one's ever said to me before."

His laugh circled around me and squeezed.

Slipping off my flip-flops, I rested my feet on the dashboard. I felt calmer than I had in who knew how long. My head was clear, Jared was tracing circles on the back of my hand, Thirty Seconds to

Mars was playing on the radio. The few days away were exactly what I needed to recharge and redirect.

I suddenly turned in my seat to face Jared.

A big smile grew on his face. "What?"

"You should do it."

"Do what?" He turned down the radio.

"Open a place. Get your chef on."

"You're crazy!" He laughed and turned the volume back up.

I pressed the radio off and said, "No, really. Look. I have money. I can invest. I talked to my dad, he's interested. I called Berk—"

"Wait, what? Mel, no." He took off his baseball hat and threw it on the dash.

"You're talented. Look, that dinner you made for everyone? They can't stop talking about it. Every time you walk in a kitchen, your eyes light up. I can tell, you're in your element. It makes you happy."

"Maybe I'm happy because of who's in the kitchen with me."

I couldn't keep the grin off my face and it was so big, my cheeks hurt. I linked my fingers between his.

"Really. Listen. Berk is looking for locations near my apartment and your sister's. He has some leads, just depends on your thoughts about size and location. I have the money. Like I said, Dad wants in, and Berk is interested in investing, too."

"What about my real job? You know, the one I start on Tuesday? The one that will pay me actual money?"

"Up to you. Keep it until all this materializes. Either way, Berk said the job is yours now or later. Whatever you want."

"That's crazy. He'd do that for me? He doesn't even know me."

"He'd do it for you because of me. Because I asked him to do it for you."

"For real?"

"Yep."

"I don't know, Mel. I don't want it be some crazy restaurant that's open all hours of the night. The point of my own place is to not have to live at work. I was hoping to start it out only for breakfasts or lunches and move from there. Not sure I'd make a lot of money or anything in the beginning, if ever. I mean, I would totally pay you and your dad and Berk back—"

I placed my finger over his lips. "Shh. Relax. One step at a time. And I am investing. Not loaning. You can do this."

"We can do this." He bit the tip of my finger.

I turned the radio back up, rolled down my window, and smiled the entire ride home.

* * *

"Why does your suitcase feel ten times heavier than it did when we left?" Jared hefted the last bag to the landing as I unlocked the door.

"Little stressed? You should expel some of that." I giggled.

"Oh no. You don't get to do that. I'm fine. I am in control of my boner."

"Clearly." I looked down at his basketball shorts and saw he was clearly not in control.

"Shut it." He carried my bags to my room.

I kicked off my shoes and started riffling through the mail Sarah was nice enough to collect for me. Bills and junk mail. The only reason the Postal Service was still in existence. I rolled my eyes, tossed the junk, and stacked the bills for tomorrow. Still on my mini vacation high, I didn't need to be bothered with real life just yet.

"Holy shit, Melody! You weren't kidding!" Jared yelled from my bedroom.

"I wasn't kidding about what?" I walked into my room and stopped short a few steps in. On my bed was a large pile of vibrators, dildos, porno mags, and various other accoutrements I'd used to spice up my now-on-hold sex life. I waved my freak flag on the regular, but for some reason seeing Jared with evidence of my fucktastic lifestyle kind of made me ill. "Why are you going through my drawers?"

"Well, my dear"—Jared walked over with a pair of handcuffs dangling from his finger—"I figured you had a naughty drawer. I had no idea you had an entire shop in your bedside table." He laughed and picked up my wrist, fastening a cuff to it before moving on to the other. The snap of the metal locking made me feel flush.

"You see"—he walked me over to the bed and sat me down—"there are rules to this challenge of ours and I didn't want you to be tempted. I, however, didn't expect to be so fucking turned on by your arsenal of toys. And this?" He held up the DVD Caroline and Sarah had given me.

"Wait, but—" I wanted to explain.

"No talking. I think we're just going to have to go through these and figure out which ones we are keeping and which ones we are tossing." He sifted through the toys in the pile. "Who needs this many butt plugs? Seriously, Melody."

"Look, I'm not going to use them. According to the rules, I'm not allowed to have an orgasm. And besides, it's not just those things you have to worry about. I don't need batteries." I gave him a two-fingered salute, highlighting that I was just as dexterous with my hands.

"Who said anything about allowing you to have an orgasm? Besides, that's easy enough to remedy. One"—he held up a finger—"no locking the bathroom door when you're in the shower. Any longer than a ten-minute shower, then the other person can come in and make sure there is no funny business. And two"—he returned my two-fingered salute—"same goes for the bedroom. No locks."

"Well, you'll be sleeping in here with me, right?" I looped my cuffed arms around his neck.

"That would be best, I think. Not sure if I can trust you to keep your end of the deal." His fingers dug into my hips.

"I am a naughty girl. You might have to punish me."

I felt his chest heave up and down and I knew he couldn't find a good rhythm to control his breathing. He pushed me back down on the bed. I guessed it was more to remove me from his space than to suggest a delicious romp.

"Let's see what this one is about." I heard plastic snapping open and a drawer sliding shut. My television clicked on and the porn DVD started playing. I refused to open my eyes. The sounds of skin slapping skin were almost more than I could handle. I started counting backward from one hundred.

"You won't break me, you know." I finally said. "All this will get to you first. I can smell your erection."

"Is that so?"

"That is exactly so. I think we better quit while we're ahead."

He looked at me, at the television, and back at me before grabbing the remote and clicking off the movie. Stuffing a hand into his pocket, he retrieved the key to the handcuffs and unlocked them. Slipping them off my wrists, he stuck them in his pocket. "These stay with me. That"—he pointed to the treasure trove of sexual exploration on my bed—"should be packed up. We wouldn't want you to be tempted to do something—"

"Naughty." I finished his sentence. He curled his lips and flared his nostrils before leaving my room.

"Where are you going?" I called after him, laughing.

"Shower. Cold." The bathroom door slammed on his words and I fell on the bed.

"Ouch!" I reached under my lower back and retrieved a large gold dildo Sarah gave me for my twenty-first birthday. I studied it and thought back on all the memories Goldie and I had shared over the past nine years. Sighing, I tossed him on the bed, got up, and rummaged through my closet for shoeboxes. By the time Jared was done with his shower, I had two stacks of boxes sitting in the hallway.

"What is that?" He pointed at the tower of sin.

"You told me to box my shit up."

He looked confused. "But why are there so many boxes?"

"Oh, that. Well, sweetie, you only checked my side table. But look, I organized them. This stack is stuff that's been used. So I guess we can throw that pile of boxes out. This one"—I stood and presented him with the second stack like I was a game show model—"is filled with lovely toys that have never been used. This pile, I was thinking, maybe we can keep."

"The stack of used is bigger than the stack of unused." His eyebrow rose as he looked at me.

"What can I say? I get bored sometimes. I like change. Oh, except for Goldie. He stays." I opened the box that held only the giant golden dildo. "It was a gift."

"I don't need to know that, Melody." He dropped his head.

"Not from a guy, silly. Your sister gave it to me." I opened the hall closet and put the keeper boxes at the back.

"Wow."

"What?"

" 'Your sister gave it to me.' Works better than 'stinky pussy.' " He pulled his shorts out and looked down. "Yep. Dead."

"I'll have to remember that. Are we staying in tonight?"

"Yes." My cell phone rang out and I danced to the happy ringtone. It was Caroline.

"Hey lady!" I wiggled my ass toward Jared to drive an extra nail into his orgasmless coffin. Who was I kidding? We were bunkmates in that coffin.

"Are you home?"

"Yep. Got in a little bit ago. What's up?"

"Can I stop by?" She sounded odd.

"Sure. You okay, Care?"

"Yeah. Good." She paused. "I'm good. I'll be there in thirty?"

"Perfect. See you then." I clicked off and stood staring at the phone, chewing on my lip.

"You all right?" Jared's hand rested on my shoulder. I looked up at him and shrugged.

"That was Caroline. She sounded really weird."

"Weird how?" He sounded genuinely concerned.

"Not sure. And"—I checked the time—"she should still be at work."

"When is she coming?" His hands massaged my shoulders, which were suddenly tense.

"Thirty minutes." I turned around and hugged him.

"What's this for?"

"Just because." I pulled up on my toes and kissed him on the chin.

"Why don't you go take a quick shower and I'll clean all this other stuff up. When she gets here, I'll run to the store or something so you two can have some privacy."

"You don't have to do that." I rested my head against his chest and squeezed him in a hug. He really was unbelievable.

"Don't worry about it. Besides, there's nothing in the fridge except a few apples."

"You." I kissed his shoulder. "Are." I kissed his other shoulder. "Awesome."

He cupped my rear end and lifted me off the ground. "Well, just remember, if all goes well, in thirteen days you'll literally be fucking awesome." He dropped me, smacked my ass, and walked away.

I strolled down the hall and it was a few steps before I understood the joke. "Ha. Ha! Not funny. Torture the girl with no orgasm. I'll remember that."

I laughed and closed the bathroom door.

By the time I finished showering and getting dressed, Jared was on his way out the door, grocery list in hand.

"Need anything?"

"You mean besides a good dicking? No thank you."

"Try not to think about it. I did notice you were low on gummy bears."

I whipped my head around. He'd found the stash I keep in the spaghetti pot in the cabinet under the counter. Of course, I never cooked so there would be no need for me to go in that cabinet other than to procure a handful of those tiny German gummies. Of course Mr. Chef Extraordinaire would be drawn to unused pots and pans.

"Did you actually fill the spaghetti pot with them or—"

I kissed him on the lips to keep him from talking. It was embarrassing enough to have him find out I stash food, it was even more embarrassing to think he'd find out how much I stash. "Don't you worry about that."

"I was just thinking that if you were worried about thieves running off with your candy, I figure they'd snag that sixty-inch screen you have on the wall."

"I'd be lost without my gummy bears."

"Would you like me to pick you up some more?" His snaked his hands around my waist.

"Yes. Please. And I would think it best you and I not discuss this matter in the future." I was dead serious but the look on his face told me he was having a difficult time understanding the gravity of the situation.

"I assure you, I will do my best to see that your gummy bears are replenished and the mission remains a covert operation. "

"You joke. Gummy bears are serious."

"I can tell." He kissed the tip of my nose. "By the way, why do you have such a big television? It's high def, all the bells and whistles."

Hand on my hip, I answered bluntly. "Two things in life deserve to be seen on a high definition big screen: football and porn."

He blew out a breath. "Jesus Christ, Melody."

I shrugged. "You asked."

"Fuck me, I sure did." He bounced up on his toes a few seconds before saying, "Be back soon." His hand found mine.

He opened the door just as Caroline was about to knock. I quickly let go of his hand, hoping she hadn't noticed and kind of wishing I hadn't been so hasty to let go. I wanted to talk to Sarah about Jared and me first. Her eyes were red and puffy. Definitely not a good sign.

"Hi," she mumbled and walked into the apartment, barely making eye contact as she headed for the kitchen, stopping at the wine fridge for a bottle of white and an opener.

"She okay?" Jared nodded toward Caroline.

"Don't think so. I haven't seen her like this since she found her fiancé inside the intern."

"What?"

I shook my head. "Never mind. Long story." I placed a hand on his chest, my fingers grazing across his nipple. The two of us shuddered at the same inappropriate time. It was certainly no time to be muttering about stinky pussies and blister dicks. Both of us knew it the moment we made eye contact.

"Well"—Jared kissed me chastely—"I'll leave you two to talk."

"Thanks." As I closed the door, I noticed him adjusting his pants and smiled.

Turning around, I yelped. Caroline was standing toe-to-toe holding an overpoured glass of wine in my face.

"What was"—she pointed between me and the door with her eyebrows hidden in her hairline—"that about? You banging Sarah's brother?"

"I am not *banging* Sarah's brother." Not for at least another thirteen days but I couldn't tell her that. "Not everything is about sex." I took the glass from her and settled on the couch.

"Since when?" She plopped down next to me, crossing her arms over her chest.

"I will gladly have this conversation with you. I am *dying* to have this conversation with you. But first, I want to know why you"—I swirled my finger in front of her face—"look like someone killed your bunny."

She did nothing but twiddle her thumbs and stare blankly ahead.

"Okay. Let's drink our wine, loosen our lips. We apparently have quite a bit to catch up on. Give me your glass. I'll refill you."

I stood in front of her and held out my hand while doing my best to remove the contents from my glass. A few seconds passed before I realized she wasn't handing me hers.

"Where's your glass?"

She shook her head.

"I didn't pour myself one."

"What?"

"I didn't want any."

"You didn't *want any*?" The idea was unfathomable to me. "Since when do you not drink wine?" I snorted and finally drained my glass. I held it up and looked at it in the afternoon sun that streamed through my living room window. "What, are you pregnant or something?" I laughed and headed toward the kitchen. "As if."

Caroline didn't laugh back. She didn't say anything. I froze and slowly turned on my heel. A tear fell down her cheek and she looked down at her hands.

"No." Visions of screaming babies and smelly diapers rushed through my head and I hit the brakes before I said something stupid. "You're pregnant? As in, like…" I held my arms out in front of my stomach.

"Yep."

"Holy shit." I'd never said three syllables so slowly before in my life. I sank nearly as slowly into the couch.

"You can say that again."

"Holy shit. Does Brian know?"

"No. Not yet." She shook her head.

"Why the fuck not?"

"I didn't know what to say."

"How about 'Hey Brian, there's a tiny human growing in my belly and guess what? It's yours!'" I rolled my eyes. "What did Sarah say?"

"I didn't tell her yet." Caroline bit her fingernails until I swatted her hand away from her mouth.

"So you told me first?"

"Yep."

"Why?"

Caroline snapped her head in my direction and gave me a look that told me she didn't understand the question.

"I didn't mean that like it came out. I just figured, out of all of us, I wouldn't be the one people necessarily would go to in an emergency."

"That isn't true, Mel. You make really shitty decisions for yourself, I mean *really* shitty—"

"Thanks!" I huffed, though I knew she was right. Then again, maybe that tide was turning. I didn't think Jared was a shitty decision.

"Let me finish. But for the rest of us, you tell it like it is and snap us out of our delusions. You honestly give the best advice."

"Well, thank you, I guess."

"With that in mind, what the fuck do I do?"

I pulled her hands into mine. "No brainer. You tell Brian."

"I can't tell Brian."

"Why not?" I've never understood people who keep shit from one another. I didn't figure Caroline to be one of those people who did.

"I don't know."

"Do you want to keep it?"

Her eyes widened and her hands flew to her stomach and I realized she'd never even contemplated getting rid of the baby.

"So we know the answer to that. Do you love him?"

"Of course I love him."

"Does he love you? Not for nothing, we all know the answer to that but I want you to say it."

She cracked a smile and said, "Yes, he does."

"Do you picture yourself with him for the rest of your life?"

"Yes."

"Then what the fuck is the problem? I swear, Caroline. Sometimes the answer is right in front of your face and you fail to see it. You come in here weepy and argumentative and for what? Because you're pregnant? I'll give you the benefit of the doubt and blame it on hormones but, seriously, shit happens and you're lucky it happened with someone you love and who loves you back.

"You're an amazing, amazing woman, Care. Sure, you've been through some shit. And sure, you and Brian have been together for only six months or whatever, but sometimes, as much as we plan and plan fate comes riding in on her red tricycle and runs over all our plans. And before you protest at all, I know that you'd rather have had a wedding before a baby. It would be the most ideal, right?"

She nodded and smiled.

"Well, tough shit. You've got a bun in the oven and a guy who loves you more than anything in this world. Embrace it. Fuck all whatever anyone else has to say. Sure, Sarah will preach for a minute but she'll get it."

Caroline fell into my shoulder and wrapped me in a tight hug.

"Happy tears?" I asked when she continued to cry. She nodded and sniffed loudly.

"You're gonna get really fat, you know." I started to tear up, realizing that our little group was changing, growing. For the better. My own small changes were part of that growth.

"I know." She laughed as snot bubbled out of her nose.

"You're going to blow out your vagina when you push it out."

"I know." I think Caroline choked on her own snot.

"They can stitch that shit up, though. Right?"

She nodded. "I think so."

"You are a mess." I held her at arm's length. "Clean yourself up, take a shower if you have to. And march on over and tell Brian."

"He's working tonight."

"So. Tell him there. Why not? It's where you two met, right? If you want, I'll get everyone together. Make it a bigger surprise."

"We can do that."

"We can. Now go shower and get your skinny ass ready before that baby turns you into a Weeble."

She left me alone and I shed a few more happy tears for my friend and a few for inevitable change. But the tide was changing for the better. For at least a few of us.

Chapter Twenty-One

Caroline eventually left to *prepare herself*—her words not mine. Apparently telling someone you are pregnant is an emotional feat, one that I'm not looking to partake in any time soon.

Not sure exactly when I fell asleep on the couch, but it couldn't have been too long. Jared was putting groceries away when I opened my eyes.

"Hey you," I muttered in my sleepy voice.

"Hey. Go back to sleep. I'll wake you up when it's time for dinner."

"No. It's okay. I'm up." Pushing myself up off the couch was a chore. I hadn't realized how tired I was. Maybe going out wasn't the best idea, but I'd promised Caroline. "We're going out tonight. Staying in canceled." I popped a grape in my mouth as I settled at the counter.

"We are? I was thinking we could watch a movie." He held up my DVD copy of *9½ Weeks*.

"Do you really think watching a movie about sex is what we need right now? I swear I've done more jumping jacks in the past few days than I have in my whole life, thanks to you." His eyebrow rose. "So if I took off my shirt"—he pulled his shirt over his head and tucked it in the back of his shorts—"it would be difficult for you to resist me?"

I was entirely too tired to play his games but I decided if he was going to fuck with my libido, I was going to fuck with his. Without saying a word, I lifted my tank top over my head, unhooked my bra, and dropped both to the floor. Popping a few grapes in my mouth, I leaned back and stared at him.

His face scrunched up for a second and his knuckles whitened as he fisted the dishtowel. "So this is how we're playing this?"

"You started it."

"But I don't have tits."

"Ahh." I hopped off the stool and walked around the counter. "But you have these." I grazed the muscles right above his hipbones, the ones that highlighted the way down to the promised land, making sure to press up against him enough so that he'd feel my nipples harden against his skin. He sucked in a breath. "And this." I slid my fingernails through the small patch of hair that ran from his belly button and disappeared beneath the waistband of his boxer shorts. I shuddered. Maybe I should have kept the counter between us.

"Everything okay?" Jared smirked and tucked my hair behind my ear.

"Fine." Everything was certainly not fine. What the hell was I thinking? We still had thirteen more days to go and I was frolicking half naked in the kitchen, touching muscles and imagining the pot of gold at the end of his happy trail?

"Fine? Because I am not fine." He lifted me up and placed me on the counter, wrapping my legs around his waist. Still keeping his eyes on mine, he leaned down and flicked his tongue against my nipple.

I gasped and he chuckled.

Bastard.

"I don't think this is what we should be doing right now." My head fell back as he ran his tongue across the hollow at the base of my throat.

"On the contrary." His teeth grazed along the line of my jaw. "I think this is exactly what we should be doing."

Our lips touched briefly before parting and allowing our tongues to mingle. The butterflies that stirred whenever Jared kissed me made me feel like I'd never been kissed before. It was addictive and I couldn't get enough.

I tightened my legs around him and pulled him in. My arms wrapped around his neck and I pressed myself closer. His hands fisted in my hair as he moaned into my mouth.

Just as I thought I was about to lose it, the door buzzed.

"Ignore it," I said between kisses.

"Okay." His thumbs rubbed my nipples.

The door buzzed again.

"Maybe they'll go away." I slid my hands down the back of his shorts and gripped his ass.

"Maybe." His hands tightened around my thighs.

Buzzer number three. And it was a long one.

"Fuck." He pulled back, lips swollen and red, hair mussed. Jesus. He was sexy.

"Damn it." I strode to the intercom and clicked, "Who is it?"

"Floral delivery for a Ms. Ashford."

"Come up." I pressed the buzzer to allow the deliveryman to

come up. Jared tossed me my tank but pocketed my bra with a wink.

I caught a glimpse of myself in the mirror by the door. My face was red from rubbing against his face, his five o'clock shadow bordering on midnight. My lips were puffy and red enough to almost pass for purple, and I had teeth marks on my collarbone.

"Teeth marks? Really?" I quickly fluffed my hair and draped it in front of me before grabbing a five out of my wallet.

He shrugged. "Those aren't teeth marks, they're love notes."

"I'll fucking show you love notes," I muttered, much to his delight as I opened the door right before the flower guy knocked.

"I heard that!"

The flower guy handed me the largest arrangement of flowers I'd ever seen.

"Thanks." I handed him the five-dollar bill and closed the door as I turned the bouquet to find a card.

"Who's it from?" Jared asked.

"No idea. I can't find a card."

"Here it is." He bent down and retrieved it from the floor. It must've fallen.

"Open it," I told him.

"You sure? You don't care if I see who sent you a monstrosity of a floral arrangement? What if it's a former lover?" The way he drew out the word *luvah* made me giggle.

"No. And besides, the word to focus on is *former*. And there is no current. At least not yet." I winked and placed the arrangement on the table. "Read it out loud."

"Oh look!" he exclaimed. "They're from your work." He tossed the card on the table and went back to putting groceries away in the kitchen. "And it's not even your birthday yet."

"No!" I picked up the card and read it out loud: "Melody, Best wishes on your birthday. From everyone at Waterman Financial." I tilted my head. Why was I getting a bouquet two weeks before my birthday?

I crumpled the card in my fist and dropped it to the floor. "Oh that's nice. This bouquet is bigger than last year." I looked over at Jared, who was busying himself with getting dinner ready. He was doing everything but looking at me. "Jared." He didn't answer; instead he chopped an onion. "Jared." I injected a bit more oomph into my voice. He tossed the onions in a pan.

"Yo! Jared!" I yelled. He stopped and looked at me. "You know these are sent to everyone at the company, right? These aren't from Zac. You know that, right?"

"Yeah. I mean, it's okay. We're just getting to know each other."

"Are you jealous?"

He gave me an are-you-crazy look and resumed chopping vegetables.

"You're totally jealous! You thought they were form Zac!" I laughed and effectively diffused the tension.

Jared frowned and chopped with a bit more vigor, but I could tell he was annoyed by the tenseness in his shoulders.

I hopped up on the counter, leaned across, and kissed him on the cheek. "Don't worry, baby. I only do jumping jacks for you."

I laughed and sat across from him before he relented, leaned forward, and returned the kiss.

"How can I help?"

"Can you tear lettuce?"

"Can I tear lettuce? Of course. These fingers"—I wiggled my fingers like jazz hands— "were made for tearing lettuce."

"You're crazy."

"You love it."

"Sure do." He winked and I tore lettuce.

* * *

"So why are we going out instead of staying in and making out all night?" Jared asked as he stood in the doorway to my room, watching as I figured out what to wear.

I was standing in my room wearing a silver sparkly bra and panties set Jared had found somewhere in my drawer. I guess he figured playing dress up was as close to the real thing as he was going to get. The tags were still on them and I didn't remember buying them or receiving them as a gift. I had a lot of lingerie items that fit that came-from-outer-space bill.

"Because I am tired of doing jumping jacks. And I promised Caroline." I caught myself in my floor length mirror. "Why am I wearing this? I look like a disco ball." I turned side to side, watching with interest as the fabric caught the overhead light and reflected back. "You won't even get to appreciate them." I sucked in my gut. Dinner had proven that my eyes were indeed larger than my stomach. If he kept cooking like that, I was going to gain at least ten pounds in the next month.

"Hush. I'll appreciate them. I'll know what's under whatever you decide to wear. And why is it taking so long?" He stepped to my closet and started looking through my clothes. He pulled out a red floral baby doll dress circa middle school.

"No. I wore that when I was thirteen."

"Oh. Why do you still have it?"

"Who knows?"

He continued to push hangers aside and produce clothing that I had no intentions of ever wearing again. I'd calmly shake my head no and he would calmly move on to the next piece.

After ten minutes he held up a pair of black leather mini shorts and a slinky white sleeveless tank.

"Bingo!" I snatched the shorts and stepped into them.

"I like those," Jared said as I slipped the tank over my head. "And I like this." He brushed the material with his hand.

I fluffed my hair before pulling it back into a ponytail and kept my makeup simple with sheer gloss, mascara, and a small bit of blush across my cheeks. Jared watched the entire process with interest and a bit of lust in his eye. I made quite sure to slow down and prolong what needed to be prolonged. He wanted to watch; I made sure I gave him a hard-on.

Slipping my feet into a pair of four-inch yellow pumps, I checked the mirror one last time.

"Jesus, you have great legs." Jared's low whistle put a smile on my face.

"Easy, big fella. Put your tongue back in your mouth. We have a bar to get to and babies to celebrate."

* * *

By nine thirty the last of our crew had arrived. Siobhan, Brian's sister, scuttled in making apologies for her lateness and promising juicy tabloid fodder. I was definitely intrigued.

"Sorry I'm late everyone!"

"Better late than pregnant, am I right?" Berk snickered.

Berk and I played darts, and Jared, Sarah, and Drew chatted at the table while Caroline and Siobhan chatted by the bar. I caught Caroline's eye from across the room and tilted my head. She gave me a thumbs-up and whispered to the waitress.

"So…" Berk sang.

"So?"

"So what's going on with you and Hottie McHotterson over there?"

"What do you mean?" I threw a dart.

"I mean, normally you call me and dish all the dirt. The guy goes away with you to your parents' house for a few days and I hear nada. Not one phone call. Not one text. Is he gay?"

"He is most *definitely* not gay." I grabbed a beer from the waitress's tray.

"Too bad." Berk tilted his head and nodded toward Jared. He was standing with his back to us. "He has a perfect ass."

"Yes, he does," I said dreamily.

"So you *have* seen it."

"I have."

"You slept with Sarah's brother? Does she know?"

Caroline walked up and joined the conversation. "I knew it!"

"Hold on. You know nothing. I did not sleep with Sarah's brother"—I placed my hand over Berk's mouth—"and before you get all into semantics, I did not bang him, blow him, fuck him, screw him, or any other kitschy euphemism that involves penises or vaginas."

"Tongues?" Berk asked.

"No. No tongues either. Unless you think kissing counts. But I'm not counting it."

"I don't understand." Berk took my beer and drank it down.

"He and I are withholding sex. For now."

"Oh my God, why?" Berk's hand flew to his heart and he stumbled backward a few steps. "Are you ill?" He felt my forehead with the back of his hand.

"You really aren't sleeping together?" Caroline looked astonished.

"Who's not sleeping with who?" Siobhan joined us.

"Melody isn't sleeping with Jared." Berk filled her in.

"Why not? Is he gay? Berk, you should ask him out. He's cute." Siobhan sipped her cocktail.

"No. Stop." I held up my hands in an attempt to corral the conversation away from crazy. "He is not gay. He and I are just taking a break from sex—"

"No!" Siobhan and Berk exclaimed together.

"But you're—"

"Melody, how am I supposed live vicariously through you and your conquests if you are not"—her arms flailed as she looked for the word—"conquesting anything?"

"I don't think that's a word," Caroline said to Siobhan.

"I don't care! Melody's not having sex! Do you know what this means?" Siobhan said a bit too loudly.

"Hell has indeed frozen over?" Berk offered.

"So you're *not* banging my brother?" Sarah appeared.

"No. I am not banging your brother."

"Why not? He's a catch, you know! You'd be lucky to find someone like him."

"Whoa. Relax, sister. Jared and I are just taking it slow."

She narrowed her eyes at me. "Why?"

"Okay. Look. Remember when we decided I would take a break from sex until my thirtieth birthday?"

"Yes." Four people spoke in unison.

"Well, Jared and I kind think we may have somewhat of a thing for each other."

"A thing?"

"We like each other, okay?"

"Well, what's the problem then? I mean the withholding was really to keep you away from Zac and—"

"Right. I know this. But,"—I looked over at Jared—"I like him."

"You like him? Or you *like him* like him?"

"Both." I turned back to my friends. "We decided neither of us have our heads on straight—"

"Which ones?" Berk laughed.

"Ha ha. But exactly. Our heads are not on straight and we are using this challenge as a way to get to know each other without all the—"

"Sex?" Siobhan interrupted.

"Yes. So we are taking it slow. Going on dates. Holding hands. Getting to know each other until my thirtieth birthday and then we can go from there."

"Foreplay," Caroline said.

"It is foreplay." Berk nodded in agreement.

"How is it foreplay?" I asked.

"All the buildup and anticipation? Foreplay."

"Operation Foreplay." Berk winked. "I changed the name of it, remember? It was my idea!"

"So you are in a relationship with my brother?"

"I guess, yeah."

Sarah eyeballed me. "I mean, good for you but it's my brother."

"And?"

"And don't hurt him."

"I'm not planning on it."

"When do you ever?" She walked away.

"What's going on?" Jared entered the conversation, handing me the Snake Bite I'd been promised. I grabbed his hand and squeezed. He looked at me with a worried expression on his face. Probably because my hands were slick with sweat. This was not the way I'd wanted to talk to Sarah about this.

I'd had enough. "Caroline. Please?"

"Oh, right."

On cue, Brian strolled over and kissed Caroline on the cheek before flipping his towel onto his shoulder. "What's up? We're getting slammed at the bar."

"Well"—she looked around at everyone before stepping in front of Brian and taking his hands in hers—"this bar, with these people, is where you and I first met. And it was the best thing that ever happened to me. It may have taken me a bit to figure it out but you knew all along that we were supposed to be together."

She took a deep breath and I looked around. Sarah and Drew were holding hands. Berk draped his arm around Siobhan and whispered, "Is she proposing?"

"No," I whispered back as I stood, fingers locked with Jared's.

"What's going on?" Brian whispered nervously, looking around at everyone in the circle for an answer that no one had. No one until his eyes locked with mine. I smiled knowingly and he searched my face for what I wouldn't say.

"Brian"—Caroline smiled widely—"you and I—" She paused for

dramatic effect. Good to know some of me had rubbed off on her. "We are having a baby."

Other than the background noise of the other patrons of the bar, there was silence in our circle. Until there wasn't. Everyone yelled congratulatory praise at the same time.

"We're having a, a, uh—"

"Baby!" Caroline yelled.

"Are you sure? How do you know? When did this happen? Holy shit. Am I really going to be a father?"

Siobhan rushed over and hugged her brother.

"I am sure. I went to the doctor. I'm about eight weeks along. Holy shit is right. And yes. You are going to be a daddy."

Brian picked Caroline up off the floor and spun her around. And for the rest of the night, we all anticipated a new addition to our small group.

Chapter Twenty-Two

"Good morning," Jared whispered as I nuzzled deeper into the crook of his arm.

I stretched my legs, pointed my toes, and wrapped my leg around his body. He dragged his fingers down the length of my body, pausing at the thin fabric veil of my panties. He tucked his fingers into the waistband before sliding his hand in and around to my ass. I breathed out audibly and I could feel the smile spread across his face. Tilting my head up, I leaned in until my lips touched his.

"Good morning," he repeated, before taking my bottom lip between his and tugging gently.

"Thank you." I rocked into him, rolling him onto his back with his hand still cupping my ass. "I don't want it to be morning yet." I stretched and yawned. "I'm so tired."

"But you still look sexy on a few hours' sleep. I'd do you." He nipped my earlobe.

"Do you think we can forgo the challenge for just today? I mean, what kind of guy would you be if you didn't let me blow my load?" I batted my eyelashes and he laughed.

"Blow your load?" He pulled his head back and made a weird face before smiling. "Sometimes I swear you're a man trapped in a woman's body."

"Why sugarcoat it?"

He gripped my ass tighter and pushed up into me. I felt his dick twitch and my inner walls pulse.

"We can't keep waking up like this." I closed my eyes as his tongue slid up my neck.

"Who says?"

I lifted my head. "Um, I think *you* said. And besides, you're going to have to go back to Sarah's place soon."

He frowned. "My sister says I can come back to her place today."

"Today?" I sat up, feeling the bulge in his boxer shorts throb a bit more. "You can't leave today."

"I have no intentions of leaving today." He kissed my forehead. "I figure I'll head back tomorrow."

I knew he couldn't stay. I knew the living arrangement was temporary, but I wasn't looking forward to waking up in my bed alone.

"I guess so." I lay down on top of him and snuggled into his chest and he rubbed my back. "I could help you."

"I only have a couple of bags. You don't have to."

"Maybe I want to."

"Then it's settled. You'll help me bring my two bags to my sister's apartment." He pinched my butt.

"It's not funny. I'm kinda used to you." I picked up my head and looked at him.

"I'm kinda used to you." He kissed the tip of my nose.

"Where are you going?"

"I'm going to make you some breakfast."

I finally rolled out of bed and walked back out to the smell of coffee brewing and Jared working in the kitchen.

"Whatcha making?" I took the steaming mug he handed me as I walked in.

"Banana pancakes." He nodded toward the counter.

"I love banana pancakes." I picked up a banana and began peeling it as I admired the shirtless view.

"I know you do. I'm sorry we didn't get a chance to have them in Wildwood."

I licked the tip of the banana. "I bet yours will be better."

"I don't know. Not much beats memories when it comes to food and how it tastes, but I'll do my best." He looked up and his mouth dropped.

I kept my eye on him as I pushed the banana between my lips.

"What are you doing?" He swallowed.

I pulled the banana out and licked up the length of it. "Eating a banana."

"You're doing a good job." He adjusted his pants.

"Yeah?" I opened my mouth and shoved the banana to the back of my throat, pulling in and out slowly.

"Son of a bitch, Melody."

I bit off a piece and smiled. "What?"

"Stop playing with your food." He took the remainder of the fruit from me and tossed it aside before leaning across the counter and grabbing me by the back of my head. He kissed me hard and I almost forgot to breathe. When he pulled away it was a moment before my heart regulated itself again. "Next time I won't be so gentle." He winked.

Knowing I wouldn't win the morning innuendo battle, I rolled my shoulders and asked, "What can I do?"

"Well, you can go put some pants on. Can't take the distraction right now. Working on making your breakfast." He winked.

"You're no fun." I laughed and headed to my room and put on a pair of yoga pants.

My cell phone buzzed with a text. Berk was downstairs.

"Make extra pancakes," I said as I walked to unlock the door. "Berk is coming up."

"I forgot he was coming over."

"Yep!"

"You excited about dinner tonight?"

"Eh." I caught his raised eyebrow and figured I needed to explain. "I mean, dinner is going to be great but I don't really know if I'm in the mood to go out." I refilled my coffee mug. "I was kind of hoping for something simple. Small." I stretched up on my toes. "Intimate."

"Happy Sunday, bitches!" Berk entered the apartment with his usual flair. "Good lord, look at those cum gutters." He stopped short in the middle of the living room and pointed at Jared. "I am jealous."

"Look at those what?" Jared and I said in unison as Jared looked down at himself with his arms held open.

"Cum buckets."

"Cum what?" I asked.

"Jesus. You'd think you'd listen when I speak." He unbuttoned his khakis and pulled them down a bit. He flexed his stomach muscles. "Cum gutters." He trailed his finger near the waistband of his Calvins and highlighted just above the hip.

I laughed so hard I had to cross my legs.

The ever lovin' victory muscle.

The muscle that screams "Victory!" to any woman lucky enough to bed a man with one, providing the perfect indentations to put your thumbs when your hands are resting on his hips when your mouth is otherwise engaged.

"You don't even have to flex to get them. What's your secret?" Berk reached out and touched Jared's cum buckets. The look on Jared's face took all sound away from my laugh.

"Good genes and lots of planks?" Jared answered.

"Perfect. We should work out together." Berk poured his coffee. "Are you a morning guy? Nighttime?"

"I, uh, usually work out whenever I have time. Doesn't matter when."

I doubled over.

"Why the fuck are you laughing?" Berk yelled at me.

"Cum gutters!" I could barely get the words out.

"Why is that funny?"

"Who calls them that?"

"Um, I do. What do you call them?"

I straightened up and put on my best serious face. "The victory muscle."

Jared spit out his coffee. "Are we really discussing my abs?"

"What?" Berk and I asked.

"They're a perfect representation of what all men should strive for. Really." Berk saluted him with his coffee mug.

"And the perfect resting place for my elbows." I sipped my coffee.

"Oh, I didn't think of that. Cheers." Berk and I clinked mugs.

"Elbows?" Jared seriously looked confused.

"You know, when we sixty-nine." I bobbed my head back and forth.

"Whatever, stinky pussy, I'm putting on a shirt."

"Don't you dare!" Berk and I said in unison, again, before looking at each other and falling into each other, laughing.

"You're both fucking nuts. Sit down and eat your birthday pancakes."

Berk leaned in. "You have a stinky pussy?"

"No, I have a blister dick." I smiled. "Long story. I'll fill you in. What's in the bag?"

Berk held up a brown shopping bag. "All the ingredients for the most delicious birthday drink ever."

"Ooh!" I clapped my hands. "What is it?"

"Bacon Bloody Marys."

"Yes fucking please."

* * *

"Are you sure you don't want to bang before we go? I mean, your balls have got to be the size of grapefruits by now." I opened the bathroom door and leaned against the doorjamb as he showered after a trip to the gym.

"Can we not talk about the size of my balls? I'm all soapy."

I checked out my eyebrows in the mirror.

He moaned.

"What are you doing in there?" I pulled back the curtain as he lathered up his stomach. His cock was at full attention. I thought I was going to pass out.

"Trying to wash my cock and balls without shooting a load."

"Fuck." I dropped my head and walked away, muttering about blister dicks all the way back to my room.

***

"Don't forget the wine!" Jared yelled from the bedroom.

"Got it!" I yelled back and shoved the bottle in my oversize bag.

"You two are too fucking adorable," Berk said.

He'd decided to ride with us to dinner instead of taking a cab. He wanted to experience the sexual tension, and he was particularly interested in our obvious issues with the withholding of orgasms and such.

"Yeah. Yeah. Adorable. We'll see what happens." I rolled my eyes.

"You totally dig him in a way I've never seen you dig anyone. I think it's cute. Sickening enough to make me want to vomit but cute." He took a sip of his beer.

"I go from smokin' hot twenty-something vixen to cute, orgasmless thirty-year-old? Great." I slid gloss across my lips.

"Maybe tonight will be the night."

"Nope. We have twelve more days."

"Whose moronic idea was this again?"

"His." I rubbed my lips together.

"Honestly. I never thought I'd see the day when Melody Ashford gave up sex. And Jesus Christ. Have you *seen* him?" Berk leaned in and whispered, "I get a full-on chub every time I'm in the same room with him. How can you stand it? If I were you, I'd want that man's scent slathered all over my body."

"I know, right? It's not easy. I swear to God I've had a hard-on since the first time I saw him in my apartment."

"And you can't even get yourself off." He shook his head.

I rolled my eyes. "Don't remind me."

"That shit better be worth it, that's all I'm saying."

"You're not fucking kidding."

"Ready?" Jared walked into the kitchen and took the beer from my hand and drank it down while giving me a look I'd grown to both appreciate and dread. The look that made my lady parts sing rounds of hallelujah and shit.

Fuck.

"Let's go!" Berk jumped up and danced his way out the door singing about bringing sexy back.

"Hey, Mel." Jared put his hand on the crook of my arm as I hopped off the stool.

"Yeah?" I turned.

He leaned down and I felt his breath on my neck. I closed my eyes and thought about what Berk had said about rubbing his smell all over my body. He was right. I wanted to bathe in it, drown in it.

"It will be so fucking worth it." He winked, smacked my ass, and walked away.

So much for clearing my head the rest of the night.

* * *

Jared parked and took my hand as we crossed the street to the restaurant. It wasn't something I'd even thought about until Berk eyeballed me as Jared spoke to the hostess and whispered, "Someone's falling in love."

"Shut up! I am not," I hissed.

"I'm going to use the bathroom. They won't seat us until everyone is here." Jared kissed the top of my head and walked away.

"Whatever, sister." Berk poked me in the shoulder. "I know googly eyes when I see them and you have them. Certainly not something I thought I'd ever have to point out to you, but I'm happy for you just the same."

"First of all, ouch." I rubbed the spot he'd poked. "Second of all, I am not falling in love. It's me! Melody! You know me. This here"—I waved between myself and Jared—"is a challenge that I have accepted. Someone called me out and I have to defend my honor. And of course see where things go after I've won the challenge."

"Your honor?" Berk scoffed. "Face it, sweets. Jared's got you all pretzeled up and you don't know what to do about it. That man has a hold of your heart and *that* puts you in unfamiliar territory."

"*Please*. Unfamiliar territory?"

"What's going on between the two of you has absolutely nothing to do with sex. Yet. So all that fangirling you're doing is coming from a place that isn't physical."

I didn't know what to say. I didn't want to admit that what he said made sense but more so I didn't want to even think about the *L* word, so I responded the only way I knew how when I was called out on my bullshit. "Fuck you."

"You're welcome. And congratulations on climbing on the bus to relationship town."

"Bite me."

"If I were straight, you'd be the first person I'd want to taste." Berk winked and walked outside to meet our friends, who were just arriving.

* * *

"Did you have a good day?" Jared asked as he gently pushed me against the door of my apartment.

"I had a great day." I kissed his neck. "Thank you. And it's not Sunday anymore."

"It's not?" he asked between kisses.

"Nope. It's Monday. Do you know what that means?"

"Eleven days." He pushed the collar of my shirt aside and nipped at my collarbone.

"Eleven days." I repeated between tiny moans.

He stepped back suddenly. I hated when he did that. "I have something for you."

I pulled back. "You do?"

"Yeah. Just something small." He inserted the key, unlocked the door, and pushed it open as he wrapped his arm around my waist. "Be right back." He deposited me on the couch.

"What is it?" I asked when he returned carrying a small wrapped box.

"No big deal. I just thought you could use it. Open it."

I pulled the ribbon and carefully unwrapped the box. My heart thudded when I saw it was from a jewelry store. "Jared?"

"Just open it." He laughed.

Inside was a silver watch with a black face. "I thought maybe you'd want a new one since, you know, you threw the other one out the window."

"Definitely." I kissed him and turned my wrist over so he could latch the new watch.

"What's this?" His thumb ran over the small tattoo I had on the inside of my wrist. He hadn't seen it since it had always been covered by a watch or bracelet. "Believe?" He read it and looked at me.

"Yeah. I got it when I graduated college. Just a reminder."

He unbuttoned his shirt, pulled it open, and pointed to the Chinese character on his ribs. "Believe."

I ran my fingers over it, then touched my own. My heart tripped and in that moment I knew Berk was right. I was falling. Hard. Fast. And against my better judgment.

My eyes were locked with his, almost as if we were trying to find some way to disprove what we were both feeling.

"Come on." He stood and held out his hand, breaking the connection. "Let's go to bed."

I handed him the watch and held out the wrist without the tattoo. He smiled and closed the latch before taking my other hand and looking at the word on my skin.

"Is something happening here?" I asked tentatively.

"Yeah. I think so," he replied and took my hand.

Chapter Twenty-Three

And after a long day of movie watching and procrastinating, Jared and I finally brought his two bags to Sarah's apartment and settled him in.

He looked around the room. "It'll do, I guess."

Sarah punched him in the arm. "It had better do. You're lucky I'm letting you crash here, little brother. Look, I'm going to order some pizza. Still like extra cheese, sausage, and peppers?"

"Always," he responded with a smile. God, I loved that smile.

"Well"—I grabbed my purse—"I guess I'll be leaving. You two have fun catching up." I kissed Jared on the cheek before he grabbed my arm.

"Where are you going?"

"I figured you two haven't had time to catch up properly. No big deal. I can see you tomorrow or something."

"Um, you can put your purse down and have pizza with us," Sarah chimed in as she grabbed the strap of my handbag and tossed it on the couch. "You two hang, I'm gonna take a shower while we're waiting for the delivery guy. He should be here any minute, I ordered a while ago. Money's on the counter. And Jared"—Sarah turned to him—"*I* am paying this time. Got it?"

"Got it." He saluted her as she skipped down the hall.

"Well, this is weird," I said when we were finally alone.

"Weird?" He opened and closed cabinets, looking for plates. I reached around him, opened the correct one, and stepped back. "Thanks."

"Yeah." I uncorked the bottle of wine Jared had picked up on our way over and poured myself a glass. "I don't know. You're here and I'll be, well, *there*. You know. Without you, I guess. Weird. I got used to you." I hopped up on the stool and looked away. I refused to make eye contact for fear of tears spilling down my face.

I rolled my eyes at my ridiculousness. "But at least I don't have to clean up your dirty underwear off the bathroom floor anymore."

It was official.

Jared Myers held my lady balls in his hands.

He took my glass from me and drank deeply. "I thought you liked picking up my dirty underwear." Positioning himself in front of me, he continued, "You know, it's not like we won't see each other again. And it isn't like we are in the type of relationship where we live in fear of the dreaded breakup."

"True. And I guess maybe *not* seeing each other every minute might make it easier to last—"

"Eleven days."

He handed my glass back to me. "Eleven. Saying it doesn't make the time pass any faster, huh?"

"Nope." I smiled.

"Good thing I can imagine what you look like naked anytime I want."

"Good thing I can actually remember what you look like naked."
I winked and handed him his own glass of wine.

"See, that's not fair. We still haven't remedied that situation."

"How about this? I'll send you pictures. A photo a day until—"

"Until I can see for myself."

"Right. And you can send me pictures." I giggled.

"That sounds like a good idea."

"It is." We clinked glasses and I winked.

He refilled my wineglass and said, "Sexy phone pics."

"And sexting," I added.

"Most definitely sexting."

"So how will I know you won't take care of business when you aren't under my watchful eye?" I teased.

Raising his eyebrows, he asked, "You don't trust me to keep my dick hands-free?"

"I don't think trust is the thing in question, to be honest. I mean you aren't the least bit worried I'm going to cave and take care of business?"

"You wouldn't." He sounded sure.

"How do you know?"

"You're too curious to see what it will be like after denying yourself for so long."

"That's an awfully bold statement." I pretended to be insulted.

"Am I wrong?"

I looked down at my feet. "No."

"But to make you feel better"—he held up his pinky—"why don't we pinky promise?"

"Pinky promise?"

"You can't break a pinky promise." He wiggled his eyebrows.

"I guess you can't." I locked my pinky around his. "I pinky prom-ise I will not pleasure myself."

"Ditto." He smiled and kissed me hard on the mouth. The door-bell rang before I could react.

"Perfect timing!" Sarah walked out in her pajamas, drying her hair with a towel. "What's going on?" She settled onto the stool next to me and poured herself a glass of wine.

"Nothing much. Just discussing how awesome finally having my apartment to myself again will be. I can't wait to stretch out on my bed with no one to steal the covers."

"I thought Jared was sleeping on the couch? You guys were doing the no-sex thing." The resemblance between Sarah and he brother when she raised her eyebrows over her wineglass was uncanny. And it took me back to the time she and I made out back in college. She was a good kisser, though Jared's lips were tastier. I shook it off.

"He was, he did. And we are." Stammering did not help the situ-ation.

"Mel's talking about the time we watched a movie and I fell asleep on her bed. And before you ask, no, nothing happened." Jared set two pizza boxes on the counter.

"I wouldn't think so. Melody's panties are all in a bunch over the fact that the two of you are holding out on each other in some sort of test of wills. Bunch of weirdos." She shook her head, grabbed a slice of mushroom, and moaned as she chewed. "I love mushroom pizza. I never ordered it when Caroline lived here, with her crazy mushroom allergy. I swear, I could bathe in it now."

As Sarah concentrated on her slice, Jared handed me a plate with two slices of mushroom, then bit into a piece overflowing with sausage, peppers, and extra cheese. Looking from his to mine, I thought my tiny mushroom slices looked pitiful, so I did what any-one would do. I reached up and grabbed his slice out of his hand. I savored the mouthgasm that followed the entirely too large bite I took. I knew I had cheese stuck to my chin and sauce dripping down the corners of my mouth but I didn't care. When I finally opened my eyes, I saw Sarah staring at me open mouthed and Jared stifling a laugh.

"What?" I asked as I took the napkin Jared handed me.

"Real fucking ladylike." Jared laughed.

I batted my lashes and asked, "What do you mean?" I took an-other bite and rolled my eyes in ecstasy, moaning before I said, "This is the best pizza I have ever had."

"You've sworn off sex. Anything you eat now will be the most de-licious," Sarah said matter-of-factly enough that I nearly choked on a gob of cheese. She smacked me on the back, a little harder than I thought she should have, while Jared uncapped a water bottle.

"You okay?" he asked once I was finally able to speak.

"Yeah, I'm fine. Thanks."

"No one likes a spitter, Mel." Sarah laughed.

"That's what her dad said!" Jared laughed.

"Wait, what?"

"You had to be there." I laughed.

"You two are meant for each other, for real."

Jared rubbed his sister on the top of her head before heading to the bathroom. As soon as the door clicked closed, Sarah pounced.

"So what exactly is going on? Are you two really dating? And you're not bang buddies? Is he just a fling? Because I'll be honest, I don't know if I want you flinging my brother."

"I am not *flinging* your brother, first of all. Second of all, calm down." I leaned back and checked the hall to make sure Jared wasn't listening in. "Look, I really like your brother. Like, really like him. I hate the fact that I am not going to wake up next to him tomorrow—"

"But you said—"

"Yeah, yeah. We aren't fucking if that's what you are thinking."

"Um, gross but okay."

"You asked. I love being with him. I love being around him. I want to get to know him better. And I am terrified if I open myself up I'll get stomped on. Just like Zac stomped on me."

"Let me stop you right there." Sarah held up her hand and lowered her voice but it was no less critical. "Zac did not stomp on you. You did not *love* Zac. You loved Zac's dick and the orgasms it gave you. Do not compare your feelings for my brother to those you had for a married man who fucked you senseless every now and then. Jared is a good guy and you would be lucky to have him."

I think my eyes may have bugged out of my head momentarily. I closed them tight just to make sure one didn't go rogue across the floor. "Slow down. That isn't what I meant."

"You don't really have a great track record, Mel. Don't hurt him. As much as I love you, he's my brother."

"Gotcha." I snapped my fingers and stood, knowing Sarah was in a mood and at the rate she was drinking wine, it was bound to go sour faster than usual. "Well, it's getting late. I'm going to go."

I pulled my purse on my shoulder as Jared walked back in the room carrying a bottle of shampoo. "I think I stole your shampoo." He laughed and looked up. "Where are you going?"

"I'm just going to get out of here. I have an early morning. Your first day is tomorrow, plus we have to go look at locations tomorrow night, right?"

"You okay?" He looked from his sister to me.

"I'm fine. Great, actually. I get to sleep in my big bed all by myself, after all." I felt how awkward my smile was. "Look"—I walked over and kissed him on the cheek—"you hang here with your sister. You two haven't spent much time together. I'll call you before I go to bed."

He placed his hand over mine, leaned in, and asked, "You sure everything is okay?"

"Everything is perfect. I'll call you."

I turned to leave. Sarah sat on the stool avoiding eye contact. Jared remembered what was in his hand. "Wait, your shampoo."

"*Your* shampoo, sweets. I bought one for you and put it in your bag."

"That's funny, because I left my White Castle T-shirt on your bed because I know you like to sleep in it."

His smile quickened my heart and my mouth dried. I kissed him quickly on the mouth and whispered, "Thank you," before leaving.

As I stood outside the apartment with my hand on the door I heard Jared ask, "What happened, Sarah? What did you say to her?"

I didn't want to hear my friend's response, partly because I knew she was only looking out for her brother and partly because she had a point. I had absolutely nothing to compare Jared to. I was in unchartered territory.

Chapter Twenty-Four

My key was barely in the door when a text came through.

Jared: *Where's my pic?*

I smiled.

Me: *What pic?*

Jared: *Don't mess with me woman*

I dropped my keys on the table, kicked off my shoes, and took off my shirt.

Me: *Oh. You mean the naked pic?*

Jared: *Yes*

Me: *K. Hold on*

I proceeded to snap a half dozen half-naked selfies before I found one decent enough to send. I stared at my phone, waiting for his response.

Jared: *Wtf Mel?*

Me: *What?*

I knew exactly what.

Jared: *Seen more of you in a bathing suit.*

Me: *Sorry. Not sorry.*

Jared: *Whatever.*

I tossed the phone on my bed. While I was brushing my teeth, I heard another text come through.

Jared: *still 11 days*

Me: *too many*

Jared: *I know. Tired*

Me: *go to bed*

Jared: *K. Good night*

Me: *Good night*

* * *

I woke up utterly exhausted and curled up on his newly minted side of the bed.

Late-night texting and a naked selfie didn't make up for the fact that I'd still had to crawl under the covers the night before without him. I didn't like it one bit. So I grabbed the one thing out of my closet that would improve my mood.

My bright yellow stilettos.

I loved those shoes. They were guaranteed to brighten my mood no matter what the issues. And, with a tiny spring in my step, I made my way to the train station.

"Good morning, Melody." Manuel, the coffee guy, smiled as he handed me my morning jolt. I loved the fact that I didn't have to order anything, he always just knew.

"Morning, Manny. *Gracias.*" I replied with the extent of what I'd retained from high school Spanish. Of course, Manny would never hold my shitty pseudo accent against me.

"De nada." His smile was genuine.

On the platform, I leaned against a pole and shuffled through my neglected e-mails.

"Good morning." A voice wrapped around me like a blanket and I straightened up.

"Good morning, yourself."

Jared stood in front of me in a suit, scruffy beard trimmed and neat. An involuntary shiver made me gasp and him smile. He closed the gap between us and placed his hand on my cheek and kissed me. It was soft. It was quick. And it was enough to stir my lady parts.

"I like it when you blush." I heard the words but was focused on the way his lips moved when he said it.

Clearing my throat, I shoved my phone back in my bag and stepped toward him as he took a step back. "I"—I tiptoed up and bit his bottom lip—"don't blush."

"Sure you don't. And you don't have a stash of candy hidden in your unused pots and pans, either."

I whipped my head back and forth and placed a finger on his mouth. "Shh. We don't talk about that in public."

He took the coffee from my hand and sipped the hot liquid. "Strong."

"Manny knows how I like it."

Jared's eyebrows shot up. "Does he now?"

I smiled and winked and stepped toward the train that had just pulled up. "Time to go."

"After you." Jared gestured, grabbed my briefcase, and handed me back my coffee.

We settled in the only two open seats we could find near each other. Thankfully it was summer and we didn't have to deal with oversize coats and winter wear. Jared sat across from me, my briefcase settled on the floor between us.

"Want the rest of my coffee?" I took one last sip before I offered it to him.

He took it and drank while I dug in my purse for a compact and lipstick. Carefully I lifted one leg up and settled it on Jared's seat, between his legs. I lifted the other and crossed it carefully over the first. I closed my eyes when I saw him look at me and shift forward in his seat.

I popped open the silver compact, twisted the tube of red lipstick, and carefully slid the color across my lips. Flicking my gaze over the mirror, I watched Jared watch me. And then I stretched and pointed my toes.

It was difficult to stifle my laugh as he jerked back with his eyes wide.

"Melody."

"Jared." I mimicked his deep voice.

"This is not helping things."

"What things?"

"You certainly know what things." He pulled his keys out of his pocket and jingled them before dropping them on the floor. Leaning forward to pick them up, his hand slid along my leg until his fingers disappeared under my hemline.

Immediate lady boner.

It was my turn to jerk back and pull my feet off the seat as I smacked his hand.

"What?" He smiled and leaned back in his seat.

"You know what." I adjusted my skirt, crossed my legs, and folded my hands in my lap, suddenly very aware of them. "Are we still on for tonight?"

"Yeah. Berk said he'll meet us at the place. Still not sure about a city location. I kind of wanted to be closer to home."

"We can just look. Berk knows you'd rather stay local. Speaking of home, has your sister talked to you about what Drew has proposed?"

"He proposed?" He sat straight up.

"No. He asked her to live with him."

"Really?" He settled back in the seat. "I wouldn't be surprised. She's there all the time anyway. Hey. How come he never stays at her place?"

"Because you're there." I smiled.

"He doesn't like me?"

"It really doesn't have much to do with you other than the fact that you're *there*."

"I'm not following."

"Well, let's just say—" I paused, attempting to come up with the right words. "Your sister and Drew are a bit *adventurous* in their escapades—"

"Stop!" He held up his hand and scrunched his face. "I do not want to hear about my sister and her boyfriend in that way. She is my sister and she is a nice girl."

I burst out laughing loud enough that the entire car looked up. "Oh my God! Grow up. You don't think your sister has—"

"Nope. Stop. We will not talk about this."

"Okay."

"Seriously."

"I got it."

"I'm not kidding, Mel."

"Sheesh. I got it. We won't discuss how your sister ties Drew down—"

"No!" He leaned forward and clapped his hand over my mouth. "Please. Stop. Talking. I'm going to take my hand off. Do you promise not to mention that thing you were mentioning ever, ever again?"

I opened my eyes wide and nodded slowly.

"Promise?"

I garbled "I promise" through his hand.

He released his hand from my face and pulled back slowly, hesitating as if he were waiting for me to say something I shouldn't.

I grabbed his tie and pulled him close, meeting him halfway. "I'm sorry." And I planted a big kiss on his mouth.

"Are we doing dinner before we meet with Berk?" he asked.

"Sure. Meet me at my office?"

"Your boss won't have me escorted out?" He smiled.

"I don't think he'd come out of his office if you're there."

"No? Did I scare him off?" He rubbed his nose against mine.

"Probably." I nipped his bottom lip before pulling back and gathering my things. "Let's go."

We shuffled out of the train onto the platform, following the narrow space to the out-of-order escalator to the main floor of Penn Station. I looked around and for a moment I thought I'd lost Jared, until he grabbed my hand and steered me toward the coffee stand.

"Be right back," he said and disappeared into the small convenience store located nearby. I casually looked around while I waited, taking in the people walking past.

I was lost in my thoughts when he returned, surprising me with a large plastic bag of gummy bears.

"I refilled your stash at your apartment but I wasn't sure if you were running low at work."

"Have I told you how amazing you are?"

"Not today."

"Well you are. Amazing." I tiptoed up and kissed his mouth with full lips, lingering a beat longer than usual.

"Keep kissing me like that"—he pulled me into a hug—"and I may not make it through the end of the day without you near me."

"Well, we should get going. We both need to be at work."

"Work." He screwed up his face as if trying to remember.

"You know, the place that pays us money?"

"Oh right, right."

He took my hand, leading me to the stairs and then outside to Eighth Avenue. We didn't say much as we waited in line for a cab. Since we'd both end up in the same vicinity, we shared the ride. He promised to call me later and meet me after work as I was dropped off first. I stood on the sidewalk in front of my building with a coffee in one hand and my briefcase and a plastic bag full of gummy bears in the other. It was as I watched until the taillights disappeared that I realized I'd fallen. The *L* word even sat on my tongue.

My phone signaled a new text message, pulling me out of my thoughts. It was Jared.

10 more days.

Yep. It was bad.

Chapter Twenty-Five

Thursday, Berk sat across from me as I barreled through yet another working lunch. I'd barely touched my dumplings and was concentrating on making imperfect numbers perfect.

"You need to relax."

"What?" I looked up, my glasses perched on the end of my nose.

"You're getting those wrinkles between your eyes." His chopsticks pointed at me. "You know the ones you get when you furrow your brow too much?" He scrunched up his face to demonstrate. "I know someone who sells that super wrinkle cream. Let me know if you need the number."

"How would you like it if I pointed out every new wrinkle you got?" I closed my eyes tight, willing the impending headache to dissipate. "My eyes fucking hurt."

"Of course they hurt. How long have you been staring at spreadsheets?"

"Too long." I poked at a dumpling, pushing it around in the soy sauce I'd flooded the bottom of the takeout container with.

"I'm just saying. You need some sort of release. A shopping spree. A massage. A mind-blowing orgasm. Something."

"God, I wish." My head fell back and I tried to remember the last time I'd had an orgasm but all that filled my head were images of Jared. I had to tighten my legs to subdue the sudden throb.

Berk seemed to notice the difficulty I was having keeping it together. "How many more days?" His snarky smirk didn't escape me.

I threw my glasses on the desk and watched them skitter across the paperwork haphazardly strewn across the top. Leaning back, I put my hands over my face and muttered, "Eight. Eight more days."

"How long has this been going on?"

"Seven days. Well, seven since we made the bet."

"Seven days just since the bet? And longer since you last had sex?" A strange look of horror passed quickly across his face before he recovered. "You haven't cheated just a little? You haven't, you know"—he held up two fingers and made a clicking sound—"one-clicked the clit?"

"No!" I drew out the *o* sound long enough to make it sound like a moan.

"Sweetie, I've seen you in some pretty precarious predicaments in the months we've been friends. I've seen you low and I've seen you on top of the world. But I have never seen you like this. For god's sake, renegotiate or something. You are my friend."

"One of my best friends." I batted my eyelashes.

"You'll never make it."

"I'd like to officially thank you for the vote of confidence." I rolled my eyes.

"I call 'em how I see 'em. And you are a mess." He shook his head and chuckled. "You should go to the gym. Burn through that stress."

I stood and stretched, attempting to rid myself of all the tightness that made me ache. "I've been going twice a day for the past three days. I'm like a walking livewire. It's like I am in lady boner hell."

Berk snorted.

"What?"

"Lady boner."

"Well, what would you call it?"

"I wouldn't. Remember? I'm gay. I like my boners manly."

My phone rang and I shuffled through the mess of papers on my desk looking for it. I answered without looking at who was calling. "Hello?"

"Hey you."

It was Jared.

"Hey." I tilted the phone and whispered to Berk, "It's Jared."

"Hey sexy!" Berk yelled through a mouthful of vegetable lo mein.

"Is that Berk? Tell him I said hey."

"Jared says hey." I plopped down in my chair and took a sip of my orange-flavored seltzer.

"How's your day going, beautiful?"

"Long. Tedious. Slow moving."

"Sounds like a party."

"Well, I'd like to think of this phone call as the sunshine in my cloudy day."

"Is he going to the gym later? I need a workout partner," Berk asked.

I held out the phone. "Are you going to let me talk to my boyfriend or do I need to hand you the phone?"

"Your what?" I heard the question in stereo and froze, my mouth hanging open, mirroring Berk's. I was met with silence but could feel

Jared's smirk reach out and smack me through the phone. I cleared my throat and stammered a bit before regaining my composure and shooting the stink face at Berk.

"So what's up?" I injected an overdose of cheerfulness and non-chalance into my tone to mask the fear that I'd spoken too soon. Or the fear that I finally had a boyfriend. Either way, I was terrified.

"Well, uh"—I listened as Jared regained his composure as well—"I wanted to know if you were free tomorrow night for din-ner?"

"Yeah, we can do dinner. My place? What were you thinking? Pizza? I'm having Chinese today so I won't really be in the mood again. But if it's really what you want—"

"Melody. No, that's not what I meant. I meant would you like to go out to dinner. Like out somewhere. Like a restaurant. Like a date. No cheeseburgers this time."

My throat went dry. "You are asking me out on a date? Like get dressed up and go out?" Berk jumped up and leaned across the desk as I held the phone so he could hear, too.

"Well, yeah. Technically, this would be our first official date but I mean, we can just say we are hanging out or whatever you are com-fortable with. I mean, pizza and Chinese sounds great, too. "

Berk and I stared at each other. I'd never considered the fact that he and I had never gone on a real date before. I guess cheeseburgers really didn't count.

"Mel? You there?"

"Yeah. Yeah. I'm here." I shook my head and watched as Berk slow-motioned his way back to sitting position, leaning too far for-ward in his chair, as if a strange and foreign scene was unfolding in front of him and he couldn't look away. "Tomorrow sounds perfect."

"You sure, I mean we can—"

"Jared." I cut him off. "I would love to go out on a date with you."

"Okay, good."

"Okay, good," I repeated with a smile that hurt my cheeks.

"I'll pick you up at seven tomorrow night."

"Seven it is. I look forward to it." Berk stared at me with eyes wide.

"I'll call you later, then. Tell Berk to call me if he wants to work out tonight."

"I'll do that."

"Okay."

"Bye, Jared."

"Bye, Melody."

I clicked off the call and placed my phone on the desk in front of me like it was fragile piece of china.

"A date?" Berk asked.

"A date," I repeated, suddenly quite pleased with myself.

"When's the last time you went on a date?" He poked one of my dumplings with his chopstick and shoved it in his mouth.

"I've been on dates." I reached for his lo mein.

"Let me rephrase. When's the last time you went out on a first date that mattered?"

"Touché," I replied after I slurped up a stray noodle and handed the container back to him.

"What are you going to wear?"

"Something new, obviously." I waved him off. "Oh, and call him if you're going to the gym."

"So we both get to date the guy with the fabulous cum gutters?"

"Hands off my man!" I laughed.

"Your man? Don't you mean your *boy*friend?"

"Shut up." I threw a balled-up napkin at him, but for the life of me I couldn't wipe the smile from my face.

"Hey. At least one of us has someone to go on a date with."

"I thought things were good with you and David?"

"Eh. He and I aren't as compatible as I thought."

"I'm sorry to hear that. He's a nice guy."

"He is. But the age difference really is too much for me. I'm tired of being treated like a kid. I know he doesn't mean it, but it is what it is."

"I'm sorry, Berk. I know you liked him."

"It's okay. Besides, I have a date with that hot waiter we met at brunch a couple weeks ago."

"Oh. He was hot! What's his name?"

"Mario."

"As in Mario and Luigi?" My snicker was met with his stare.

"As in you are voluntarily cutting yourself off from sex so you have no room to make fun of anything."

I considered his words for a minute and repeated my earlier sentiment. "Tou-freaking-ché my friend. Tou-freaking-ché."

Chapter Twenty-Six

I made sure to get my workout in early the next morning. Sarah and I took a forty-five-minute boot camp class that was supposed to hit all the basic workouts in a shorter amount of time. Unfortunately, the entire class had my mind in the gutter and Sarah giggling at my reactions.

Music filled the space and we all got into our positions and jogged in place. Scott, our instructor, bounced around and slapped everyone a high five.

"High knees in five, four, three, two, one."

"High knees." I snickered. Scott heard and blushed.

"Jesus fuck," Sarah said as she worked her knees as high as she could. "I really need to get a better sports bra. My tits are banging against my kneecaps."

"No they aren't!" I giggled, messing up my concentration, causing me to double high knee my left leg.

"Yes, they are. Look." Sarah pivoted so she was high-kneeing in front of me and sure enough, she drove her knees high enough to hit her boobs.

"Oh my God, Sarah!" I nearly fell over. "Stop doing that!"

"I can't help it."

Scott saved her by counting us down to stop. After a short stretch we worked our legs with squats, lunges, and the ever-enjoyable round of burpees. By the time we whipped through that quick set, we were panting and on the floor. Which was good considering the next round was abs. I hated ab workouts.

"On your backs. Knees bent. We're going to start off with thrusts."

For sixty seconds I pulsed my groin to the ceiling while muttering nonsense about blister dicks.

"Stop thinking about fucking my brother."

"I am not thinking about fucking your brother."

"You most certainly are. You don't think I remember the blister dick, stinky pussy story?"

"I can't help it."

"For fuck's sake. You two live in the same pea pod, I swear."

"Okay. Spread your legs wide into a vee while lying on your back. Your legs and your body will form a triangle. I want you to sit up and slap that triangle as hard as you can!"

"Slap the what?" I said a bit too loudly.

"Slap the tri—never mind." Scott turned beet red and turned away. "Sit up and slap the center, between your legs."

"Seriously, Scott?" I raised an eyebrow as I attempted to remove the pornographic images from my head. They were doing nothing to help my celibate situation.

"On the floor. The space on the floor that just so happens to fall between your legs."

"What the hell is wrong with you?" Sarah whispered.

"I think I am going crazy." I sat up and slapped the space on the floor that just happened to fall between my legs.

"No shit you're going crazy. You two are making me crazy. I swear he's more nervous about this than when he was waiting to hear about his scholarship to college." She shook her head as she sat up.

"He's nervous?" I froze mid sit-up and fell back when my midsection began to cramp.

"Hell yes, he's nervous. And so are you. You'd think the two of you were competing for gold or something. God. It's just sex."

I pulled my legs in and grabbed my water bottle. "No. It's not just sex." I stood.

"That's what he said. What the hell did you do to my brother?" She continued with her sit-ups. "The more disturbing question would be what the hell did he do to you?"

"That's what I'd like to know." I took a swig of water and headed out the door fifteen minutes before the end of class.

* * *

Work, of course, limped along. Other than having to deal with answering my own phones and getting my own coffee, it was quite uneventful. I couldn't wait for Jenny to come back from her vacation. I hadn't realized exactly how much she did for me.

I quickly hopped online and ordered her a bouquet of thank-you flowers with my corporate card. She really did make my life easy.

I hadn't heard anything about her interview and made a mental note to talk to Zac about it at some point during the day, but when I finally got around to it, I found out he'd left early.

Lunch consisted of a giant apple and a few tablespoons of peanut butter when all I really wanted to do was eat a pizza. An entire pizza. By myself. I thought the nervous eating ended in college. Apparently it hadn't. At least I had the sense to make better food choices.

The date with Jared weighed on me. The closer it got, the more I panicked. It hadn't dawned on me that we hadn't gone on a date. The night before, as I shopped for something new to wear for the occasion, I mentally flipped through the times we'd spent together. I probably would have chalked them up to dates if someone had asked but I never thought about the formality of asking someone out on a date. Had it really been so long since I'd been treated to a proper evening out with someone who expected nothing physical from me in return for a meal and some drinks?

I did what I could to shake off the thoughts but Jared had shaken up my idea of fabulous and I was a little out of my element. A good night's sleep and a decent workout had me looking at things with new eyes. Fabulous didn't need to be larger than life. Fabulous didn't need to be lonely. Fabulous could be low-key. Fun. Quiet. Fabulous could be Jared. And me.

* * *

I was ready to go by six o'clock. Showered, hair curled loosely, lightly made up, dressed in a non-cleavage-baring dress with brand-new heels on my feet, sitting on my couch, glass of wine in hand, exactly one hour before Jared would be there to pick me up.

What.

The.

Fuck.

I leaned back, pulled a pillow onto my lap, and flipped through the channels. When I was sure it was almost time to go, I checked my phone and saw only fifteen minutes had passed.

Entirely too keyed up, I called Caroline.

"Hey."

"Are you eating?" My stomach growled.

"Yes. Pizza. So good." She moaned. "What's up?" She sounded happy.

"Brian off tonight?"

"Yep! We're going to curl up on the couch, eat lots of pizza and popcorn, and watch a movie. When is Jared picking you up?"

"Seven."

"Don't you need to get ready?"

"I'm ready."

"What?" She coughed.

"I've been ready since six." I stared at my nails, happy I'd decided to leave work a bit early for a mani-pedi.

"But what about your hair? It takes forever to straighten."

"I left it curly."

"Makeup?"

"Done and understated."

"What are you wearing?"

"Baby blue boatneck A-line dress."

"Does it at least fall above your knees?"

I laughed. "Yes. And I'm wearing brand-new, cream patent-leather peep-toe wedges."

She was silent a beat longer than she should have been.

"Hello?"

"Two things. One. You really like this guy. And two. I want to borrow those shoes."

"One, don't act all weird. It's no big deal. It's just a date. And two, no problem."

"No. Not 'no big deal.' You *really* like him."

"I'd rather talk about shoes."

"Melody Ashford!" Her voice didn't quite reach stern.

"What?"

"Admit it."

I sighed. "Fine. I like him, okay? Happy now?"

"That makes my heart happy."

"Yeah?"

"Yeah."

"He's just a guy! I am such a goopy puddle of mush over him. It's strange."

"You love him."

"I haven't known him long enough to love him."

"You think love has a timeline? Or in any way takes your feelings on the subject into consideration?"

"Well, I wish it would."

"It doesn't. Sorry, babe. You've been smacked in the face with the frying pan of love."

"Nice visual."

"It's the truth. And you wanna know the best part?"

"What's that?"

"You fell in love without sex."

"A seemingly impossible feat, and you're crazy."

"Too true."

The doorbell buzzed. "Hold on. Who is it?"

"Jared."

"Where's your key?" I'd never taken back the key from when he was staying with me.

"I thought since it was a date, I should pick you up like it was a date. It's okay. I'll use the key."

Tears pricked the corners of my eyes. Giddy butterflies danced in my stomach.

"No! Hold on, I'll buzz you in." I pushed the button before returning to Caroline. "Did you hear that?"

"I heard that!" she squealed.

"I have to go." There was a knock at the door.

"Is he knocking?"

"Yes." I looked through the peephole and smiled. He was shifting from leg to leg and adjusting the collar of his shirt. "He has flowers!" I whispered.

"Flowers? Brian, he brought her flowers!"

I heard Brian mumble "Great" on the other end.

"He looks nervous." I chewed on my thumbnail as I one-eyed the peephole.

"Oh my God! Go have fun and call me tomorrow. I want to hear all about it."

"Okay. Love you, Care."

"Love you, too, Mel."

I clicked off, tossed my phone on the couch, smoothed my dress, and opened the door.

* * *

"I am having such a great time."

We walked hand in hand down Nassau Street in Princeton. We walked from restaurant to restaurant, from bar to bar, stopping in for a small appetizer and drink at each.

"So am I. What's been your favorite so far?"

"The empanadas from that first place. They were so good!"

"They were!"

"What about you?"

"The paella from that Spanish place."

"I loved that. And I loved sitting out on that rooftop terrace. Looking over at everyone walking around. And the sangria! I need more of that in my life."

"I'm glad you're having fun."

"What made you think of Princeton?"

"My grandparents used to live in Lawrenceville before they died. They used to bring me here for ice cream when I was a kid."

"Ice cream?"

"Yes. And that is where we are headed."

"So that's Princeton University?"

"Yeah."

"It's gorgeous. So old and regal looking. I would love to smell their library."

"I'd never have pegged you as a library girl."

"Yeah. I get it. Most people don't peg me as smart." I turned my head, suddenly aware that I cared more than I thought about how Jared saw me.

"Hey." He stopped walking and stepped in front of me. "First of all, a thirty-second conversation with you would prove to anyone halfway educated that you are very intelligent. And second, I was referring to the fact that you're a math girl. Usually numbers and words don't stay connected for too long."

"Oh." A crack in the sidewalk suddenly looked quite interesting. "I didn't think of that."

"Frankly, I'm a bit concerned you think I'd think that way of you."

"Well, no. I didn't mean that...I don't know what I thought."

"I also find it quite amusing that Ms. Melody Ashford, Queen of Sarcastic Wit and Self-Confidence, has somehow turned into a puddle of goo."

"I'm not goo. Maybe pudding, but not goo." I smiled.

"Good thing I like pudding." He placed a hand on either side of my face.

"Good thing."

The feel of his lips on mine made every nerve in my body sing.

My eyes were still closed when he stepped back. "You ready for that ice cream?"

"What?" My eyes flicked open. "Right. Ice cream. Onward."

I gripped his hand and side glanced at him, my heart swelling at the sight of his sexy smirk.

The line at the small ice cream shop snaked outside and across the street.

"Why is the line so long?"

He smiled. "Because it's the best ice cream on the planet."

"Seriously?"

"Seriously." He suddenly looked concerned. "Do you not want to wait?"

"No no! Of course I do! I've just never seen a line this long for anything other than the Cronut."

"Well, the sweet cream ice cream here puts the Cronut to shame."

"Big words, my friend. Some would say fighting words."

"It's a fight I'd be willing to participate in."

By the time we made it in the door, we'd had fun checking ourselves out in the funhouse mirror outside the shop.

"Oh my God! Look how short I look!"

Jared stepped into view of the reflection. "We look like we have huge asses!"

I turned to check out the view. "It's like a hundred years of squats in one rectangular reflection."

He stepped back and snapped a photo of the mirrored scene. "I love this pic."

"Let me see." I leaned over and checked out the shot. "Send that to me."

"Yeah?"

"Yeah. I want to send it to my dad."

"I can send it."

"You have my dad's number?"

"Yeah. He gave it to me in case I had any trouble satisfying an Ashford woman." He laughed.

I smacked him on the arm. "Shut up! He did not!"

"He really, really did." He swiped and scrolled through his phone. "See?"

Jared held up his phone and sure enough, my dad had recently sent him a text message: *just checking in.*

"I can't even." I held my arms out wide. "That's my dad."

"I think it's great." He attached the photo and sent it off. "All he wants is for you to be happy."

"Well, you make me happy." I stared at the menu, trying to decide if I wanted a cone or a cup, peanuts or sprinkles.

"You make me happy, too." His hand squeezed mine and a smile crept across his face as he joined me in looking at the menu. It was as if we were a couple of awkward teenagers.

* * *

"I had a great time." We stood outside my building.

"So did I."

"I can't believe this was our first date."

"I know, right?" His laugh was easy.

"Do you, uh"—I pointed my thumb toward the door—"want to come up? For coffee or something?"

Jared stepped forward and kissed me, hard.

"I would love to." He finally said as he stepped back and took my hands in his. "But I won't. Not today."

"Oh."

"I want to remember this as our first date. Not as anything else." He smiled. "I mean, if you asked me, it was a pretty perfect first date."

"It *was* a pretty perfect date. But now that I think about it, cheeseburgers counted."

"Cheeseburgers counted, huh?"

"Yeah."

"And you agreed to come anyway?"

"Yep."

"So you'd be willing to go on a third date?"

"I'd be willing to think about it." I teased.

"I'll take it." He walked me up the stairs to the door.

I pulled my keys from my purse and passed them from hand to hand. I didn't want the evening to end, but I more than understood the need to preserve the evening as it was. Innocent. Amazing. Memorable.

"So, call me?"

"Absolutely." He kissed me softly on the lips. "Good night, Melody."

I opened the door to the building and stepped inside. "Good night, Jared."

He was standing at the bottom of the steps when I closed the door. I took off my shoes and headed toward the stairs. The walk back to my apartment was slow; I wanted to rewind the evening.

I was at my door when my phone rang. Jared.

"Miss me already?" I smiled and pushed the key in the lock.

"Miss you always. So, how 'bout that next date?"

"You don't waste any time." I tossed my purse and keys on the table.

"So is that a yes?"

"Yes." I grabbed the vase with the flowers he gave me earlier and carried it to my room, placing it on my dresser.

"Sunday?"

"Let me check my calendar." I giggled as I placed my shoes in my closet.

"I'll wait." He hummed the *Jeopardy!* tune.

"Oh, look at that! I *am* free."

"Good! I was worried. I'll call you."

"I'll answer." I sat on my bed.

"Perfect. And Mel?"

"Yeah?" I slid my hand under my pillow and pulled out his White Castle T-shirt. I'd worn it every night since he left and had yet to wash it.

"I had a really great time tonight."

"So did I. Thank you."

"Good night, sweetheart."

"Good night."

I fell back on my bed, arms outstretched and a perma grin on my face. I'd just had the best night I could remember with the most amazing guy. And for once, I didn't think of sex once the entire night.

Chapter Twenty-Seven

Saturday night, Sarah and Caroline came over for some much needed girl time.

"How long has it been since we've done this?" Sarah asked as she placed a plate of cheese and crackers on the coffee table and sat down on the floor.

"It feels like forever," Caroline said while she carried a bottle of sparkling water and three wineglasses to the table.

"I know, right? This summer is already flying by and I feel like so much is changing." I poured Sarah a glass of Prosecco and topped it off with a few ounces of grapefruit shandy. "You"—I pointed to Caroline—"are pregnant and you"—I nodded toward Sarah—"are contemplating moving in with Drew."

"Don't remind me! It's bad enough he brings it up all the time." She took a sip of her drink. "This is good! Where'd you get the recipe?"

"I was surfing around on social media after my date last night and came across it."

"Speaking of dates, how'd your first date with Jared go last night?" Caroline smiled. "And I want all the details."

"I'd rather you spare the details, thanks." Sarah crinkled her nose. "But with the way my brother was floating around the apartment last night, I can kind of guess you two threw the challenge out the window."

"Actually"—I spread fig jam on a cracker and topped it with a slice of Brie—"it was our second date—"

"When was the first? Why didn't we know about it?" Caroline interrupted.

"Cheeseburgers in Wildwood. And I didn't think it *was* a date. Not then anyway."

"That's cute." Caroline popped a grape in her mouth.

"Thanks. And for the record, Sarah, we haven't thrown away the challenge."

"Then why was he all swoony and weird?"

"He was swoony and weird?" My heart grew five sizes.

"Yeah. I don't know what you did"—she pointed a slice of cheddar at me—"and normally I'd blame it on the magic of your vagina, but that boy is bananas over you."

"Well, I know for a fact she is bananas over him, too."

"I know. I can tell. Eh"—Sarah shrugged—"she could do worse."

I smacked her with a pillow. "Hey!"

"I'm kidding. I haven't seen him this happy in a long time. If you're what makes him act like a love-struck loon, then by all means, you have my blessing."

"Thanks, that means a lot."

"Still doesn't mean I want to hear all the sordid details."

"I do." Caroline raised her hand.

"You got it. You and Berk get the details on the bumping and grinding, and Sarah, you get to live with a boy. Cheers!"

"I don't like cheersing with sparkling water." Caroline frowned.

"Don't cheers to that!" Sarah yelled.

"Why not? I live with Brian and it's great."

"You have a bun in the oven."

"So?"

"So it's different. You're getting all familied up and stuff. My living with Drew would just be—"

"We weren't familied up, as you say, until recently."

"When Jared lived here, it wasn't so bad."

"Are you kidding, you two bickered the entire time he stayed with you."

"That wasn't bickering," Caroline added, "that was sexual tension."

"No it wasn't!" I laughed.

"Oh, hell yes, it was. You two wanted each other from the moment you saw each other on the stairs the day he moved into Sarah's place."

"I'd have to agree with her." Sarah nodded.

"Shut up. Now way."

"Oh yes. Honestly, I think his moving here gave you a little push to end it with Zac."

"Jared had nothing to do with that."

Sarah held up her hands. "I'm just saying."

"I'm just saying, too," Caroline added.

I rolled my eyes. "You two are always just saying."

* * *

It was nearly midnight by the time I finished putting the last of the dishes in the dishwasher. I grabbed a blanket and clicked on the TV. I wasn't yet tired and figured I was due for some nineties sitcoms.

I was nearly passed out on the couch, a few episodes in, when my phone rang. I blindly searched around me and found it under my arm.

"Hello?" I hadn't bothered to check the caller ID.

"Hey beautiful." Jared's voice stirred me awake.

"Hey yourself. What time is it?" I couldn't make out the time on my watch in the dim light.

"Almost one."

"That's it?" I sat up. "I feel like I've been asleep for hours."

"I can let you go. You can go back to sleep."

"No. No. It's good. I want to talk to you." I pulled a pillow off the back of the couch and put it behind my head.

"I want to talk to you, too."

"I'm assuming that's why you called?"

His laugh was soft. "You'd assume correctly. Are you in bed?"

"On the couch. I fell asleep watching *Friends*." I muted the TV after pulling the remote from between the cushions. "Are you in bed?"

"Yeah. Early night. Drew and I went to a Yankees game then came back here."

"I know. Did they win?"

"Nah. It's okay though. I'm more of a Mets fan."

"I'm going to have to break you of that habit."

"Take it up with my dad."

"I might have to."

"So"—I could hear him shuffle the covers—"how was your night with the girls?"

"It was good. Great, actually. I found out an interesting tidbit about my friend's smokin' hot brother."

"Yeah? What did you learn?"

"I hear he's got himself a girl and this girl has him all swoony. Apparently he's bananas over her."

"Is that so?"

"I mean, I can't be sure, since I heard it form a third party but"—I stretched—"that's what I hear."

"Well, if the sister is to be believed and a girl has him all— What was it?"

"Swoony."

"Right, swoony. If he really is all swoony over a girl then he's a goner."

"A goner, huh?"

"Yeah. Hard to come back once you've gone swoony."

"Good to hear."

"So did your friend tell you anything about how this girl feels about the smokin' hot brother?"

"As a matter of fact she did." I was smiling so big, my cheeks hurt. "She digs him, too."

"She digs him?" I could picture his smirk, the lift of his eyebrow.

"Yeah. Apparently she can't stop thinking about him. I'm pretty sure she's gone bananas, too."

"Well, at least they can be bananas over each other together."

I paused, unsure if I should get clarification on the thoughts running through my head. It didn't take long for my mouth to spit it out. "She keeps calling him her boyfriend."

"Oh, well that adds to the story, now doesn't it?"

My stomach pitched. "Seems to add something." I hoped he was getting where I was coming from.

"If you ask me"—he cleared his throat—"if he's as swoony and bananas as you say, then I'm pretty sure she's right."

"She's right?"

"Well, yeah. I mean I'm sure if you asked him, he'd say that he thought of her as his girlfriend."

"Just like that?"

"Just like that. Two peas in a pod."

"At least they seem to be in pretty good company." I yawned.

"Go to sleep, Mel. I'll pick you up in the morning. We can go for a run before breakfast."

"I wish you were here."

"Me, too."

"Use your key."

"Okay."

I stood and folded my blanket. "So I'll talk to you tomorrow then."

"It *is* tomorrow."

"Six days." I smoothed the front of the White Castle T-shirt I was wearing.

"Six days." I heard him blow out a breath. "Good night, Mel."

I crawled into bed. "Good night, Jared."

* * *

As promised, Jared was at my apartment early. I woke to him crawling into bed next to me.

"Better make it fast, my boyfriend will be here soon." I teased as his hands slid over my thighs. It felt good calling him my boyfriend. The thought didn't have me wanting to run for the hills like it once did.

"I can take him."

"I don't know. He's a pretty big dude."

"Yeah?" He brushed my hair from my face.

"Crazy, too." I smiled.

"I want to kiss you."

"Then kiss me."

"I think I'll have a hard time controlling myself." He brushed his lips against mine.

"That makes two of us." I rolled so I was lying on top of him. I kissed each side of his face softly as my hands slid down his sides and slid under his ass. "I thought we were going running?"

He shifted as I secured my legs on either side of his hips and tucked my feet under his thighs. "It's raining." He pushed my hair off my face and gripped a handful behind my head.

"Is it? I hadn't noticed." I ground my hips down into him and heard him inhale sharply. I watched his eyes widen.

I gasped when he pushed against me and tugged my head back, exposing my neck to his mouth. His lips trailed across my throat and his teeth grazed the tender skin below my ear. His hand fisted my hair tighter.

"You want to play it this way?" I smiled before scraping my nails across his chest. His grip let up and I used the opportunity to bite his nipple.

"Fuck," he growled out as I ran my tongue over the bite. "I think you should be careful."

"Of?" I sat up and squeezed my thighs together. I could feel his excitement grow under me.

"I'm barely holding on here." His voice was breathy, gravelly. Goose bumps littered his chest and sweat slipped from his brow. He gripped the hem of my shirt until his knuckles were white. I knew it wouldn't take long to push him over the edge.

"It's okay." I rolled my hips.

He grabbed me tight and tossed me to the side as he shifted on top of me. "We made a deal." He bit my bottom lip. "We aren't doing this yet." He pushed himself up on his hands, holding himself above me.

I tugged at the bottom of his shirt. "Yes we are."

"Mel." His grabbed one of my hands and pulled it away. "I can't believe I am even saying this, but we can't." He pulled my other hand away and held both above my head. "Not yet."

"You're kinda being a buzzkill."

"Believe me, I know." He rolled over and lay next to me, muttering under his breath.

"Why did we agree to this again?" I turned and looked at him. His profile was beautiful. With a slight bump in his nose, stubble across his jaw, and a full bottom lip, I found him perfect.

"Because we need it. We needed the break." He rolled and propped himself up on his elbow. "Right?"

I reached out and ran my hand along his face. "Yeah, sweetie. We do."

When his lips pressed against the palm of my hand, I clamped my legs together. The next five days might actually kill me.

Chapter Twenty-Eight

4 Days

It was noon and I was still throbbing from the day before. I woke up in the middle of the night drenched in sweat. Apparently sex with Jared in my dreams was just as good as I imagined it would be in real life.

I was jonesing.

Hard.

Honestly, I felt like my vagina was going to pack up her shit and leave. She was tired of the deprivation. I was tired of the deprivation, and if Jared's snark was analyzed, I'm sure I'd find he was tired of it as well.

My phone interrupted thoughts that should have been on the spreadsheet in front of me. "What?" I cringed.

"Nice. So I guess my brother isn't the only one with a shitty attitude today."

"Sorry."

"Yeah well. The two of you are acting like you haven't gotten any in…wait, you haven't." Her laugh pierced my soul.

"Nice."

"I'm kidding. Kind of. I'd ask how you're holding up but—"

"I'm not." I threw my pencil on the desk. "Seriously. I'm over this."

"Come on. How much time? Four days until your birthday?"

"Yes." I stood and stared out the window, watching the cars below me snake along.

"You can do anything for four days."

"Fuck, Sarah. It's more than sex."

"Maybe I'm not the best person to discuss this with." I could hear her sipping something through a straw. "You know, you could go take a yoga class. Meditate or something. Go hiking."

"Hiking?"

"I don't know. I watched a show yesterday on how to be one with nature and how people destress by hiking and shit."

"I'm not hiking."

"I didn't think so. Anyway, I'm calling because I am assuming we are celebrating your birthday Saturday?"

"Why Saturday?"

"Um, for reasons I refuse to discuss with you."

"Oh, right. Yeah. I don't want to do anything crazy. We can just go to the bar or stay in." I riffled through my drawer looking for an unopened bag of gummy bears.

"Who are you and what have you done with my friend?"

"What?" I found one and fell back into my chair.

"You've always been the center of attention, Mel, because you demanded it. I'm not complaining, I'm stating fact, and now you want to *stay in* for your birthday celebration? You feeling okay?"

"I'm fine. I just don't see any reason to go crazy over a birthday," I reasoned through a mouthful of chewy bears.

"You're turning thirty. You've had this day on countdown since you turned twenty-one. Seriously, you've got it bad and unfortunately the only cure is to get it good."

"Unfortunately, huh?"

"Forget it. I can't believe I never thought about how perfect the two of you are for each other."

"He is kinda perfect."

"And so are you. And I told him so."

"You did?"

"Yeah. He's not the only one who got the warning. If he hurts you, I'll make his life miserable."

"Well, thanks."

"You're welcome. Now, why don't we all do early dinner on Saturday, then come hang here? Have some drinks. Play Pictionary. Whatever."

"Sounds perfect."

"Good. I'll make the calls. Later, babe."

"Later, babe."

* * *

3 Days

"What are you doing?" Jared asked as I made my way down to the yoga studio.

"Heading to a yoga class. I figured I had nothing better to do on my lunch break."

"Maybe eat lunch?"

I pressed my phone to my ear as I pushed through a throng of suits on their way to lunch, meetings, and wherever the hell else people went in the middle of the afternoon on Tuesday. "No time for lunch. I need to get out of my head. Lunch doesn't do that."

"My sister told you to meditate, huh?"

"Yeah. She told you, too?"

"After she told me she'd find someone to chop off my balls if I ever broke your heart."

"Aw, that's so sweet of her."

"Because they aren't your balls."

"I don't know if I want to talk about your balls right now."

"Too right. You go meditate. I'll go have a working lunch with Berk and decide if the clients can afford the monstrosity of an apartment that they are fighting for."

"Okay. Tell him I said hi. Dinner tonight?"

"Yes. Chinese?"

"Yes. Sleepover?"

"We'll see. I'll meet you at your house after work."

"We'll see?" I smiled, knowing he was having as much difficulty as I was. Thank God there were only three days left.

"I might have to stand under the shower with the water running ice cold."

"We can stand in there together. Then we can wash each other. Get all soapy and slippery—"

He growled and muttered a curse under his breath. "I'm so happy I get to go into this meeting with a raging hard-on. I'm sure everyone will be so pleased to see me."

"Berk will be happy." I pointed out. "Besides, how do you think I feel? Downward dog is going to kill me."

"True. And it does give me some satisfaction to know that your boner will be giving you as much trouble as mine. Maybe I can take care of it in the bathroom—"

"Don't you dare! Unless, of course, you want me to take care of things on my end."

"No. Definitely not. That's something I've been looking forward to taking care of for a while now. Don't take that from me."

"Ugh." I moaned. "Goodbye Jared."

"See you later, Mels."

I hung up the phone as I reached the yoga studio. I pulled open the door and climbed the flight to the small second-floor space. I was going to need to scare up some extra Zen. And something to bribe my bits from packing up and moving on.

* * *

2 Days

I walked up to Jared and noticed how his khakis hugged his ass and how his light blue shirt, rolled to the elbow, strained ever so slightly across his shoulders.

I called out. "No suit?"

He turned and his smile stopped my heart for a moment. When a guy smiles like that at a girl, she better grab on with both hands—and I was so happy I had.

"Not today. Easy day, just working numbers in the office."

"I like your tie." I ran my hand over the fabric as he leaned down to kiss me. His lips lingered and I snaked my free arm around his neck. Just as the kiss began to take on an urgency, he pulled back and hopped up and down a few times.

"You okay?" I laughed. I felt it, too, but my lady libido was lying in wait. I think I'd finally convinced her that something amazing would happen soon enough.

"Barely. You?" He grabbed his wallet to pay for two cups of coffee.

"You know what? I'm good today." I handed Jared his cup as we made our way to the platform. "I didn't have any weird, sweaty sex dreams last night. I'm good. I think I have a handle on this whole no-sex thing."

"It only took you how long?" He laughed.

"Shut up! I slept like a baby last night. I'm going in to work to kick ass and make another client a lot of money and then I'm going to come home and fill the bathtub with bubbles, pour a nice big glass of wine, and read a smutty book."

"Be careful." He placed his hand on the small of my back as I climbed onto the train and walked toward the back to find a seat. "Smutty book, huh? What kind of smutty book?"

"Oh, you know. Girl meets boy, boy digs paddles and rope, girl likes it, hardcore fucking ensues. They live happily ever after."

"Sounds"—he paused and shifted his briefcase between his feet and moved his coffee to his other hand—"interesting."

"Not so much interesting as relaxing."

"How many yoga classes have you taken?"

I laughed. "Only a couple." I stretched my legs before crossing them and leaning my head back on the seat.

"Tired?"

"Yeah. I shouldn't be. I got plenty of sleep."

He slipped his hand around mine and squeezed. I slid my fingers between his and squeezed back. I leaned into him and dropped my head onto his shoulder.

"We should go somewhere," he said after a few moments.

"Yeah? Where do you want to go?"

"I don't know. Maybe just somewhere for the weekend."

"This weekend?" I picked my head up and looked at him.

"No. God, my sister's already annoyed she isn't celebrating with you on your actual birthday. Imagine if I took away the weekend?"

I laughed. "Don't mess with your sister."

"Ha. Don't I know it?" He raised our clutched hands and kissed my knuckles. "Maybe next weekend or the weekend after. What do you think?"

"I think a whole weekend away with you sounds amazing."

"Where do you want to go?"

"Surprise me. You seem to be good at that." Of course I was referring to the way he dropped into my life and flipped my whole view on relationships. He was the best kind of surprise.

"Likewise." He pressed his lips against my head.

* * *

1 Day

I was antsy. I came home from work and paced. Nerves were getting the best of me and it drove me nuts. Of all things I should be anxious about, sex was not one of them. Sex was no big deal. Sex was something I did to pass the time. Something that got me off. Something that I was very good at. And instead of getting ready, I was wearing a hole in the hardwood and sipping Chardonnay a bit faster than I should.

I knew Jared was on his way over and I couldn't unknot my stomach. I was afraid of changing what we had and hoped that what was between us didn't hinge on anticipation. The door buzzing knocked me out of my thoughts. *Odd*, I thought. Jared had a key.

"Hello?"

"Hey sweetie! Surprise!" My mom's voice shouted through the speaker.

"We came to visit for your birthday!" My dad added.

What the everloving fuck.

"Oh that's great," I managed to squeak out. I squeezed my eyes shut and pressed my head against the wall. *This isn't happening.*

"Are you going to open the door?"

"Yeah. Sorry." I buzzed them in and opened my apartment door.

I was sitting on the arm of my chair when they walked in, with Jared bringing up the rear. His eyes were wide and he could barely contain his laugh.

"Look who we found!" My dad thumbed toward Jared.

"We can all have dinner together," my mom added.

"Hey! I didn't know you were coming." I hugged my dad.

"Well, it wouldn't be a surprise if we told you," my mom clucked and walked to the kitchen. She immediately grabbed a sponge and did the few dishes that I'd left in the sink.

"Mom, you don't have to do that."

"It's okay, sweetie. Go get dressed. We will go out to dinner and maybe tomorrow we can have a girls' day and get our nails done."

I stared at Jared and he shrugged before dropping his head.

"You're staying?"

"Yes. I mean, we didn't get a hotel. I figured we could sleep on the couch or a blow-up mattress. You have one of those?"

"No, Mom. I don't. I didn't have one the last time you dropped in either."

"Oh, well your father and I can make do. I can sleep on the floor." And the guilt was suddenly very thick.

"You guys can take my bed. I'll sleep on the couch." I grabbed my mom's bag and carried it to my room. "Jared, can you grab my dad's bag and bring it in here?"

"On it." He all but jogged the few steps to my room.

"What the fuck is happening?" I whispered.

"I don't know. But it's pretty comical."

"What is comical about this?"

"To be honest, after this long waiting, a few more hours won't kill us."

"A few more hours? They are sleeping over. In my room. In my bed."

"Are those new sheets?"

"Yeah. I got them…Focus. What are we going to do?"

"Not each other. At least not in the immediate future." His laugh was shallow.

I smacked his arm. "Be serious."

"Look"—he placed his hands on my arms—"it's okay. It's a bump. We can handle bumps. And you know what?" He pulled me in to a hug.

"What?" I wrapped my arms around him and pressed my cheek against his chest.

"I think that waiting a bit longer will make it better. Instead of waiting for the clock to hit midnight, we can maybe take our time. Make it special."

"You're right," I mumbled into his plaid shirt. "I hate that you're the voice of reason."

He lifted my chin. "If you hear me muttering about stinky pussies too loudly at dinner, promise you'll kick me in the shin."

"I promise." I kissed him, nipping his lip before I pulled away. "Let's go bring the folks out to dinner."

Chapter Twenty-Nine

Jared stayed until the clock struck midnight and wished me a happy birthday. My parents were fast asleep and unaware of the wicked make-out session that was going on in the next room. My lips were still sore. Once he left, however, I lay wide awake staring at the ceiling, attempting to count the number of times the fan spun. I was keyed up, nervous, excited, terrified. The ache that had disappeared days ago suddenly returned with a vengeance.

By the time the sun rose, I was dressed and out the door. My parents were still asleep and I decided to go for a run. But not before I called Berk and convinced him to meet me at the diner. He wasn't happy, but after I pointed out what day it was, he was out the door before he clicked off the call.

I was a sweaty, starving mess by the time I found Berk sitting in a booth, two coffees poured, sweetened, and creamed. Berk very well may have been my soul mate.

"Happy birthday, sweaty bitch! I ordered your coffee." He pulled me in for a hug so tight I thought my head would pop off.

"Happy birthday! Thank you." I plopped into the booth. "You're in a good mood."

"I got laid last night but I don't think that's why you called. I feel like you're going to tell me a juicy story. Spill. You and Jared did the deed! Don't leave out any juicy detail."

I held up a finger and drank deeply. I could feel my eyes focus. I needed that moment, that small minute sitting across from my friend. Thankfully he was patient.

"We did not do the deed. I have no juicy details unless you count the fact that my lips are still swollen from the marathon make-out session we had on my couch last night. "

"Wait. What happened to banging at midnight? Did his cock turn into a pumpkin? Did you lose your shoes?"

"Well"—I sighed and dropped my head to the table—"my parents showed up last night. Took me and Jared out to dinner. Slept over."

"No!"

"Yes. It was a 'surprise.'"

"Wow."

"Why are you laughing?" I tossed a balled-up napkin at him.

"It's funny."

"It's not funny."

"It's a little funny."

"Fine. It's a *little* funny."

The waitress delivered our meals. Berk had opted for healthful oatmeal and fruit whereas I had ordered a plateful of eggs, bacon, potatoes, and toast with butter.

"I can't believe you are going to eat that." He made a face.

"You know I eat when I'm stressed."

"What are you stressed about?"

With my mouth full, I answered, "Weareshuposedhavseshtoday."

"I'm sorry I couldn't hear you through the amount of food falling from your mouth."

I chewed, swallowed, and took a large gulp of coffee. "We are supposed to have sex today."

"Didn't we just cover that?"

"Yeah."

"Then this is not news. What's tripping you up?"

"I think I love him."

His coffee cup held steady halfway to his mouth. "Come again?"

"You heard me."

"You think or you do?"

"Want to. Don't look at me like that."

"If he said it right now, would you say it back?"

"What?" I shoved half a piece of toast in my mouth.

"Attractive. Pretend I'm him." Berk puffed up his chest. "I love you, Melody."

"Ha ha. Funny." I downed a glass of orange juice.

"Seriously. What would you say?"

"I don't know."

"You do know."

"I guess I'd say it back."

"You guess or you know?" His cocked eyebrow was really annoying.

Without missing a beat, I replied, "I know."

"When are you seeing him?"

"Tonight. Mom is taking me out today for some girl time."

"Then get out of here, go hang out with your mom, and when you see him later, tell him."

"I can't do that." I fiddled with my fork. "Can I do that?"

"People do it every day, apparently."

"So I should tell him I love him. Just like that."

"Yes. And then call me tomorrow and tell me what happens. I mean, I don't need to know the ins and outs"—he wiggled his eyebrows—"of his response, but still."

"Perv!" I threw my napkin at him.

"You love it. Go before I make you pay for this meal."

"Fine." I jumped up, walked around the table, and kissed Berk on the cheek. "You're the best."

"Yeah, yeah. You're giving me a big head."

* * *

I ran all the way home only to find my parents awake. The sheets and blanket I'd used were folded neatly on the arm of the couch. Coffee was made, my favorite cup sitting in front of the coffeemaker.

"Hey Dad." I kissed him on the cheek as he read the paper.

"Hey. Your mom is getting dressed. Jared stopped by."

I whipped my head around. "He what?"

"He left you a note." He held up an envelope.

I opened the bottom cabinet, lifted the lid of my spaghetti pot, and reached in to grab a handful of my favorite candy. Then I flipped open the envelope and unfolded the piece of paper inside.

Happy birthday. Have a great day with your parents. Dinner tonight? My place? Pizza? Six? Nothing too fancy. See you then. ~Jared

I popped the last of my gummy bears in my mouth and stared at myself in the mirror. I still had eight hours before I had to be at his house. So I did what any sane thirty-year-old woman who had just realized she was in love would do at ten in the morning. I opened a bottle of champagne and made a mimosa.

Chapter Thirty

My stomach was churning and I wasn't sure if I should turn around and walk back to my apartment or knock to let Jared know I was there. Behind me was my life. Currently happy and robust and full of everything I could want. He and I were in a good place. A place I never thought I'd be. But there I was. Nervous over what was about to happen. Had we built it up so much that all we were headed for was disappointment? Had we been thinking too much about it? Not enough? Would the reality be so disappointing that I would lose the most important thing to happen to me since I could remember? Beyond his door was something new, unexpected, frightening, and, if I was being honest, sexy as fuck.

With my eyes closed, I blew out the breath I'd long been holding and rapped my knuckles on his door.

I barely remember his face as he opened the door wide enough for me to step in. I barely remember the sound of the lock engaging.

What I do remember, what I could still see and feel, are the few seconds I spent standing in front of him. Heat spread throughout my body and for a moment it felt as if I'd caught on fire. Only a couple inches separated us as I watched him lick his lips, and I bit down on mine. I wanted to live in that moment. That small moment right before the kiss. One that filled me with so much anticipation it hurt.

Two deep breaths.

In. My eyes shifted to the door.

Out. I closed them and wiped it all away.

In. I opened my eyes. He was closer than he was a breath ago.

Out. A ball of nerves caught in my throat.

And then his mouth crashed on mine, my hands clutched his face. My body pressed against him as his pushed me to the wall with a step.

Jared's lips pressed against my neck and my head fell back against the wall. His good hand fisted the fabric of my skirt and slowly pulled the floor-length cotton up over my thighs. Fingers explored me, pressed against me, entered me.

I laid my hands on the top of his head as he dropped to his knees and pulled my lace panties to the side. His tongue darted out, snatching the strength from my legs. His grip on my hips nearly immobilized me. My foot rested on his shoulder, opening myself up more, giving him more access.

Slowly, slowly I slid down the wall.

Slowly, slowly I lost the ability to stand.

"Bedroom," I breathed, unable to form more than two syllables.

He took my hand and pulled me to my feet. "I missed you."

"I missed you, too."

"I had a plan." He kissed my mouth, my face, my neck.

"A plan?" I unbuttoned his shirt as we shuffled toward his room.

"Romantic." His good hand gripped the back of my neck.

"Do you want to stop?" I kicked off my flip-flops.

"No!" he exclaimed and pulled his head back. "Do you?"

"No! But, I mean, if you had plans—"

"Fuck the plans." He pulled me back in just as we reached the bedroom door.

The backs of my knees hit the bed and I fell on the bed, Jared landing on top of me.

"Ow!" He pulled his hand in.

"Are you okay?" I froze. He had a splint on his finger.

"Good. I'm good." He rolled over onto his back. "I broke my finger today playing basketball during my lunch."

"Oh my God! Are you okay?" I stood.

"I'm good. I'm good. It just kind of sucked explaining to my boss that I need to take the afternoon off to go to the emergency room after I'd been there only a few days." He reached for me and I held out my hand. He grabbed it and pulled me toward him. I straddled his lap, my face an inch from his.

His hand tucked a strand of hair behind my ear. "So, how was your day?"

"My day was good. I ate all the gummy bears."

"We'll have to get you more."

"I love you." I held my breath.

He stopped moving. My heart stopped beating. A slow smile curved across his face. "I love you, too."

"You do?" My heart started beating again.

"I do," he said before his mouth collided with mine.

His arm gripped my waist and he stood and turned around, depositing me on the bed. Kneeling down in front of me, he tugged the waistband of my skirt down and slipped it off. I pulled my tank over my head.

"Gorgeous." His hand grazed my shoulder before sliding across my cheek. I scooted back on the bed as he leaned into me, crawling along with me until my head was on the pillow.

Our kiss deepened and took me to a place of utter contentment. The urgency disappeared and our movements slowed.

He was propped up on his elbows above me, his hips settled between my thighs, his lips and tongue grazing my neck. My hands burrowed under his shirt, my nails slowly trailing along his back. He pressed into me and rocked forward and I gasped.

When his hand splayed my neck, I could feel the tightening of anticipation in my stomach. He slid the fabric that covered my breasts to the side and flicked my nipples with his tongue. They tightened to erect buds and he pulled each between his teeth. His lips clamped down and pulled back.

Unable to take much more, I rolled us over so I was straddling him. Sitting up, I reached behind me, unhooked my bra, and dropped it to the side of the bed. Leaning down, I traced tiny kisses along his jawline, across his chest, and down to his stomach. I undid his pants and tugged them over his hips. I continued to trail small kisses down his body, his legs, until I slipped his pants off entirely and crawled back up until my lips once again explored the small trail of hair that led south from his belly button.

"Melody," he breathed as I licked the skin above the waistband of his boxers and blew gently.

"Shh," I whispered, and slid the tips of my fingers under his waistband and slipped them down, too.

Taking him in my hand, I maintained eye contact for a moment before slipping him between my lips. With one hand on him, I slid him in and out, stroked him up and down, watching him the entire time. I could feel him throb in my mouth, feel him tense when I took as much of him as I could, until he grabbed my head on either side and pulled me off, tugging me back up toward his face.

"Come here." He kissed me hard and tore my lace panties with his good hand while his other arm wrapped around my waist.

He was pressed against me and all I could think of was what he would feel like inside me. I knew I was wet, I could feel the slick heat between my thighs. I ground my hips against his.

"Fuck, Melody."

"Condom" was all I could squeak out.

"Table."

I reached over and grabbed the foil pack. I fumbled with it and dropped it on his face. "Sorry." I laughed.

"Let me do that."

I fell to the side and watched with interest as he opened the foil and rolled the latex down his length. He rolled over so his hips were once again settled between my legs.

"You okay?" he asked as he was poised just outside my body.

"More than. You?"

"I have never been more perfect."

I shifted a bit so his tip was touching me. The ache was nearly unbearable.

And then he slid slowly into me, catching my gasp with his mouth. Slowly rocking back and forth, fingers interlocked. I pulled a leg up and wrapped it around his waist.

At first our movements were slow and deliberate. Our rhythm in perfect sync. But before long, slow and deliberate became hungry, and hungry became ravenous. Every thrust rocked me to my core. Our breath was ragged, our hearts racing. My hips bucked against him, his ground down into me. My hands clutched his back, nails dug into his flesh. His teeth nipped at my neck, his hand cupped my breast, fingers pinching and pulling.

"Melody. Oh my God," he breathed out.

"Please. Oh please!" I whispered.

I couldn't get enough. He couldn't get far enough inside me. I couldn't open wide enough to pull him in. He grunted my name, I moaned his. Faster and harder we danced.

Heat spread from my toes, shot up my legs, and exploded between my legs as I cried out, wrapping my arms and legs tight around him as an orgasm racked my body. I knew it was coming but wasn't prepared for the intensity.

"Jared! Don't stop. Fuck," I nearly screamed.

He picked up the pace, slamming into me until I stopped shaking.

I tried to catch my breath and he held himself above me, slowing pushing in and sliding out. He dropped his forehead to mine and kept my gaze. Each thrust was slow. I slid my fingers down his back and he gasped.

When I clenched around him again, he smiled. He'd just shattered me and was in the process of rebuilding me with every push of his hips. I could feel myself begin to throb each time he pulled himself out of me, then clench as he slid back in. Unlike the last explosion, this orgasm was a slow simmer. It was almost unbearable. When he grabbed my hands and held them above my head, my stomach knotted.

"Melody."

I couldn't answer. I couldn't breathe.

"Melody. I love you."

"I love you." I could feel my climax rise but it wasn't fast enough. It tormented me, I felt it everywhere and it took over. My toes began to curl and my thighs began to shake.

"I can feel you." He increased his pace. "I can feel everything."

I was pinned down by my own release and I opened my mouth to scream but his lips claimed mine as our orgasms vibrated through us. It was the most erotic thing I'd ever experienced.

I'm not sure how long it was before I was able to relax my legs enough to unwrap them from around his waist but when I finally did, they lacked the strength to do anything but flop to the side. He rolled onto his back and we both lay staring at the ceiling for what seemed like forever.

"That was—" he breathed.

"Awesome." I finished his sentence.

"Totally," he responded.

I was still coming down from my high, body still trembling.

He reached down and took my hand in his. We fell asleep that way, reenergizing for the next round. We never did end up eating dinner that night and we missed breakfast the next morning. With the way things were shaping up, there'd be time for that later.

Chapter Thirty-One

W hat took you so long?" Sarah jumped up and pulled me in for a hug as Jared and I walked through the door of the restaurant.

Jared gave me a quick kiss on the cheek and a quick squeeze of my hand before heading over to talk to Drew and Brian.

"Um, do you really want her to give you all the dirty details?" Berk stepped in and pulled me away before whispering, "*I* would like to know all the dirty details."

"Noted," I whispered back. "We'll have brunch tomorrow." I handed him a small wrapped box. "Since I forgot to bring this to you yesterday."

"Happy birthday!" Caroline rushed up and gave me hug before handing me a gift bag. "Come on. We need to eat. I am starving!"

Jared pulled out my chair and handed me a beer before sitting next to me.

"Aw," Caroline cooed. "You two are so cute."

"Get a grip, Care. He pulled out her chair, he didn't save her kitten," Sarah reasoned.

Berk and I snickered while Jared turned a lovely shade of hot pink.

"Shut it," Sarah sniped while we all laughed.

"Let's talk about food." Caroline changed the subject. "What are you all having? I am—"

"Starving." Sarah and I finished her sentence.

"What are you having?" Jared asked as he perused the menu.

"I don't know. What looks good?"

"Everything." He handed me the menu.

"I'll have a cheeseburger."

"You always have a cheeseburger." Brian laughed. "I even have one named for you at the bar. It's a pain in the ass to make."

"Sounds about right," Berk quipped.

"Hey! Watch it!"

Jared leaned in and whispered, "You're not a pain in the ass."

"Thank you." I leaned in and kissed him. "You're not too bad yourself."

"Do you think," he continued, "we could fake food poisoning so we could go back to your place?"

I smiled. "Wait it out a bit and I promise, I'll make it worth your while."

"You already have." He squeezed my hand and kissed me again.

* * *

Two weeks later I came home from work after a particularly long day to find Jared sitting on my couch with a big smile on his face.

"Hey you." I leaned down and kissed him.

"How was work?"

"Exhausting. Seriously." I plopped down on the couch next to him. "I'm as tired as a vibrator that got snuck into a women's prison." I kicked off my shoes and turned, dropping my feet onto his lap. I wiggled my toes. Thankfully he took the hint and began massaging them.

His laugh boomed through the room. "Wow. I've never heard it described quite that way." His thumbs screwed into the balls of my feet and I moaned.

"Careful," he said as he shifted in his seat.

Smiling, I opened my eyes and noticed a packed bag sitting next to him. "What's going on?" I pointed with my toe.

"What do you mean?" His eyes were closed as he leaned his head back on the couch.

"You packed my bag?"

"Oh yeah." He smiled. "Get changed. We're going."

"And where are we going?"

"Does it matter?"

"Not really." I stood and stretched.

"Can we get cheeseburgers on the way?"

He swatted my ass. "Go get changed."

"Want to help?"

"There will be plenty of time for that later."

"Fine." I pouted, pulled my shirt over my head, and threw it at him.

"God, you're such a tease."

"Who's teasing?" I called from the hallway as I tossed my panties into the living room.

* * *

"Rub me?" I handed Jared the sunscreen and smiled.

"Again?" He wiggled his eyebrows and I am sure he was thinking about our time in bed earlier that morning.

It had been two weeks since my birthday. Two weeks since I told him I loved him. Two weeks since he said it back. Two weeks. I pinched myself daily.

"Get your head out of the gutter and rub me. I don't want sunburn."

"But rug burn on your knees is okay?" He laughed as I looked down at my knees and smiled. It had been a fun night.

He finished rubbing lotion on my back and lay down next to me. "Hey."

"Hey." I leaned in and kissed him quick. "Do you think your sister is going to have Drew move in with her?"

"I don't know. It would be nice. He told me I could take his apartment. Otherwise I need to start looking."

"Living with your sister isn't cutting it?"

"It's putting a damper on my sex life."

"It's such a full life, too."

"It is now." He smiled. "I mean, it's just hard when I feel like I'm sneaking around."

"It's not like she doesn't know."

"I know."

"But I know what you mean. I'll talk to her if you want."

"I don't know if it will do any good. That poor guy has it bad and she acts like it's no big deal."

"She doesn't think it's no big deal. She's just used to having things her way."

"Yeah, I guess." He sat up and squinted toward the ocean. "Want to go swimming?"

"I could get wet."

He sucked in a breath. "Tease."

I rolled over and removed my sunglasses. "Let's go then," I said as I took off toward the water. He chased after and tackled me into a wave.

"No fair." I laughed and wiped water from my face.

He treaded water a few feet from me and said, "All's fair. Remember?"

"Better watch your step, Myers. We may just have to revisit our little challenge."

"You wouldn't." He swam over and his hands showed me exactly why I wouldn't.

"You're right." I wrapped my arms around him. "How did I ever go about my days without you in them, Jared Myers?"

"I don't know. And I don't really want to find out." His kiss warmed me to my toes.

"Want to go in a bit and get something to eat? I'm starving."

"We didn't eat breakfast, did we?"

"Well, we were busy."

"Yes, we were. Come on. Let's go get some breakfast then." He swam toward the shore.

"It's after noon."

"Is there really a cut off for banana pancakes?" He turned to me.

"I guess not."

We held hands as we walked back to the small bed-and-breakfast he had found online. It was cute and right on the beach. And, as promised, it was a surprise. I knew we'd discussed a getaway, but I hadn't heard a peep until I came home from work the day before and my bags were packed.

We dropped off our stuff in the room before heading toward the small diner on the corner. After the waitress delivered two tall glasses of milk and two big stacks of pancakes, I took a second to appreciate where I was and what it had taken for me to get there.

I leaned across the table and he met me halfway. We kissed softly. "I love you."

I smiled. "I love you, too."

I smiled because I'd never thought I'd say the words. I'd never thought I'd find someone worth it. But sitting across from me, eating banana pancakes with a sexy smirk on his face, was someone worth waiting for. Worth finding. Worth keeping. It had taken me only thirty years and a wicked round of foreplay, but I was in love. And it was the best feeling I'd ever experienced.

Cocktail Recipes

Adios Motherfucker

- ½ oz. vodka
- ½ oz. rum
- ½ oz. tequila
- ½ oz. gin
- ½ oz. blue curaçao
- 2 oz. sweet and sour mix
- 2 oz. lemon-lime soda

Instructions:

Pour all the ingredients except the lemon-lime soda into a glass with ice. Top with the lemon-lime soda.

One Night Stand

- 1 oz. Kahlúa
- 1 oz, Cape Velvet cream liqueur
- ½ oz. Cointreau
- 2 oz. cream

Instructions:

Pour all the ingredients into a shaker with ice. Shake well. Pour into a martini glass or shot glasses.

Cock-Sucking Cowboy

- 2 parts butterscotch liqueur
- 1 part coffee cream liqueur

Instructions:
Layer the ingredients in a shot glass.

Mimosa

- Equal parts dry Prosecco or Champagne and orange juice
- Splash of orange liqueur

Instructions:
Pour the Prosecco or Champagne into a glass; fill to the top with orange juice. Add a splash of orange liqueur.

Bend Over Shirley

- 1½ oz. raspberry vodka
- 5 oz. lemon-lime soda
- ¾ oz. grenadine
- Cherry

Instructions:
Pour vodka into a highball glass filled with ice. Add the lemon-lime soda. Top with the grenadine. Drop a cherry into the glass.

Sex on My Face

- ½ oz. whiskey or bourbon
- ½ oz. coconut rum
- ½ oz. peach liqueur
- ½ oz. banana liqueur
- Splash of cranberry juice
- Splash of apple juice
- Splash of orange juice

Instructions:
Pour all the ingredients into a cocktail shaker with ice. Shake well. Pour into tall glass with ice or serve as individual shots.

Blue Balls

- ½ oz. blue curaçao
- ½ oz. coconut rum
- ½ oz. peach liqueur
- ¼ oz. sweet and sour mix
- Dash of lemon-lime soda

Instructions:
Pour all the ingredients into a cocktail shaker filled with ice. Shake well. Strain into a shot glass.

Suck Bang Blow

- 1 oz. orange-flavored gin
- 1 oz. peppermint liqueur
- 2 oz. lager
- 1 oz. herbal liqueur
- 3 oz. tequila
- 1 oz. Hpnotiq liqueur
- 1 oz. vodka
- 1 oz. lemon vodka
- 1 oz. orange liqueur
- 1 lime, peeled
- 5 oz. strawberry daiquiri mix
- 2 cups cranberry juice
- 1 cup sugar

Instructions:

Pour all the ingredients into a blender with ice. Blend until smooth.
Pour into a hurricane glass and serve.

Leg Spreader

- 1 oz. coconut rum
- 1 oz. citrus vodka
- 1 oz. Midori
- 1 oz. peach liqueur
- Splash of sour mix
- Splash of pineapple juice

Instructions:
Pour all the ingredients into a cocktail shaker filled with ice. Shake well. Strain into a shot glass.

Too Fruity

- 2 oz. coconut rum
- 1 oz. lime rum
- 2 oz. cranberry juice
- 2 oz. pineapple juice
- Lime wedge

Instructions:
Pour all liquid ingredients into a pint glass filled with ice. Top with squeezed lime wedge.

Snake Bite

- ½ pint lager
- ½ pint hard cider

Instructions:
Mix the ingredients and serve in a pint glass.

Bacon Bloody Mary

- 15 oz. tomato juice
- Hot sauce (to taste)

- 3 shots bacon-infused vodka (recipe follows) or bacon-flavored vodka
- Sea salt
- Black pepper
- Lemon juice
- 1 strip cooked bacon
- Lemon wedge

Instructions:

Fill a cocktail shaker halfway with ice. Add the tomato juice, hot sauce, vodka, a pinch each of salt and pepper, and a generous squeeze of lemon juice. Shake well. Pour into a pint glass filled with ice. Sprinkle more pepper on top and add the slice of cooked bacon and lemon wedge for garnish.

Bacon-Infused Vodka

- 7 strips bacon
- Vodka (enough to fill the size jar you choose)
- 2 glass jars with lids (any size)

Instructions:

Cook the bacon until crispy and drain. When cooled, crumble bacon into one of the empty glass jars. Pour the vodka over the bacon and tighten the lid. Shake the jar once daily for seven days. Strain the vodka into the other clean glass jar. Store in a cool, dark place for up to one month.

Please turn the page for
an excerpt from Christine Hughes's
previous sexy romantic comedy,

Operation One Night Stand!

Chapter One

I had commandeered the sofa. The beautiful, butter-yellow sofa Sarah had purchased when she first moved to her amazingly spacious two-bedroom apartment almost three years ago now probably had a permanent imprint of my ass. The cushions had become a wasteland overflowing with wads of snotty tissues, and creamy brown stains from my new, aptly named addiction—Pint of Tears—smeared the arm. My trusty sidekick, Mr. Bibbles, a childhood stuffed thing—I wasn't sure anymore if he ever really was a bear—lay oddly contorted at my side.

For five years, Steven and I dated. Lived together. Worked together. Dreamed together. That was before it all went to shit. That was before I found him in *my* bed with Betsy the Intern. That was before he figured it was okay to forget about the fact that he was my fiancé. That was before I found myself homeless, refusing to ask my parents for help. I showed up with nothing but a suitcase full of crap—and Mr. Bibbles—at Sarah's door. I didn't even have to ask. Within twenty-four hours, my room was decorated, my bed was made, and I was moved in.

For the past six weeks, I'd lived with Sarah. My best friend, my trusty confidant, and, probably, the only person on earth who'd have put up with my shit for as long as she has. Besides the other third of our trio, Mel. My nightly crying fits, my refusal to leave the house for anything other than work, and my newly minted status as Ice Cream Dreams's most valuable customer wore on my friends.

Every day on the way home from work, before I planted my growing ass on the once beautiful sofa and cried, I stopped at a tiny little ice cream shop called Ice Cream Dreams. They pride themselves on making any ice cream concoction to fit any mood. The first day I walked in, the girl behind the counter took one look at me and Pint of Tears was born. Chocolate on chocolate mixed with chocolate, gummy bears, marshmallow, and peanut butter. It became their best-selling ice cream flavor of the fall. Probably because of me.

Me and my ever-growing, ice-cream-eating, tear-shedding, sofa-arm-smearing ass.

I would silently curse Sarah as she invited me out every Friday. Every Saturday. I would inwardly cringe at the ten pounds I'd gained—while simultaneously thanking my speedy metabolism that it wasn't more—as I watched from my perch on her butter-yellow sofa while she left for the gym with yoga mat in hand.

All I needed was a spoon, a pint, and a remote control.

My new life.

Sucked.

I'd taken to sitting on the couch and watching every single de-pressing break-up movie ever filmed. Multiple times. From black-

and-whites, animated, Ryan Gosling, Jack and Rose to addictions, affairs, Ryan Gosling, Jack and Rose. Oh, and by the way, Rose, I call bullshit. Jack would have pulled your ass from the frozen waters of the Atlantic and shared some space on that door or whatever the hell you were floating on. Then again, maybe you knew something we didn't. Maybe he deserved an icy, watery grave. Maybe you were on to something. Men.

Fuck 'em.

Sideways.

One particular Friday night, I was in the middle of another round of "Which Movie Is More Depressing?" (*When a Man Loves a Woman* was winning, by the way) when I heard Sarah's key in the lock. At the time, I wasn't fazed. We'd gotten into a routine. She'd come home from her date or the gym or dinner out with friends, ask me how I was, ask me if I needed anything, and, when I said no, she'd say good night and go to bed. Once in a while she'd sit on the couch with me, eat out of her own pint of Support System (yeah, another flavor), and watch me as I worked on my ugly crying face. I was pretty sure it was the ugliest crying face ever. I was giving that actress from *Homeland* a run for her ugly crying face money. Which is weird, because without the ugly crying face, she's beautiful. She never would have let Jack sink to the icy depths.

Then again, better to sink than live with the daily heartbreak of a roaming dick.

Instead, Sarah walked in with backup. Melody stormed into the room, ripped off my blanket, and threw Mr. Bibbles across the room. Sarah calmly walked over, grabbed my ice cream and spoon, and placed them on the kitchen counter.

"What the hell?" I shrank into the sofa.

"This is an intervention."

"Mel, you threw my bear!"

"Screw your bear, Caroline. Enough is enough. So Steven cheated on you. That doesn't mean you have to become an ice cream swilling hermit! What the hell happened to you?"

"You are a hot mess, doll face," Sarah quipped as she pulled a new pack of baby wipes from her purse and began wiping the chocolate off my face. Maybe I was.

"I'll see your hot mess and raise you a walking disaster. At least that's what she'll be if this shit keeps up."

"Leave me alone. And don't talk about me like I'm not here." I tried to retreat as far into the corner of the sofa as I could. Unfortunately, the more I squished in, the more tissues squished out.

Sarah hung up her coat before sitting on the coffee table across from me. "Sweetie, we know you're hurting. But it's time to move on. You're still working with him, you're reminded every day of what happened. No wonder you're stuck. You need to get up, get out, and find a new job. Move past this."

"How am I supposed to move past anything? I see Steven every single day. It's not like I can magically unsee him." I fingered the engagement ring I wore around my neck as fresh tears spilled over. I couldn't bring myself to get rid of it. Unfortunately, Steven still worked at the law firm, so I couldn't escape him. Who was I kidding? His daddy *was* the law firm.

"I know it's hard. I can't imagine having to see the two of them day after day," Sarah said, reminding me that Betsy and her welcoming vagina worked there, too.

"Every day I walk in and try to keep my head high but I keep running into her stink eye. She won't stop fucking staring at me." Sarah dodged my wild hand gestures. "Like I'm the one who ruined *her* life by walking in on them." Melody held the box of tissues and I yanked a bunch out and wiped my face. "Not to mention that everyone knows Steven and I broke up. Like anyone in the office needed anything else to gossip about."

"Fuck them. They're a bunch of middle-aged leeches who aren't happy unless someone else in unhappy. And fuck her. Punch her in the face," Melody suggested. "She's just mad she can't fuck the boss's son anymore."

"Right. I know they're still boning like they're the last two people on earth." I blew my nose. "Probably still doing it in the bed Steven and I bought when we moved in together." I could no longer breathe through my nose. "I bet they have sex in the office, too."

Fuck them both.

"I am sure they are not having sex in the office." Sarah laughed as Melody pursed her lips and checked out her fingernails.

"You think they're having sex in the office?" I asked her.

"Of course she doesn't. Right Mel?" Mel didn't answer, so Sarah threw a pillow at her. "Right?"

"I don't think it matters if they are still boning."

"Of course it matters! He begs for my forgiveness every single day. 'Oh, Caroline, forgive me.' 'I love you so much.' 'She means nothing.'" It made my skin crawl. "Bahhh. I want him to shut up. Just shut up!"

"Well, that's something," Melody piped up.

"What?" I asked.

"Mad. Mad is better than what you've been doing."

"And what have I been doing, Melody? I mean besides mourning the loss of a five-year relationship with my fiancé who cheated on me? Besides walking into a work every day and having people actually stop talking the second I come within earshot? Turning it over and over in my head, trying to figure out what *I* did wrong when I know Steven made the decision to cheat, not me?" I stood and threw my tissues. "How should I be dealing with it, Mel? Tell me. I'd love to take advice from a bed hopper who wouldn't know a relationship if it kicked her in the twat." Immediately my hands flew to my mouth.

"Nice." Melody smirked and Sarah gasped.

"I'm sorry. So sorry. I don't know what—"

"Stop. It's fine. I kind of like the sass." Mel winked. "Glad to see you fired up over something other than ice cream and Leonardo DiCaprio's icy death."

"Rose should have made room," I mumbled.

"Holy shit. Enough. I will cancel cable if you don't stop." Sarah rolled her eyes.

"Sorry."

"Look, don't be sorry. Be brave. Be strong. Be happy. Be amazing. Don't be sorry." Melody handed me another tissue.

"Exactly. You need to get up, get out, and meet some people."

"People." Melody waved Sarah off. "Pssh. She means men. You need to meet some men. You need to get your lady parts ready"—Mel grabbed her crotch—"and give them some love."

"My lady parts are fine the way they are."

"Shriveled up?"

"They are not shriveled up."

"When's the last time you had sex?"

"What does that matter?"

"The fact that you answered my question with that question tells me 'too long.' You need to get out and meet someone."

I dropped my head between my knees. "What if I can't? What if no one else wants me?"

Sarah dropped onto the couch next to me and rubbed my back while Melody headed toward the back of the apartment. In that moment I knew I had hit rock bottom and there was nowhere for me to go but up. But up to where? What or who would be waiting for me at the top of whatever?

The answers were sitting next to me rubbing my back and walking back into the living room, bathroom garbage can in hand.

"Look," Melody began as she placed the garbage can on the coffee table and sat next to it, "you're beautiful, talented, and smart. Who wouldn't want you? I mean, shit, you're only twenty-eight years old and the world is your oyster! You've had, what? Two, maybe three, boyfriends in your life? How many one night stands? How many nights of just fun? How many nights that were all about you and what you want? Now isn't the time to wonder who will want you, now is the time to take what you want."

"I've never had a one night stand." I crinkled my nose in mock disgust to mask the embarrassing lack of experience in that department. In truth, it had always been something I was too nervous to do, something other people did. I was a "relationship girl." Always with a boyfriend.

"Now is the time for you to live your life. Start over."

"With a one night stand?"

"Sure. Why not?" Sarah asked.

"That's just not what I do." I shook my head.

"You need to do something. Tell Steven to fuck off. Put the damn ring away." I clutched it and Sarah rolled her eyes. "I don't mean get rid of it—"

"I say sell it," Melody added.

"What I mean is take it off, put it away. Kick up your heels. Step out of the shadow Steven kept you in. Christ, Care." Sarah threw her arms up in frustration. "I need wine. Anyone else need wine?"

"You need to ask?" Mel laughed.

"Look, I appreciate what you're trying to do, but I can't just go out and date someone. I can't just go and talk to strange men. That's not me. I've slept with exactly two people and both were boyfriends."

"We are not saying you have to go bang every guy you meet but what's wrong with a one night stand?"

"Steven said—"

"What the fuck?" Melody grabbed her hair. "Who the fuck cares what Steven said, Care? Really? I don't mean to be a bitch here but, seriously, I am pretty sure you need to stop with the Steven references. He's lucky I didn't castrate his cheating ass."

"But—"

"But what?"

"I don't want people to think I'm a slut."

Melody laughed. "I had a one night stand last weekend. Does that make me a slut?" Melody stared at me.

"That's not really a good example, Mel." Sarah handed her a glass of red before handing me mine. "You had a one night stand the weekend before that, too."

"And the weekend before that," I added.

Melody opened her mouth and closed it quickly before shaking her head and taking a large swallow of wine. "Look, my point is that you can." She stood and plucked the wadded-up snot rags from the sofa and tossed them in the trash. "There comes a time when you need a reality check. Realize this truth: you'll never be good enough for some people. Say it over and over again until it sinks into your sad little skull." I ducked away when she rapped her knuckles on my head. "And when you realize that, ask yourself whether it's your problem or theirs."

The harsh bitch of reality coldcocked me across the heart. I wasn't ready to realize anything. Fresh tears spilled down my face. "Mel, I just want to move on. I want all this past me."

"Of course you do. And we'll help you. Come on, get up." Melody put down her glass and grabbed my arm, yanking me out of my seat. I looked back longingly at my spot before turning to face her.

"Drink the wine."

I took a sip.

"No. Drink the whole thing."

I looked to Sarah and she nodded. I brought the overpoured glass to my mouth and drank. I drank and drank until the glass was empty and Sarah took the glass from my hand.

Wiping the tears from my cheeks and brushing the hair out of my eyes, Melody continued, "We have a plan."

"Yes. We've got it all figured out." Sarah smirked as they walked me down the hall.

That plan began with a very invasive cold shower and a loofah, quite a bit of complaining on my part, and fresh pajamas. When I was finally cleansed of tears, snot, and sticky trails of ice cream, the girls sat me on the couch—Mr. Bibbles was nowhere to be found—handed me another glass of wine, and laid out their plan. I sat and listened. And drank. And tried to understand. All I ended up doing was drinking more.

"You want me to what?" I reached forward and tried to pour the empty bottle into my glass. Melody hopped up and ran to the kitchen. I held my finger to my lips until my glass was filled. I needed the silence to process this plan.

"We'll go to a bar—" Sarah began.

"Someplace new," Melody interrupted.

"Yes. And we'll scan the crowd. Look for someone take-home worthy. When you find him, nominate him as the target."

"And do what again?"

"Flirt. Pick him up. Do what you need to do." Sarah was way too into this.

"So what you're saying is, I walk into a bar, point at a hot guy, and declare that I am bringing him home."

"Yes."

"Why can't I just get his number?"

"Because this is Operation One Night Stand, not Operation Get His Number."

"What if I can't find anyone take-home worthy?"

"Then you don't. That's the point. There is no timeline."

"Right. We just go out and watch you troll for the one."

"I'm supposed to marry 'the one.'"

"Not this one." Melody high-fived Sarah.

I rolled my eyes, stood, and paced the room. "Let's leave that alone for a bit. Tell me about the plan. There has to be more to this plan than me getting it on with a hottie stranger guy." I needed the subject to change, even if only for a minute. I wasn't that girl. I didn't sleep around. But, holy hell, I really wanted to be.

"Right. More about the plan." Sarah refilled her glass before handing Mel the bottle. "We need to rip this Band-Aid off. We need to get free and clear of all this"—she waved her arms around, sloshing the red liquid onto the hardwood—"*shit*."

"Shit." I nodded my head and continued to pace. "Remove the shit." I was pretty sure I needed more wine. "Pour me." I held out my glass and Melody poured.

"Are you ready to hear this part?"

"Rip off the Band-Aid." It was my turn to slosh.

"You need to"—Sarah paused—"why don't you sit down for this?"

"Sit down?" I pointed to the couch.

"Yeah. That would be good." Melody agreed. "Drink."

The three of us drank deeply before Sarah continued.

"Youneedtoquityourjob."

"I'm sorry—what? It sounded like you said I need to quit my job." I laughed and took a sip.

When neither one of them corrected me and, instead, averted their eyes and busied themselves with refilling their wineglasses, I nearly choked.

"You can't be serious? I can't quit my job! How would I pay for anything? How the hell would I make rent, Sarah? You gonna foot the bill on your teacher's salary?"

"Wait, wait. Settle your tits, doll," Melody reasoned. "Are you really going to subject yourself to working alongside Steven and his fuck toy? Around all those miserable people? When was the last time you didn't dread going to work? All the Steven business aside, when?"

"That isn't the point."

"It is the point. There is no way you are going to get past this un-less you make a clean break," Sarah said.

"How am I going to find a new job?"

"The same way everyone else finds a new job. You look for one. You use your network. Mel and I will help you, and I am sure your parents will help you, until you get on your feet."

"My mom never liked Steven," I mumbled and chewed on a fin-gernail.

"Neither did I," Melody blurted. "What? I thought we were be-ing honest."

"We are." Sarah pointed between herself and Melody. "We need Caroline to be honest."

"Me? About what?"

"What you want. Do you want to stay in Steven's shadow? Do you want to stare at Betsy the Intern all day long? Do you want to work someplace that chews away everything great about you until you become an empty shell? Or do you want to take life by the balls and live a little?"

"It's a lot to take in so fast."

"So fast? You've become part of the decor, darling. Get your sweet ass off my couch before I remove you from it myself." Sarah smiled.

"And you think I need to have sex with a stranger?"

"I think you're looking too much into it."

"I don't know. I need time to think."

And I did think. And partake in numerous talks about the ins and outs of dating and one night stands—I mean, I had been out of the game for five years. We took a trip the next day to a hair salon and Fred Burke's, a high-end boutique store, and even squeezed in some much needed fat burning with spin class on Sunday. In between all of it, my ice cream was thrown out, Ice Cream Dreams was asked not to sell my ice cream to me anymore, and my résumé and cover letters were revamped. All I needed to do was rip off the Band-Aid. Easier said than done.

About the Author

Christine Hughes is a former middle school English teacher from New Jersey. Her first novel, *Torn*, a YA paranormal, was named a 2012 Hollywood Book Festival finalist and a 2012 RONE Awards finalist and has been released by Crushing Hearts and Black Butterfly Publishing, as has its sequel, *Darkness Betrayed*. Her stand-alone NA romance, *Three Days of Rain*, was a finalist at the 2013 Paris Book Festival and also has a home with CHBB.

Learn more at:

Christine-Hughes.com

Twitter, @HughesWriter

Facebook.com/ChristineHughesAuthor